Lying to You

Amanda Reynolds lives in the Cotswolds with her family, where she writes full-time. Her debut novel, *Close to Me*, became an e-book bestseller. *Lying to You* is her second book.

'Gripping, claustrophobic and often deeply unsettling, *Close To Me* exerts a magnetic pull from its first pages' – Kate Riordan, author of *The Girl In The Photograph*

'Taut, compelling, well-paced. ADDICTIVE' – Will Dean, author of *Dark Pines*

'Keeps you guessing, and then just when you think you know, you find another twist in the road. Gripping and suspenseful' – Michelle Adams, author of *My Sister*

'*Close To Me* reveals itself like a buried memory, the details peeking out and keeping the reader guessing until all is discovered in the shocking conclusion . . . sure to have readers thinking about the story and how much they can trust their own recollections long after the final page' – Cate Holahan, author of *The Widower's Wife* and *Lies She Told*

'An intriguing, well-told, tightly knit story that will hold you to the last page and make you put one hand on the banister whenever you're at the top of the stairs' – *SHOTS Crime & Thriller Ezine*

Lying
to
You

AMANDA REYNOLDS

WILDFIRE

First published in 2018 by
WILDFIRE
An imprint of HEADLINE PUBLISHING GROUP

1

Cataloguing in Publication Data is available from the British Library

ISBN 978 1 4722 4517 5

Typeset in Dante MT by Palimpsest Book Production Limited,
Falkirk, Stirlingshire

Printed and bound in Great Britain by
Clays Ltd, St Ives plc

Headline's policy is to use papers that are natural, renewable
and recyclable products and made from wood grown in sustainable forests.
The logging and manufacturing processes are expected to conform to
the environmental regulations of the country of origin.

HEADLINE PUBLISHING GROUP
An Hachette UK Company
Carmelite House
50 Victoria Embankment
London EC4Y 0DZ

www.headline.co.uk
www.hachette.co.uk

To Dorothy and Vincent – both writers before me

The lies we tell ourselves are the worst kind, for we have all the time in the world to convince ourselves they are true.

Jess

Sunday, 4th December 2016 (Morning)

The chirpy ringtone reverberates around my tiny two-roomed flat, working its way inside my head and fixing on a spot somewhere behind my eyes. I squint at the screen to see if it's Mum, reluctant to allow in her chaos, but it's not a number I recognise. She could be calling from a different phone, of course, but it's a couple of weeks until our monthly duty call, and Sundays normally pass her by. I hesitate and the call ends, but when it rings again I pick up.

'Jess? Is that you?'

I haven't spoken to Will in over a year, almost two come to think of it, but I'd know his voice anywhere. My brother's accent is even stronger over the phone, the same as everyone's where we grew up, the vowels lengthened, as though there's no rush to get the words out, time less of a luxury back home than it is here in London.

'Yes, it's me.'

'Are you on your own?' Will asks.

'How did you get my new number?' I reply, ignoring his question.

'Mum's address book,' he tells me, then he interrupts my rant about how I can't trust her to keep anything secret. 'Jess, listen, I've got some bad news. I'm sorry, but Mum passed away last night.'

'You mean she's *dead*?'

'Yes.' His tone is matter-of-fact. 'She collapsed in the street outside the pub.'

I stand and take the three paces to the window, staring down at the traffic of people and cars two storeys below. A steady flow, even on a Sunday morning.

'Jess, you still there?'

The rickety dining chair hits the wall behind me as I sit back down. I rock it back and forth, tapping a key on my laptop so the screen lights up, bright but out of focus. 'Yeah, I'm still here.'

'You okay?'

'I don't know, you?'

'Yeah, I am, but I need you to come home. Soon as you can.'

I sit up; only then aware I'd slumped down. 'I can't, Will. You know I can't.'

'Someone has to sort things out,' he says, as if it was already decided. 'I promise he won't give you any trouble, if that's what you're worried about. I won't let him.'

'No, it's not that,' I say, as if I can dismiss Will's concerns, and mine, so easily. 'I've got appointments, clients – did I tell you I've got a new job? I can't take time off without any notice. It's important. I'm a qualified counsellor, and I have a supervisor. I see her once a fortnight. It's part of my accreditation. I can't just—' There's silence at the other end. 'Mum's really gone?'

'I know it's hard to take in, but yeah, she is.'

'When's the funeral?'

'Don't know yet, a week or so? But you need to come back straight away. There's loads to do . . . the house, and forms to fill in . . . You know I'm useless at that kind of stuff.'

'I'll be there for the funeral, of course, but—'

He's not listening, telling me his regulars won't wait for jobs he's already booked in. He has lawns to trim, trees to cut back. Yes, even in winter. His excuses about work commitment are no different than mine, and he only lives around the corner, whereas I'm a hundred miles away. He reminds me he has a child, a one-year-old, who's teething, and Becky's working full-time now.

'I need you here, Jess. Please come home.'

We both know I won't refuse him, although I try to find alternatives.

'What about Mick and Tony? Can't they help?'

'They're still away.'

'In prison?' I ask, as if there would be any other reason why our older twin brothers might be 'away'.

'No, they're on a world cruise, Jess. Of course, in prison.' Will sighs. 'They'll try to get compassionate leave for the funeral, but it'll only be a few hours at most. And I'm warning you, the house is a right tip. Mum had pretty much given up on it after I left.'

'Great! So that's it, I have to come?'

'No, you don't *have* to, but it would be really appreciated if you could.'

'Fine.'

'Great. Text me what time train you're on and I'll pick you up from the station.' There's a pause before he asks, 'Is that OK? I know we haven't seen each other for a while, and it's going to be difficult for you, coming back, but I won't let him near you. You know I won't.'

'Yeah, course,' I tell him. 'I'll see you tomorrow.'

Jess

Monday, 5th December 2016 (Lunchtime)

I'm checking my phone for the third time when I spot the train in the distance, a surge of passengers moving forwards on the crowded platform. I join them, hoping Will has seen my message, even though he hasn't bothered to reply. It was a rushed text, sent from the back of the taxi. Then I'd rung work.

I'd hoped to leave a message on the answer machine, but my boss had picked up straight away, his annoyance quickly replaced with condolences, advising me to take as long as I need. I'd wanted to correct him, tell him I'm fine, more inconvenienced than grief-stricken, but even in my head it had sounded wrong, and I didn't want him to change his mind about the time off. I suppose it was reasonable to assume I'd be upset, given my news, but Mum wasn't your typical mum, and I haven't seen her in ten years. My emotions are hard to fathom, let alone share.

I haul my bag up the step and on to the luggage rack, bracing my knees and ignoring the nausea that swells in my stomach as the journey begins. I haven't reserved a seat and the train is packed, but I don't mind standing, prefer it in fact, a cold breeze siphoning in through the cracked window and the toilet nearby should I need it. I should have booked my ticket last night, but I'd opened a bottle of wine instead, raising a glass or two to Mum's memory.

The train is quieter after the first hour. I grab a seat near my bag, not that there's much of value in the scruffy holdall, just a few changes of clothing and my best suit, luckily a dark colour so it will be fine for the funeral. I've folded the jacket around my black heels, the ones I bought before the trial when I thought I should look more sophisticated for the jury. I wore flats in the end, on James's advice. The last time I wore heels was the day of my interview, although I was massively over-dressed, the other candidates in jeans and sweats. Still, it got me the job. I haven't had time to try on my outfit for the funeral, but I haven't gained weight, lost some if anything. Maybe when I get back I'll try to look after myself a bit better, eat more and drink less, but even as I plan how I can shop for fresh ingredients, I know I won't. I've never cooked from scratch; wouldn't know where to start.

I glance at my table companions, an elderly couple in matching anoraks, and a woman to my left who must be about Mum's age. Her hair is dark and it looks freshly blow-dried, sleek and neat, the antithesis of Mum's dirty blonde. Mum dyed hers every fourth Tuesday to cover the distinctive red that runs through our entire family. Or at least, she used to.

6

I have no idea what colour it was last week, or last year. Somehow a year apart has turned into ten, but she never offered to visit, and I wasn't going to go home. I drag my fingers through my matted curls, which reminds me I haven't packed my straighteners, or my hair dryer.

Peering through the murk of a December day, I press my face close to the window, watching as the high-rise offices thin out. I haven't left London for . . . must be at least five years. A terrible weekend away with a married man who cried when he came, then told me how much he loved his wife. I fight a moment of panic, breathing in and out fast so the glass fogs and I have to wipe away the condensation with my palm. The buildings disappear, expanses of green and mud-brown opening up, the sky almost white. I shiver, imagining the train speeding into the distance, an endless hurtle into a blanket of nothingness. I wrap my coat around me, leaning away from the woman and her perfect hair until the hypnotic rhythm of the train takes over, an image of Mum falling-down drunk for the final time, cartoonish and unpleasant, playing on a repetitive loop in my head, in time with the thrumming of the train tracks and the bass of someone's music behind me. For some reason it bothers me a lot that I don't know if Mum's hair was blonde, or red, or grey, everything else overshadowed by that irrelevant detail. I rang her once a month for a five-minute call, shorter sometimes, and I hated every second.

As the train slows at the next station my phone buzzes loudly. I slide the button on the side to mute, then read the email from my supervisor. The last time we met I'd been upset, disappointed by what she'd decided for me. I know she thinks it's for the best, but I can't imagine starting all over again, raking over the past with yet another stranger. I shared everything with her, the whole truth, but it still wasn't enough. She reminds me about our final appointment, scheduled for the thirteenth of this month. I want to go, but I'm angry with her. She's let me down, like everyone does. I reply, but briefly, informing her of my mother's death and that I hope to be back in time for our final meeting, although if that's the date of the funeral I'll have to postpone.

For now, all my plans are on hold.

Six Months Before . . .

Supervision Session #1 – Jessica Tidy – Tuesday, June 21st, 2016

(Jessica Tidy, known as Jess, age twenty-six, contacted me via email last week. She's a newly qualified integrative counsellor, working at a practice in Central London. Today's meeting was to discuss the nature of her supervision.)

Full notes in client file ref: 718/16

Meeting taped, transcript of relevant section below (abridged)

Jess: Can you call me Jess, please? No one calls me Jessica, not even my mum.

Me: Of course. Tell me, Jess, why did you decide to retrain as a counsellor?

Jess: I think I said it all in my email.

Me: Yes, it was lovely. So chatty.

Jess: Sorry, it's not my strength, that kind of—

Me: No, you misunderstand, I liked it very much. I don't tend to take on much supervision these days, I'm semi-retired and I keep my client list fairly select, but I couldn't resist meeting you. Your CV is very impressive. I love the fact you started from nothing, going back to college to get the qualifications you needed for the counselling course. As far as supervision goes, you suggested we might meet fortnightly?

Jess: Yes, and I wanted to ask you about payment before we start. It's just that I don't have that much put by.

Me: I'm sure we can work something out. London is so expensive, isn't it? And the training too . . . you were self-funded?

Jess: Yes, I was a waitress; before I was a counsellor, I mean. And whilst I studied.

Me: A kind of counselling in itself.

Jess: Yes, definitely. You hear a lot of stories.

Me: Let me tell you a bit about myself, how I work. Then you can decide if I'm the right fit for you.

Jess: Oh! I thought it was all settled? I mean . . . I know it's you I want to see. You're the best. I've done my research.

Me: Why do you think I'm the best supervisor for you?

Jess: I don't know, I just got a good feeling when I found your website.

Me: Your colleagues haven't offered to supervise you themselves?

Jess: I did ask, but they're all stacked out, and I thought it was best to see someone outside of work. My boss is an idiot. I wouldn't want to confide in him, don't know how he keeps any of his clients.

Me: Oh dear. So, what are your expectations of supervision, how do you see us working together?

Jess: It's about my clients, of course, talking through their issues, making sure I haven't missed anything as I'm newly qualified, but supervision is also important for me, so I have someone I can talk to, if it's getting too much.

Me: Exactly. This line of work can certainly take its toll, so feel free to talk about anything that's bothering you, however small. I still see my supervisor once a month for that very reason. Anything you'd like to ask before we begin, assuming you're happy to start today?

Jess: Yes, definitely. Thank you, and no, nothing I need to ask.

Me: Great. I'll be taking notes, and I also tape everything on my phone, so I can transcribe sections of our conversations later, in case I've missed anything, or want to highlight something I feel is important. Is that all OK with you?

Jess: I've nothing to hide.

Me: Great. Why don't you start by telling me a little bit about your background, your family, education, that kind of thing.

Jess: I'm the youngest of four, only girl. We've got the same mum, but three different dads, although we've all inherited Mum's red hair, which is weird when you think of it, although I never have before. She dyes it blonde, so you'd never . . . sorry. The twins, Mick and Tony, they're ten years older than me, thirty-six. Will, he's closest to me in age, five years between us. He must be . . . thirty-one now. I hadn't realised he was in his thirties . . . I mean I knew, but I hadn't really . . . we've kind of lost touch over the last couple of years, but we were close when I lived at home.

He's got a long-term girlfriend, and they had a baby last December, he sent me a photo in his Christmas card. They live with her mother now, in the same village where we grew up. Sorry, is this too much detail?

Me: No, not at all. Carry on.

Jess: That's pretty much it, apart from Mum. We speak on the phone once a month. Haven't seen her since I left home to move to London ten years ago.

Me: Thank you, Jess. I'd like to move on now to why you decided to become a counsellor.

Jess: Yeah, of course. Family stuff is a nightmare, isn't it?

Me: We can talk about that if you feel it's relevant, but today I wanted to gather as much background information as I can.

Jess: Yes, of course. Sorry.

Me: No need to apologise. You said you were a waitress before?

Jess: Yes, I was waitress for years . . . hated it! Kids throwing food, rude parents, tourists who can't speak English or find the right change, and the pay is crap. I was looking for something new, more of a challenge, and I've always wanted to help others, felt I could empathise.

Me: That empathy you talk about is a common reason for people to be drawn to our profession. In fact, a lot of counsellors have received therapy themselves then decided they would like to swap chairs.

Jess: That's not exactly what happened to me, but yes, I think my background might be helpful for once. And I love studying, which is crazy as I left school with absolutely no qualifications.

Me: Sometimes the time just isn't right, then it suddenly is. You're lucky to have found your niche so young.

Jess: Twenty-six feels pretty old sometimes.

Me: Well, I can assure you it isn't. Now, let's move on to your clients. It's been a while, but I do remember how difficult those first few appointments can be.

Jess: I guess so, but I'm loving it so far.

Me: Any challenges you'd like to share?

Jess: There is one client I'm finding a bit trickier than the rest. She's very young, sixteen. Her doctor referred her for coun-selling as she was acting out at school, some alcohol issues I believe. She saw my boss first, didn't take to him at all, can't say I blame her, so he passed her on to me. Last attempt, I think.

Me: You've completed the initial assessment?

Jess: Yes . . . at least I tried to, but she's so angry . . . yeah, just angry.

Me: Were you concerned for your own safety?

Jess: God, no! Nothing like that, but I do feel sorry for her. I remember what it felt like at that age, how unfair it can all seem. I'd love to tell her it will get better, she's not always going to feel like this, but you just don't know, do you? Stupid to make promises.

Me: You can certainly acknowledge how she feels, reflect her anger, and to some extent your own feelings. I'm sure that will be a reassurance to her, but of course you'll need to tread carefully.

Jess: I'm making sure it's all 'by the book'.

Me: That's good, but what I meant was, and please feel able

13

to speak freely with me, it sounds like she may be stirring up some issues for you.

Jess: I don't think so.

Me: Let's imagine I'm her, sitting here now. What would you like to tell her?

Jess: I suppose I'd say it's OK to be angry. Anyone would, in her place. That the way she's been treated by the adults in her life was wrong. Do you think if I said all that I would be crossing any lines?

Me: No, I don't think so. *Do you?*

Jess: I don't think so either, but what if she doesn't come back? I won't get the chance to say any of it then.

Me: I'm afraid that's her choice. She's not your responsibility, Jess.

Karen

Monday, 5th December 2016 (Afternoon)

'I hope I'm not speaking out of turn, Karen.' She passes me my postal receipt. 'I thought you and Mark would want to know.'

She must have served me thousands of times over the years, every stamp or parcel fed through her bony hands as she soaks up and passes on the village gossip, but I can't for the life of me recall her name. She's someone I'd struggle to pass the time of day with if we met under any other circumstance, and right now I have no desire to continue this one-sided conversation. I open my purse to tuck the slip of paper inside.

'Dropped dead outside the pub,' she informs me as she counts out my change. 'I don't know if it's true, but someone said she was lying right in the middle of the road. The cars were all driving round her. No one stopped! Can you believe that? Funeral's probably next week, not that you'll be likely to—'

'No,' I reply, meeting her eye, 'we won't.' I take the note, but the coins slide off, tumbling between us. 'Leave them! I'll manage, thank you.'

I fumble amongst the charity collection tins and leaflets about Christmas postal dates as I retrieve my lost change, tucking the cold coins in the palm of my hand. I only came in to post back a dress; an impulse purchase I immediately regretted, especially as I had to pay the return postage. I'd hoped it might look better on my grown-up daughter than it had on me, but Frey crumpled her nose at the plain black shift.

'I didn't mean to upset you,' the woman says, picking up a pound coin and handing it to me.

I look up at her wrinkled face and bite back a reply, reminding myself how she was always patient with Mum, then I turn to the inquisitive queue, their interest clearly piqued by the exchange they've just witnessed. I hate that moment of recognition, synapses clicking, colour rising in cheeks or draining from faces, the sympathetic smile, or more often, feigned distraction. Mark tells me I'm paranoid, no one cares, not any more – it's been over ten years – but we both know he's kidding himself. Nothing that exciting has happened before or since in our small community. We should have moved away, but these things have a habit of following you around. I've reached the door when she calls after me, 'I've found another one, Karen. Fifty pence!'

The air is sharp as I walk briskly towards the supermarket, the soles of my boots tapping hard on the icy pavement, coins jangling in my coat pocket. I don't look up until I reach the steady line of cars queuing for the car park. Must be school pick-up time. I hadn't realised it had got so late, the grey sky turning to charcoal. Across town, Frey will be collecting in books from her students, although she often uses a giant computer screen linked to her laptop, textbooks utilised less often these days apparently. We'd been in the garden when she'd told us she'd got the job. It was a warm summer's day but the air had chilled a little when Mark remarked how much things had changed since he'd left teaching. The news our daughter had come to share should have been joyous, her first teaching post, due to start in the September, but it was soured by Mark's reaction. Not that he'd meant it that way, he was incredibly proud of her, and he told her so; such a prestigious school, he had no idea she'd applied. Then he glanced at me across the patio table, as if he'd worked out I'd known about the change in direction for some time. Frey was talking too quickly, garbling on about how she got in a complete muddle with the 'techy stuff' and thought she'd blown it, but Mark was staring blankly in that vacant way he has, his thoughts elsewhere.

I reach the entrance to the supermarket and stop, defeated by the noise and bustle. There are pushchairs and shopping trollies everywhere, and announcements over the loudspeaker asking for all available staff to report to the checkouts. I should have run my errands hours ago, as I'd planned, but I was waylaid by other, more pressing matters: messages to send, arrangements to finalise, and the repetitive business of simply getting up and dressed. In truth, I could have completed those tasks in under an hour, but my usual apathy has eaten into my day. I can lose a whole morning or afternoon quite easily, inertia pinning me to the bed, or leaning me against the kitchen sink, staring out at our unkempt back garden, neither of us sufficiently bothered by the mess to do anything about it.

I turn from the overflowing shop and walk back to the car, waiting in the cold gloom of the driver seat for the rush to die down. I don't cope well with crowds these days, and there's really no hurry. It's a dull view: the car park, and in the distance the local schools. Infant and Junior schools first, and behind them the huge comprehensive, a sixties concrete structure which looms over its smaller cousins, imposing and yet uninspiring. I always wondered what Mark could possibly find behind those grey walls to sustain his interest. He loved teaching, but in the last few years of his career I noticed his enthusiasm waning. I suppose he was stuck, little chance of promotion unless we'd moved away, which wasn't an option with Mum to think of.

I take my phone from my coat pocket and send Mark a message, breaking the bad news, then I compose a longer message to Frey, asking if she's had a good day, which she usually has. I don't mention anything to her about Lisa Tidy's death. No point worrying her unnecessarily, not until we know for sure Jess will be back for the funeral. I click send, rummaging in my bag for my pills and reaching into the back for the bottle of water that's been rolling around the seat for as long as I remember.

Feeling calmer, I watch the mothers returning to their cars with young children, school-made Christmas decorations clutched in tiny hands. I hadn't wanted Frey to go to the village school, a rough and tumble place, but Mark had insisted, said he couldn't pay for privilege when he taught in a comprehensive that prided itself on welcoming all; besides, we could never have afforded the fees. He assured me he would keep an eye on our daughter when she started at the comp, but she turned down her father's offer of a lift on her first day, preferring to keep her connection to 'Mr Winter' as quiet as possible. I walked her as far as the gates, watching as her new blazer was engulfed by the masses, most of them towering above her tiny frame, a flock of dark crows swallowing her up. It felt as though those first eleven years of motherhood had sped by. On the way home, a fall of leaves rustling at my feet, I passed Lisa Tidy, cigarette in hand, swaying barefoot in her front garden. 'Your girl's first day at big school too?' she slurred. I nodded back, quickening my pace. 'Makes you proud, don't it?' she called after me.

I suppose I should make a move, the rush will probably have eased by now. I'm not sure what would happen if I couldn't manage these basic things, like buying food. Maybe Mark would take over, but I doubt it. His malaise seems even more entrenched than mine. At least it's something to do; an hour killed. It's possible to lose yourself wandering up and down the aisles, and it's better than going home, especially today.

Five Months Before . . .

Supervision Session #2 – Jessica Tidy –
Tuesday, July 5th, 2016

Full notes in client file ref: 718/16

Meeting taped, transcript of relevant section below (abridged)

Jess: Is it all right if I take off my jacket? It's so hot today.

Me: Of course, and help yourself to a glass of water. How have you been since I last saw you?

Jess: Yes, good thanks. I'm settling into a pattern with my regulars, they seem to be getting to know me, trusting me more.

Me: That's great. How about the girl you mentioned last time?

Jess: *Girl?* Oh, yes. I haven't heard from her.

Me: Have you tried to contact her?

Jess: Of course, but I've been busy.

Me: Looks like a nice mix of staff specialisms where you work.

Jess: You looked it up?

Me: Don't look so surprised, Jess. I do my research too.

Jess: The website's very out of date. I keep nagging my boss about it, but he never listens.

Me: He sounds a difficult man, but the important thing is you're getting lots of client-facing hours, and plenty of variety by the sounds of it.

Jess: Yes, that's true, although I did have a sticky moment last week. One client turned up drunk, shouted the place down. She had to be escorted out. Shook me up a bit, to be honest.

Me: Was she too drunk to make any use of her appointment?

Jess: Oh yeah, believe me, I know *drunk*, and she was ready to pass out. Sorry, I should explain. My mum is an alcoholic.

Me: Must have been a horrible reminder, seeing someone in that state.

Jess: It didn't bother me that much, but I'm going to refer her to my colleague anyway. I'm not qualified to deal with addictions.

Me: Technically you are, Jess. Your training equips you to deal with all kinds of—

Jess: Alcoholism is a specialism, there's another counsellor who—

Me: If you want to refer her, you can of course do so at any point. You mustn't feel obliged to continue if you're uncomfortable for any reason. It's the same for all your clients. Nothing personal, except—

Jess: *Personal?*

Me: Maybe this woman was drunk that day and no others. To assume she's an alcoholic . . .

Jess: She was falling-over drunk. I don't think that's anything personal. What are you trying to say?

Me: There are bound to be trigger points in our work, and as you mentioned your mum's alcoholism I wanted to raise that possibility with you.

Jess: It's got nothing to do with this.

Me: You can't deny your past, Jess. That's one of the main things I've learnt over the years.

Jess

Monday, 5th December 2016 (Afternoon)

'Jeez, Will, you weren't kidding!'

I kick aside the post on the mat and cover my nose with my hand as I push my way into the hallway. The piles of rubbish and Mum's precious 'console' table are in the way, but it's the smell that's most off-putting, like the bottom of a kitchen bin. I steady myself with a hand to the clunky smoked-glass table, the dusty surface covered with Mum's extensive collection of lipsticks and an assortment of empty glasses, fingerprints and lipstick impressions clinging to their sides. A memory of her standing in this exact spot flashes up, as clear as if she were still here. A pout as she applied her 'lippy' in front of the gilt mirror above the table, outlining the feathery edges of her smoker's mouth in dark red before smacking her lips together and declaring herself 'Done!' I smooth down my crazy hair, now a mass of frizzy curls.

'I warned you it was bad,' Will says, following me in. 'Becky and I popped over yesterday, but we didn't stay long. It's not suitable for a toddler, as you can see.'

The first half of the hallway is filled with bulging black refuse bags, and beyond that a line of emptied bottles snakes its way ahead of us towards the kitchen. They're mainly clear glass, vodka at a guess, but there are a few green beer bottles too. The pattern is almost deliberate, a zig-zag line following the contours of the sticky carpet. Mum had obviously abandoned any attempt at concealing her drinking. I'm about to challenge Will on the state of the place when he says, 'To be honest,' pausing to pick up a bag of rubbish, then dropping it when liquid pours from the bottom, 'I hadn't realised it had got quite so bad.' He frowns at me. 'Don't look at me like that, you weren't here either.'

'No, but I don't live around the corner. Was she with anyone?'

'A boyfriend, you mean? No, not that I know of.' He peers into another black bag then looks at me. 'Why wouldn't you let Mum give me your new number? I asked her a few times, but she said you'd never talk to her again if she did.'

'I suppose I wanted to move on. Like you.'

He asks what that's supposed to mean, and I shake my head, covering my mouth and nose again as I pick my way between the bottles and rubbish. He reaches out and pulls my hand from my face and tells me to stop being pathetic. We both laugh, the tension broken, back to being big brother and little sis again.

Will was waiting for me in his van when I walked out of the station, his elbow resting on the wound-down driver-side window, a lit cigarette cupped in his hand. I told him off for his lack of

24

response to my message, but he reminded me he was always useless at keeping in touch, as if that were excuse enough. The stink of damp soil and cut grass in the van was overpowering, mixing with the familiar smell of Will's tobacco, but I didn't mind the stale smoke so much. I've never been a smoker myself, other than the odd one for appearance's sake as a teenager, but Will's roll-ups remind me of him, a comforting scent. 'Hey, stay awake!' Will had told me as we slowly made our way through town, the exhaustion of a sleepless night and the long journey catching up with me, but he was quiet too, glancing across as if he didn't recognise me. Once we got closer to the village, I sat up and took more notice, commenting on the new houses lining the twisting road, replacing the open countryside. The modern estate stretched back as far as I could see, side roads branching off into smart-looking cul-de-sacs with impressive homes. Will had shrugged when I'd commented on the loss of the open fields, said the new developments don't bother him, more potential customers for his gardening business. Then we were here, staring at the squalor our mother had lived in for weeks, possibly months, or even, although I hope not, for almost two years, since Will moved out.

'I'll get your bag,' Will says, tramping back to where he's parked his van at the side of the road.

I watch him from the door, afraid to explore further on my own, but when he returns it's only to drop my holdall at my feet.

'Right.' He claps his hands together. 'I'll be off.' He turns to leave, retracing his steps along the path.

'Will! You can't leave me here on my own,' I call after him. 'This place is uninhabitable. You said so yourself.'

He sighs, and looks back. 'I've got stuff to do, Jess. A tree to take down by the village hall and then hedges to cut back. It'll be dark soon.'

'What about *this* path?' I point out the weeds, some of them the size of bushes.

'I'm already behind, Jess. These short winter days are a curse to me.' He turns to leave again, then pauses, walks back, his face serious. 'You know he still lives in the same place? End of the lane by the fields. The cottage has gone to wrack and ruin.' When I say nothing, he continues, 'Mark Win—'

'I know who you mean,' I reply, interrupting him. 'He isn't allowed to come near me, you know that.'

'You probably won't bump into him, he only ever goes out to walk his dog over the fields. I've never seen him in the village, but—' Will is looking down at his heavy boots, leaving the thought hanging. 'Look, I'm busy, but if you need me—'

'I'll be fine. Like I said, Mark Winter's not allowed to even look at me.'

'If he tries anything, Jess—'

'I'll tell you straight away, promise.'

'OK.' Will puts his hands on my shoulders. 'Make a start, and I'll be back when I can.'

The house feels smaller than I remember; funny how our memories play tricks. Maybe it's the quiet that shrinks the rooms, or the mess. I never liked coming home, even when I lived here, but at least it was always filled with noise: raised voices, angry or drunken, often both. My brothers cramming the place with life. Now it's almost silent, the only sound from an occasional car or motorbike along the short stretch of road outside. I walk towards the front room, kicking aside piles of newspapers, and skirting the empty cardboard boxes, carrier bags, and bottles. The threadbare curtains are closed, the tatty sofa covered in stains. Mum's favourite chair is covered with signs of a life cut short: an overflowing ashtray on one arm, an abandoned remote control on the other, and a coffee mug near where her slippered feet would have been, the contents of the mug solidified and tinged green. I pick up the slippers and notice there's an imprint of her feet in the lining. There's an empty glass on the smeared dining table in the corner, red lipstick prints on its smudged rim. It's as though Mum has just left the room, stumbling into the kitchen to pour herself another. I try to push aside thoughts of her dead in the street, not dead-drunk, but dead. Will said the people she'd been with at the pub assumed she'd staggered home, the alarm not raised until closing time when everyone had poured out and found her. He'd glanced across at me and said it was probably instantaneous, that's what the doctor thought. No pain, just nothing. But isn't that what people always say, and how would anyone know?

I drop the slippers where I found them and follow the lines of bottles back towards the kitchen, picking up as many up as I can, armfuls of them, one inadvertently held upside down and dribbling neat alcohol down my coat as I press the light switch with my elbow. The kitchen is dark, the blind closed and the slats thick with dust. The strip light flickers then illuminates the worktops, but there's nowhere to put the bottles down, the bin overflowing, every surface piled with dirty crockery and glasses, the cupboard doors ajar and crammed with more emptied bottles. I release my hold on the ones I'm carrying, already frustrated by the task and the fact I've been left alone to deal with all this. The bottles skittle and fall, one bouncing on the lino flooring. I screw up my eyes and wait for the bottle to shatter at my feet, but it finds a soft landing on a pile of newspapers. Defeated by the sheer scale of the task, I rinse my hands under the tap, but there's no hot water, my hands turning numb. I sponge my coat with the mildewed dishcloth, wondering where Mum was found: immediately outside the pub, a slumped figure in the doorway, or in the road, cars dodging her body? I don't want to know the answer, but I can't seem to stop torturing myself with the possibilities. I wish I'd asked Will for more details, but I didn't get much chance, he was in such a rush to leave. Too busy even for a cup of tea. Maybe it was the squalor that drove him away, or perhaps the prospect of spending time with me? I shake my hands dry and pick my way out of the kitchen, climbing the stairs.

It's dark up here too, the bulb unresponsive when I try the light on the landing. The doors are closed to Mum's room and the twins' bedroom next door, blocking out any natural light from the front of the house. I wander into my old bedroom, a grainy yellow glow filling the small space as my fingers automatically find the light switch by the door. The peeling wallpaper is the same floral pattern of my youth, darker where my posters once hung. I used to spend hours lying on my bed with my legs up against Beyoncé's, listening to Will playing his music next door. He had a CD player, always turned up to full volume when he was home, heavy stuff like Muse and

The Killers. He also had a double bed and a better view over the back garden than I did. I had my eye on his room for years, but in the end it was me who left home first, Will only last year when Becky fell pregnant and they moved in with her awful mother. I sigh, noticing the curtains have fallen off their hooks above my single divan and no one's bothered to reattach them.

Will's room looks as if he might sleep in it occasionally, the double bed made up with duvet and pillows, whereas the twins' bedroom is completely empty, the huge double-decker bed they built with scaffolding now gone. I leave Mum's room until last, the stink of sweat and urine overpowering as I open the door. I always remember this room in semi-darkness, the smell unpleasant even then, sickly sweet. Mum would either be asleep or laid up for another reason: her back, her legs, her heart. I back out and close the door, crossing the landing to the bathroom, the green carpet musty with damp spores, the walls clammy. My bladder is full, but one glance down the pan and I decide I can wait. I'll need bleach, lots of it, and antibacterial spray, rubber gloves too, a few pairs, and some basic provisions: milk, bread, something for dinner, although the thought of food turns my stomach. I run down the stairs and retrieve the set of keys Will left on the console table, the letter box rattling on its one remaining hinge as I slam the door behind me.

The cold air feels good after the staleness of the house. Next door, the mirror image of ours is boarded up, their grass also in desperate need of a cut. I glance down the alleyway directly opposite, discarded drink cans and cigarette butts littering the length of the passage. It was always used as a cut-through to school, known as 'fag alley', and it looks like the tradition has continued. I cross the road and turn the corner, a red-brick building facing me, a small block of flats by the look of them, and a new roundabout. Everything else is much as I remember it: row upon row of identical houses, although the properties seem better maintained than they were when I lived here, gardens tended, windows replaced, even the odd extension or conservatory tagged on.

The first shop as I turn into the High Street is the green-grocer's, a fixture in the village for several generations. Trays of cauliflowers and apples line the path, covered by flapping parasols where the striped canopy doesn't quite reach, and there's a row of amputated Christmas trees leaning up against the wall, caught in netting as if they were snared wild animals. The smell of Christmas is released as I brush by their oily foliage, my hand trailing the spiky needles. Inside, a man balances a bag of satsumas in the scales as he chats. He looks over and smiles, a flicker of recognition travelling across his face, his mouth open to call out something. I cross quickly, dodging cars, past the chemist and the butcher's, the pizza delivery place and the vet's.

One of my earliest memories is of sitting in my pushchair outside the vet's, Mum pinballing her way between the super-market, the pub, and the off-licence. I was probably about five – old enough to know her language and behaviour were inap-propriate, and far too big to be strapped in a buggy with barking dogs at my eye level – but it suited Mum to leave me with my sensible older brother, his hands clamped tight to the curled handles. Will said my first word was 'bugger', but it could have been a lot worse. Tony and Mick's language was far more colourful than Mum's, and that was saying something. The pub is still there, and the off-licence. It's unnerving, the lack of change, as if the ten years I've spent in London haven't made any difference, everything waiting for my return.

The road is a lot busier, that's one difference, a steady line of cars as I approach the supermarket. We never had a car, but sometimes Mick or Tony would wait for me outside school in a mate's beat-up ride, front windows wound down, cigarettes between their long fingers. The twins always seemed uninterested in my arrival and there really was no point them picking me up as we only lived around the corner, but I fell for it every time, my heart lifting at the sight of them. Then I'd notice an older girl leaning in to talk, her mates laughing and flirting. I watched the way those girls moved, studied their facial expressions, copied the sound of their high-pitched giggles, and listened to the cries and moans that came from the twins' room late at night, sometimes Mick banished to the sofa, occasionally Tony.

The supermarket I knew, a low-budget discount store, has been replaced by a much bigger one, the scale of it surprising. I head towards the entrance, dodging the queuing cars, past young children piled into the back of four-by-fours, and smaller cars filled with sixth-formers driving themselves. Christmas songs greet me, and a whoosh of warm air infused with the scent of baking bread and something festive, like cinnamon or mulled wine.

The supermarket is packed, mainly mums and small children, plus some older kids from the comp, black blazers undone despite the bitterly cold day, hands crammed with sweets and cans of sugary energy drinks, just as mine once were. I find the toilets behind a dreary coffee shop, then I grab a trolley, the handle still warm from the person who must have abandoned it at the door. I don't need much, just enough to tide me over until the house is sorted, and the funeral is out the way.

I'm debating whether to buy two or three bottles of wine, slowly making my way along the length of the aisle, when I come to an abrupt halt. I look up and see a woman's slender white fingers clamped around the far end of my trolley, and there's a raised foot, clad in a smart knee-high boot, pushing firmly against the left front wheel. Dark eyes stare back at me, unmoving, focused on mine, her mouth set in a tight line, as if a marker pen had drawn it on in one fast stroke.

'Mrs Winter,' I say, my voice childish, the last ten years fallen away. 'What are you doing?'

Karen

Monday, 5th December 2016 (Afternoon)

The cottage is empty. I feel it as soon as I walk in, mine the only heartbeat, and loud in my ears, as though it were audible, the adrenalin still sluicing through my veins despite the slap of cold air when I'd rushed out of the supermarket. I drop my handbag on the kitchen table and walk back into the hall, calling up the stairs, expecting and receiving no reply. The dog would have barked if they were in. In my more paranoid moments, I wonder if my husband anticipates my return and makes his escape before I arrive. Especially today. He didn't reply to my message, no comment on the news it contained, but he must realise it's inevitable Jess will come home for her mother's funeral. What Mark doesn't know is I've already seen her, been as close to her as I dared get. Too close.

I fill the kettle and watch it boil, my coat heavy about me as darkness falls on the garden beyond the steamy window.

Mark will be home at some point, and I need to sort out what I want to share with him. The whole sorry tale? Or as I suspect, an edited version of my encounter with Jess. He will be as disappointed as I am to hear she's back, and already causing trouble, but I can't inflict too much on him. No, I shall keep my account to a minimum; if I tell him at all. He must be feeling so vulnerable, and afraid. He'd be appalled if he knew I contemplated, if only for a split second, grasping a handful of Jess Tidy's wild red hair, my hand outstretched as I walked towards her, the feel of those curls already making my hands twitch into tight fists. I didn't touch her, of course, common sense prevailing, or maybe the tablet I'd taken in the car, or perhaps because she'd then looked up, her trolley halted by my foot, her expression all doe-eyed and innocent, still deploying her trademark frightened-rabbit look, the one she maintained throughout the court hearing. I could have pushed her trolley aside then slapped her hard across the face, felt the reassuring strike of my palm across her freckled cheekbone, but the heat left me and cold shame welled to fill the void, tears suppressed as I realised how awful my actions would appear, and how far-reaching their consequences. A mad middle-aged housewife assaulting a young woman in a supermarket aisle. It was bad enough I'd grabbed her trolley, a foot raised to halt her progress, our eyes locked. *Did I look mad? Angry? Would anyone understand what had driven me to do that?* It was perhaps worse to think they might, a sympathetic bystander making the connection to our shared past. But we were unobserved, our drama playing out silently among the bottles of Chardonnay and Pinot Grigio, everyone else too

34

preoccupied with their own lives to worry about the collision of ours.

I root around in my bag for my pills, little patience for the search, grabbing the packet and pushing two into my palm through the foil. I shouldn't, not quite so soon after the last one, but the relief as I swallow them is worth it, another mouthful of water straight from the tap to make sure they're in my system, the cold spray wetting my thick woollen sleeve, my cup of tea abandoned before it's made. I wait for the effect, as though it were instant, a shot of sanity in my arm, then I pull my phone from my coat pocket and dial a number I know by heart, a diversion until Mark's return. I daren't save this number as a contact, but there's no need, muscle memory always clicks in as my thumb taps out the familiar pattern on the screen, although this time I notice a slight tremor in my hand as I wait for him to answer. I shan't confess what's happened, not yet, but I might be able to gauge from his tone if he already knows. The garden is shrouded in almost complete blackness now, the view sketched out in shadows and silhouettes. I allow my focus to blur, everything shrinking to the sound of the call, a repeating ring, summoning him to me.

'Kar?'

He's the only one who addresses me by this diminutive, and the relief I feel is immediate. He sounds the same, so he can't know what I've done. Not yet. I contemplate an early confession, the impunity of telling him myself, before I've told anyone, even my husband, but instead I hug the phone to my ear, saying nothing.

'It's difficult to talk now, Kar,' he tells me, his voice dropped to an almost-whisper. 'You OK?'

He sounds concerned, but there's a trace of impatience too. Phone messages are our preferred means of communication.

'I need to tell you something,' I say; deciding again that it's better if he hears it directly from me.

'What is it?' he asks, and I back away from my decision, a bubble of panic rising at the thought I might ruin everything.

'Nothing. I'm fine, just needed to hear your voice.' My words sound too intimate, too needy, but I can't take them back. 'Bad day,' I tell him, knowing he won't press me further.

'Can you get away tomorrow? There's a meeting in the hall about the new development. We could both go, show our faces, then disappear?'

'Yes, that would work,' I reply, trying to sound less keen than I am.

'I'll message you later,' he says, and the line goes dead.

I breathe deeply, allowing myself a smile, reflected back to me as I glance up at the kitchen window. We're still OK; for now. But the respite is short-lived, the swell of panic soon returned. He could find out at any moment, hear it from someone in the village who was in the supermarket, or . . . I inhale deeply and take off my coat, hanging it up on one of the hooks in the hall, then I pull the Hoover from the tangle of shoes in the cupboard and haul the heavy cleaner up the stairs and along the landing, past Mum's old room to the smallest bedroom, once Frey's but now grandly referred to as 'The Study'. I reach behind Mark's desk and feel for the spare socket, attacking the balled dog hair with the nozzle, sucking it from the corners where it collects. The rhythmic back and forth motion is good, the satisfying swoosh of fur being pulled up the pipe diverting enough to allow my thoughts to form, as though I were decluttering my mind with each stroke, teasing out my reactions, the white heat of emotion now less intrusive.

Jess had looked different, but she was only sixteen the last time I saw her; flat shoes and no make-up, a childish re-invention for the benefit of the jury. I've watched the last decade transform my own daughter, so I don't suppose it should surprise me that Jess has changed too, but I never saw Frey's innocence in the Tidy girl, not even in court. Nothing to be nurtured or protected, no vulnerability. Only aggression, masked as teenage angst, excused too often. Still, the contrast is undeniable, and more than that, she'd been afraid of me, her voice shaky, her expression filled with shock and surprise. I try to remember Jess Tidy as she was, picturing her as a schoolgirl, in the same class as Frey, only a month in age between them, but it's impossible to separate out the girl and the woman, the two now entwined.

I switch off the cleaner and look across at my husband's desk, the reflected light from his lamp falling across the computer screen which is dark, although there's a faint glow from the switch at the side. He must have been in here before he left with the dog. A spark of hope ignites within me; maybe he's been writing again. I jiggle the mouse and the screen illuminates, inviting me in, but before I sit down I glance out of the tiny mullioned window for signs of Mark's return, torch flickering, Walter at his heel. I want to hear him say he under-stands why I lashed out, that it's *her* fault, not mine, but the garden is as bleak and empty as the fields beyond, a cold draught slipping in through the gaps between the glass.

I sit at Mark's desk and type in his passcode, the same six digits he always uses. It's hardly the first time I've done this, but my heart rate still quickens as I scan through his search history. It began as a barometer of my troubled husband's moods, sporadic hacks into Mark's web-page history, purely for my peace of mind. Was he looking for work, taking up a new hobby, gambling, watching porn? Very occasionally it would make me feel better, moments of insight sparking a transitory hope, but more often than not Mark's online searches spoke to me only of his inability to settle on anything purposeful. Even an inappropriate download would have shown a spike of interest in *something*. I flick through again, clicking on pages he's recently visited, mainly research on Fitzgerald: Zelda, and F. Scott, which is mildly encouraging, although we've been here before; a burst of enthusiasm which burns too brightly to be sustained. *'I'm writing a critical essay,'* he'll say, or, *'I have an idea for a book,'* and then I hear no more.

I'm about to return the computer to its dormant state, mindful of the limited time I have, when I spot a new saved document, concealed under an innocuous-looking heading. I pull the chair closer, the rug rucking up under the wheels as I hover the mouse over a file entitled, 'Research for Book – Dec 2016'. It's probably exactly what it claims to be, a new writing plan which will soon be discarded, self-pity accompanying Mark's reply when I enquire how it's going, but maybe this project will be more established, something to distract him from the shock of Jess Tidy's return? I click on the file, drumming my nails on the wooden desk as I wait. The ancient system is in dire need of an upgrade – a source of constant irritation to my husband as there's no way we can afford a new computer – but I find the anticipation lifts my mood. I can't wait to see what he's planning.

When we first met, Mark fresh out of university and filled with ambition to be a teacher and a writer, he would share all his projects with me, my opinion sought and gladly given. I've never been an academic like my husband, but the weight he gave my judgement cemented our bond. I loved how he would take notes as I spoke, annotating his manuscripts and nodding when I was critical; never taking offence, although I was careful to give none. When one of his colleague's wives told me she couldn't say anything to her husband, for she knew her opinion would never be right, I'd sympathised whilst privately basking in the knowledge Mark and I were special, two sides of the same coin. The truth was I loved his cerebral side, the passion with which he spoke of language and teaching. I'd left school at eighteen, my plans for university put on hold when Mark and I fell in love and were married within a year. I immediately fell pregnant, much to Mum's disgust, but she was wrong in her assumption that Mark preferred me *barefoot and in the kitchen*. He encouraged me to read widely, and we talked about literature in a way I'd have been self-conscious of with anyone else, using words I'd previously needed a dictionary to understand but which began to feel natural on my tongue, and appropriate, as though I'd earned the right to use them. If he's finally settled to a topic for his book, it can only be a good thing.

I imagine us by the fire in the sitting room – Mark reading excerpts to me, a needle-sharp pencil in his hand, his face full of pride – and a tiny dance of excitement begins to beat beneath my heart. I stand to glance again out of the study window, closing the curtains before I sit down to read what my husband has written so far, my eyes eager to slide down the first page, hungry for something constructive to counter today's events, a project that could be cathartic for us both. I need this thread to grasp at, a flicker of hope to soften the blow of Jess's return.

Chapter One – March 2006

She was special, her admiration a light flicked on inside me. It was addictive, heady, irresistible. She was also difficult, challenging, frustrating. We were both to become victims of that contradiction, a volatile mix of vulnerability and confidence. She was a car crash and I stood, willingly, in her path, blissfully unaware of the disaster that sped towards me . . . but I am getting ahead of myself. Let me start with how I first met Jess Tidy.

The Exclusion Unit was an uninspiring place for that initial encounter, and not somewhere I'd often had cause to visit. Located at the end of a long, windowless corridor, a forgotten draughty room, it was furnished with low, tacky-topped tables; a malignant acceptance permeating its stuffy atmosphere of rejection, the view on to the playing fields offering a tantalising glimpse of freedom and fresh air. It smelt of stewed coffee and sweaty feet. Home to the disenfranchised and disruptive, a less auspicious location is hard to imagine.

Jess was seated alone at the far table, her back to me, her distinctive red hair pulled into a tight ponytail, exposing enormous gold hoops in her ears. I was hesitant as I approached, studying the back of her head, her shoulders, the mass of curly red hair, the hoops in her ears a defiant statement, a badge of honour indicating her status as a troublemaker. Should I insist she remove the jewellery, or let it go? She was on her final warning, only allowed into school for a few hours a week to study for her exams, but I needed to be careful. She was a Tidy, and it was prudent not to get on the wrong side of that family. Besides, battles should always be chosen wisely, minor infractions best ignored.

The headmistress had warned me to 'play it carefully', but only after she sold me the idea of acting as Jess's mentor. It would be a 'step up' in my personal development, she advised. Perhaps a stepping stone to promotion. On reflection, I can see she played to my many insecurities. I hadn't risen through the ranks as she had, my ambition contained firmly within the classroom. I'd resisted the few opportunities that came my way, reluctant to be promoted out of the teaching role I loved, or at least, had once loved, but I'd also stagnated, and she recognised the opportunity that presented. She held Jess up before me as a way out of that rut, a glint of light in a sea of mediocrity. 'I think you can really help her, Mark.'

In fairness, I knew the score. You couldn't walk the corridors, or pass the time of day with a colleague without hearing the latest gossip about Jess Tidy. The notorious incident which precipitated the need for a mentor had occurred the previous week, and was still a source of much talk around the school; Jess's threatened expulsion rescinded purely because her brothers arrived mob-handed and intimidated the headmistress. There was a level of fear surrounding the Tidy family which I felt keenly as I walked towards Jess for our first meeting.

She swivelled round in her chair to glance at me over a hunched shoulder, her expression one of deliberate indifference. I was struck by how tiny she was: the small, heart-shaped face, the features refined, gentle. Although some of the 'bad girl' tropes were there: her jaw muscles working hard on a piece of gum, her skirt hitched up to expose most of her bare thighs, a denim jacket over her school shirt, her tie at half-mast, in a huge knot. But there was an innocence to her that twitched at my heart, making it difficult to equate the girl before me with the vicious allegation she'd recently made against a colleague, Barry Johnson. She'd immediately retracted her claim, but the damage was done. For Jess, at least.

I took a deep breath and walked towards her, waiting for her to stand, school protocol when a teacher approached, but Jess remained defiantly seated, her eyes flicking up and over me, then she looked down at her phone, tucked into her palm under the table, her thumb tapping out something on the screen which I assumed was a message, but on closer inspection turned out to be a childish game.

'You need to put that away,' I said, taking the seat beside her. 'And next time, stand up when I arrive, OK?'

Jess got up from her seat slowly, a smile playing on her lips, as she said, 'Sorry, sir. Forgot.'

I wondered, even in those first moments together, whether Jess recognised my neediness; this arrangement as important to me as it was necessary for her.

'I know who you are,' she said. 'You teach English in lower school. You're Mark Winter.'

'Mr Winter, and please sit down.' Which she did, still smiling. 'And yes, you're right, I do teach lower school. Our paths haven't crossed before, which I imagine is why I was asked to be your mentor.'

I smiled back, already seeking that bond. 'Totally clean slate as far as I'm concerned, Jess. What do you think?'

'So, you're telling me you ain't heard nothing about me or my family?' she asked, holding eye contact.

'Well, of course, I know of . . .' I trailed off, no need to finish the thought. 'That's immaterial, Jess. And there's no such word as "ain't".'

'Try telling my mum that,' she said, picking at the red varnish on her stubby thumbnail.

'I'm here to help you,' I told her, trying to re-establish eye contact. 'It's an important time with your exams coming up.'

Jess frowned, the dark flicks at the corners of her lashes disappearing as her expression narrowed. 'You think you can help me? Make me your pet project?' she asked, the challenge delivered with little vigour, as though it was all too much effort, but her eyes flashed with anger. 'So, you can go to the headmistress and tell her what a good thing you've done, keeping Jess Tidy out of trouble, and look, she scraped a pass in some of her exams, what a fucking miracle! They don't want me here, and I don't want a babysitter.'

'You know, Jess, you and I can fight this, but it is what it is.' I leant back in my chair and stretched out my legs beneath the table, folding my arms. 'I'm not here to judge you on what's happened in the past. My job is to get you through the next few weeks and out the other side, hopefully with some qualifications. Do you have any idea what you might like to do when you leave school?'

She looked straight at me then, surprise opening her features, as if the thought had never occurred to her. It was clearly a revelation that life could offer her other options, that there might be choices to be made beyond a preordained pattern of soulless jobs, or collecting *benefit payments as she pushed out one unwanted child after another. 'How do you mean?' she asked.*

'Career choices, or higher education, an apprenticeship? Your grades aren't too bad, Jess. I think with my help we can still improve on them.'

She softened a little then, asked me tentatively what I meant, was there really a chance she could go to college? Her innocence was so touching, stirring something protective in me, the bonds already forming. Like the tentacles of a fern unfurling after a harsh winter, I could feel something opening up deep inside, something that had been closed off for too long.

I push myself back from the desk, as if the physical distance will make any difference to how I feel. The tiny dance of excitement has turned to a thunderous stamp, squashing the life from my bruised heart. I read everything again, over and over, until I see things that maybe aren't there, hidden meanings, lines that puncture me as they replay in my thoughts. *'She was special, her admiration a light flicked on inside me.' 'It was addictive, heady, irresistible.'* There's no doubt of my husband's admiration for Jess Tidy, even on the first meeting.

I've always thought we felt the same way about *that girl*: a troublemaker with few redeeming qualities, a loser who threw all Mark's efforts back in his face, leaving no good deed unpunished. I search for reasons, justifications for Mark's tone, but although they come, the sickening feeling remains. I take deep breaths, holding on to the hope that I'm wrong. I trusted him implicitly, never doubted his account of that time. If I ever felt even a trace of resentment I dismissed it at once, for his sake, and mine, and of course Frey's; years of absorbing so much emotion, the pills an ineffective antidote. He told me Jess was predatory, that he never encouraged her, never saw her as anything more than another one of his students. He said he tried his best, but she was a lost cause. He said so much, or did I only hear what I wanted to, what I could cope with?

A sound downstairs jolts me back to reality. I reach for the mouse, closing the document and every other open page, my hands shaking as I rush to cover my tracks. Then I stand, a little woozy, but I ignore that, willing myself back to normality. I switch on the vacuum cleaner, Mark's account whirling around my head, disturbing the dormant past as I push the cleaner back and forth across the rug, smoothing down the wrinkles before I switch it off.

'Karen, you upstairs? Walter, stay there! Good boy.'

Mark runs up behind his words, taking the stairs two at a time, tapping me on the shoulder as I walk towards our bedroom. 'Karen?'

I turn back, waiting for my husband to ask me how I am, to return me to that state of trust I'd taken for granted, my reply unformed until I say, 'Jess is back. I've seen her.'

'Where?' His face is pale, although his eyes are bright, searching for clues. I can't trust myself to respond, simply shaking my head. 'Sorry, that's not important,' he says.

'It was in the supermarket, if you must know.' I push past him, dragging the Hoover towards the stairs, then I abandon it at the top, running down, the dog prostrate across the hall floor, exhausted. He doesn't even bother to get up as I step over him to go into the kitchen.

I flick on the kettle to boil it again and when I look over my shoulder Mark is standing in the doorway. He still looks like the same man he was this morning, but he isn't, not to me.

'Must have been upsetting for you,' he says. 'Did she see you too?'

'Yes, she said my name, called me Mrs Winter. I walked out, left my shopping behind.'

He moves towards me, wrapping an arm around my waist, and although I stiffen, resisting his embrace, he persists, his hand in the well of my back, his shirt fresh and cold from outside as he closes the gap between us. It's so rare these days for us to be affectionate. Perhaps I've overreacted, read things into his account that simply weren't there. He's a man of words, he's bound to enhance, paraphrase, embellish. *Isn't he*?

'Why did she have to come back after all these years?' I ask, wiping my nose as he gently releases me, his eyes searching mine. 'I thought it was over, that we could finally relax.' I turn away, fussing with the kettle and teapot, my movements clumsy.

'Her mother—'

'I know about her mother!' I spin round to face him.

The teapot slips from my grasp and smashes on the tiled floor. Mark says nothing, watching as I crouch down to collect up the pieces. Then he mutters something about how he has work to do, and I hear him climbing the stairs to his study, the dog following behind.

I imagine running after them, telling Mark what I've read,

how his words have hurt me, shaken my unshakeable belief, but I can't seem to move, staring instead at the shards of brown earthenware in my hands, closing my fingers around them until they press in.

Five Months Before . . .

Supervision Session #3 – Jessica Tidy – Tuesday, July 19th, 2016

Full notes in client file ref: 718/16

Meeting taped, transcript of relevant section below (abridged)

Me: I'm interested to hear a little more about your background today, Jess. We've only touched on it briefly so far. Your mother is an alcoholic, you said?

Jess: For as long as I can remember.

Me: Must have been tough for you, growing up.

Jess: Not a lot of fun.

Me: And you have three older half-brothers?

Jess: Yeah, that's right. The twins were in prison last time I heard. Aggravated burglary, I think, but it's always something. Mum was fifteen when she had them, and their dad was never on the scene. Not that it's an excuse to rob little old ladies. Will's dad was gone before I was born. He was supposed to be quite a nice guy, but Mum met my dad and got pregnant. I guess not many men would stick around after that. I don't remember my dad at all. He was a lorry driver, used to come and go a lot Will said. There was a step-father too. Unfortunately.

Me: *Unfortunately?*

Jess: I was getting older, more interesting to him if you get my meaning?

Me: You were abused?

Jess: I could handle myself.

Me: How would you describe your current relationship with your mother?

Jess: Virtually non-existent, except for a monthly phone call.

Me: Any contact with other family members?

Jess: Will's visited me in London a couple of times, but not for ages. He sends the odd card, birthdays, Christmas, that's it. It's my fault, I made it clear I needed a fresh start.

Me: Why was that?

Jess: Don't know, guess I wanted to move on, but we were close when I was living at home. He was the only one who looked out for me.

Me: No adult you trusted enough to confide in?

Jess: Not really. I was always in trouble at school. There was this one teacher, Johnson. He really hated me and my best friend, Becky, but he was especially mean to me, calling me names. Stupid stuff, but hurtful.

Me: That sounds terrible. Did you report him?

Jess: I suppose I should have, but I don't think anyone would

49

have believed me. Becky made me say he'd interfered with me, to get him in trouble.

Me: Had he?

Jess: God, no! I don't think I was his type. I admitted it wasn't true, but the headmistress said she had 'no choice but to expel me'. The twins went to see her, threatened all sorts and I was allowed to stay, but only until my exams, and only if I had a mentor. That's how I met Mark Winter.

Me: And did you trust this mentor, Mark Winter?

Jess: At first I did.

Karen

Tuesday, 6th December 2016 (Morning)

I type in Mark's passcode for the second time in as many days, my head inclined to listen for his return as I wait for the computer to catch up. The creaks of the cottage's old timbers almost trick me into a pre-emptive click on the mouse, but when I look out at the foggy view through the study window there's no sign of either my husband or the dog. I'm quite alone.

Mark was up here for hours last night. His attempts to comfort me after I'd told him about the incident with Jess in the supermarket, or at least, a truncated version of it, soon abandoned in favour of getting a bit more *'work'* done . That's a joke. He hasn't done a day's work since he was suspended from teaching, preferring to live off my inheritance and the few benefits we're entitled to, our outgoings pared back to the bone. Mum's cottage may be falling down around us, all non-essential repairs neglected, but without it I don't see how we'd

51

have survived financially. I pause again, the document now open in front of me, but I'm ambivalent about the idea of reading Mark's book; another betrayal to add to the list. It feels like the only way to find out the truth, *his truth*, uncensored this time, but it also feels wrong. I'd been so decided last night, him up here, me downstairs imagining him typing up his account of that terrible time, but now, as my opportunity to read ebbs away, I'm less certain. There's no denying there's still an unease within me, my breath held, my thoughts and opinions whirring, but there's also the realisation I'm at the point beyond which I won't be able to turn back.

Before I can change my mind, I start to read the new pages, remaining alert for the sound of the back gate opening, signalling my husband's return.

Chapter Two – March 2006

The second time I met Jess, she seemed pleased to see me, her scowl replaced with a bright smile as she spotted me approaching from across the room. I'd intended to begin work proper that day, a sheaf of plans in my notebook – revision timetables, past papers, cheat-sheets – but Jess had something different in mind, that was clear from the off. I found her over-solicitousness more difficult than the truculence of our first meeting. She was blatantly flirty, her skirt hitched even higher, her lips formed in a mock-pout as I admonished her for not completing the assignments I'd set. She smelt of cheap perfume, but somehow the scent was as pleasurable as it was cloying. I leant away from her, reorganised my books, then stood behind my chair as I tried to instil some balance in our relationship, seeking out the higher status which should have been mine automatically. I was forced to distance myself, both physically and mentally, because it would have been all too easy to forget she was a student.

Jess was a beautiful girl, strikingly so, her hair a mass of soft curls, untethered that day, which made her look older, her eyes dark and yet filled with light, her lips soft. But I knew better than to befriend, or in any way reciprocate her adoration. I'd been targeted in that way before. It was forbidden territory, a disastrous course of action, everyone knew that. I was always scrupulous in my handling of such situations. Still, crushes developed, egos were flattered, it was part of the hormonal soup we all swam in. I was relatively young, thirty-nine at the time, and the students liked me, particularly the older girls, who loved to flirt, but Jess was unashamed, touching me on my hand, my arm, and then shockingly as I sat back down I felt the graze of her leg against mine beneath the table. I pulled away, but she pressed in again, only the thinning wool of my suit trouser preventing skin-on-skin contact. I glanced at the only other member of staff in the room, the head of the Exclusion Unit, thankfully preoccupied with a disruptive student, but still . . . I had to spell out to Jess that her behaviour was totally inappropriate. I paused, to make sure I wasn't confused and about to make things unnecessarily awkward between us, but there was no mistaking her intent, her actions designed to provoke. Which they had. She grinned at me and raised an eyebrow.

'I'm your teacher, Jess,' I stated. 'You need to remember that, or we can't carry on working together.' Then I pulled my chair back in an exaggerated move, designed to emphasise my words.

Her demeanour changed in an instant, from coquettishness to vulnerability, the hurt in her eyes too painful to witness, although I could not turn away.

'You're sick of me already?' she asked.

It struck me then how she was such a strange mix of fragility and confidence, already exhibiting far too many unhelpful behaviours at the tender age of sixteen. It was incumbent upon me, not only as her teacher, but also as an adult with morals and a sense of responsibility, to be mindful of that vulnerability, and to tread carefully with her feelings, all nestling so close to the surface, conflicting and raw.

'Of course I'm not sick of you,' I replied. 'You and I are in this together, Jess. But I'm your teacher, you need to remember that, and behave appropriately. Whatever you may think of me, wherever you might imagine this leading, it can't. Not even as a silly game, OK?'

She blushed, the only time I ever recall her doing so, and I was tempted to soften the impact, to spare her feelings, but knew I couldn't for fear it would humiliate her further, or worse, be misconstrued as encouragement. It would have been easy to misjudge her, to forget she was sixteen, and as such entirely impressionable, because she tried so hard to act beyond her years, to outgrow them and move on. She wasn't going home to stability and warmth. Her hard edges shielded her, a buffer of protection. She needed them.

It's difficult to imagine anyone more different from my doll-like daughter, the same age as Jess, but whose innocence was still preserved. Jess was already a sexual being at sixteen, possibly before. It was her currency and she derived power from it, whilst having little concept of its true potency, or how much damage it could inflict.

She was clearly trying, even on that second meeting, to reel me in, and to further emphasise that thought she leant across and told me she was no longer a virgin. Appalled, I drew back, both physically and in my comments. Admonishing her for her lack of boundaries, restating my role as her mentor, nothing more. She must speak to me as a teacher, with respect. Although, I admit there was a part of me that saw her admission as a breakthrough, and privately congratulated myself, puffed up by the recognition of the trust I'd built with her, so soon, so easily, as if—

'Karen? You upstairs?' Mark's voice cuts across his own words, startling me.

'Up here,' I call out, jumping up from his chair, my voice shriller than I'd hoped. I grab the mouse, close the document and pick up the duster I brought with me, wiping over the screen with an unsteady hand.

'Karen?'

I walk out on to the landing and lean over the bannister, glancing the yellow cloth across the peeling varnish. Mark's beneath me in the hallway, holding back a bedraggled Walter. 'Oh, there you are,' Mark says, frowning. 'What were you doing?'

'Just pottering,' I say, running down the steep stairs towards them, shaking out the duster as I go. 'Good walk?' I pause on the bottom stair, hoping any quaver in my voice can be attributed to my fast descent. 'You were up and out early.'

'Yeah, it's another foggy one, almost lost Walter at one point.' He looks at the dog, a heavy mass leaning against his leg, Mark's grip tight on his collar. 'You know what he's like with a tennis ball.' Mark smiles, although he seems agitated. 'Wouldn't give up on it,' he says, holding up the muddied ball.

'Eventually found him right at the back of a big pile of bram-bles.' He rubs the dog's domed head, the scent of wet fur wafting towards me as Walter eyes the ball. 'You got any plans for today?'

I look at my husband, imagining him seated beside Jess, her thighs on show, pressing her leg against his beneath the table as she shared the intimate details of her life. He'd told her off, said it was wrong, laid down clear boundaries, but he clearly enjoyed the attention of a precocious and attrac-tive sixteen-year-old. He was flattered, still a young man, thought her beautiful, sexual. I shake my head, as if in answer to his question, but I'm also trying to rid myself of the image of them together, touching, a shudder passing through me.

'You feeling OK?' he asks as he runs up the stairs, his atten-tion now on his open study door, within his gaze as he climbs. Walter's right behind him, the dog's wet nose almost touching the back of Mark's knees.

There are so many potential replies to his question, but I content myself with a quick, 'I'm fine,' as I look up. 'You?'

'Yeah, good. Might do some more writing.' He's directing his comments more to the dog than me, the pair of them paused halfway up, side by side now. 'Unless there's anything you need me to do first?'

'No, I don't think so.' I allow him to move up another two or three stairs before I halt him again. 'So, what is it you're writing . . . *exactly*?'

He looks over his shoulder. They're almost at the top now, the length of the steep drop between us. 'I'm not sure yet.'

'See where the muse takes you?' I hold his gaze as I shake out the duster.

'Something like that.'

I steady myself, gripping the silvery wood of the newel post, the varnish almost rubbed clean by many years of hands reaching out. 'Will I get to read it?'

'Maybe,' he replies, then he shrugs and turns away to take the final two stairs as one, his study door closing a moment later.

I walk through to the kitchen and toss the duster in the washing machine, staring at the floor for far too long. I should be used to the distance between us by now. Some days we barely connect, the business of a life shared all we find to talk about, but this hurts. I force away the shock and pain, pretending there's nothing new in what he's written, nothing I didn't already know. Jess Tidy was a tart, and he told her so. *'End of'*, as Frey would say. Ridiculous of me to care so much. It's Mark's way of recovering the truth, and he's said nothing incriminating, not really. But I know in my gut that's not true.

I go back into the hallway, to the tangle of coats hanging on the hooks by the back door, reaching inside the pocket of mine to retrieve my phone. Our elaborate plans are already in place, but I need to be in *his* world again, not Mark's, just for a moment. It's my escape. Subterfuge and sex. Not love. *Not this.* Thank God, *not this.* I send the message, then tiptoe up two stairs, then three more, reaching the midway point where I can peer between the spindles of the bannister at the closed study door, an impenetrable barrier. I wonder what Mark's writing now, what new horrors await me. I should stop reading, but I know I won't; even the sense of dread that builds inside me won't keep me away. I walk back down, my phone alive in my hand, his reply filling my screen. I have a whole day to get through first, but my reward waits, and there's always the tablets, they sometimes help. I turn on the taps in the kitchen and fill the room with steam, blotting out the grey view.

Jess

Tuesday, 6th December 2016 (Afternoon)

Pen poised over my To-Do list, I wonder again why I've been given so much unwanted responsibility. There's too much trusted to me, things I don't really understand, like finances, or lack of them, and I'm tired, exhausted in fact. It was impossible to sleep in my old room, the single bed uncomfortable, the curtains falling down. I tried my best to reattach the hooks to the inadequate fixings, standing on the bed and fighting the cobwebs and clouds of dust in the middle of the night, but it wasn't just the curtains that were bothering me. I hate being in the house alone, and I hate the countryside: the fog and the mud and the peace and quiet. I miss London, the sirens, the bars, the possibilities. I miss my tiny flat, and my sofa bed. I pick up the phone and call Will, but he sounds preoccupied, the noise of his van making conversation difficult.

'The insurance company need to know the cause of death,'

I tell him. 'Although there's probably nothing to pay out. She wasn't covered for pre-existing conditions. The salesman must have seen her coming.'

'Surprised she even had insurance, she barely had enough money to pay the rent,' Will replies, then the line breaks up.

'Car-dio-myo-pathy?' I repeat back. 'Is that what you said? Can you spell it?'

'No idea how you spell it, but it means her heart was weak, from the drink,' he says, his words half lost to the grind of the rusting engine and the loose contents of the van. 'The doctor said she'd had it for years, so that tallies with the insurance company refusing to pay.'

'Which doctor was that?'

'The one who signed the death certificate. He was in the pub with Mum before she died, which was lucky. Saved a lot of hassle. I left the certificate on the console table for you, with the keys.'

'Why wasn't I told before?' I ask, wandering into the hall to look for the certificate, Mum's name jumping out from the official document as I pick it up.

'Told what before?'

'That she had a heart complaint. I should have known.'

'You weren't here to tell, were you? You even changed your number. Anyway, you knew what she was like. She hardly looked after herself, did she?'

'No, but her heart . . . I didn't know. You could have written to me.'

'Not the kind of thing you put in a card,' he replies.

I sit back down at the table in the corner of the front room, the death certificate laid out before me. 'She used to complain about her heart, but I thought—'

'Is there anything else, Jess? I'm sorry to rush you, but I've got so much to do today.'

'Me too, Will,' I tell him, tempted to hang up. 'Me too!'

'Yeah, sorry. I'm having one of those days.'

'I thought we'd do this stuff together, Will. Not me on my own.'

'I'll try to get over later, but I can't promise . . . Oh, actually, I've got a thing tonight, maybe tomorrow?'

I was going to tell him what had happened with Karen at the supermarket yesterday, but instead I decide to punish him by withholding the information, hanging up as he says goodbye.

Sitting on the edge of Mum's bed, the lamp switched on, I turn the volume down on my phone and prop it up against the yellowing pillow. The music keeping me on hold is something classical, probably supposed to be relaxing, but it's not working. I open the top drawer of Mum's bedside cabinet and peer in, tipping everything – mainly condoms and packs of tissues, but also, disturbingly, a vibrator – on to the stripped and stained mattress.

'Hello? Mrs Tidy?'

I make a grab for my phone, holding it in front of me to speak, afraid to switch off the speaker in case I accidentally cut them off and have to start over. 'Hi, yes, like I said to the last two people I spoke to, I'm *Miss* Tidy, ringing about my mum's house. She just died, and I need to notify someone about the tenancy.'

'Please hold,' the woman's voice at the other end tells me. 'I'll try to transfer you.'

'I'm grieving, for fuck's sake!' I shout back.

'Sorry?'

'No, nothing,' I reply, sighing as the music returns.

Classic turns to pop as I throw the contents of the bottom drawer into a nearby carrier bag, then I clear the cluttered surface of the bedside cabinet with a satisfying sweep of my forearm, scooping everything into the same plastic bag. A lipstick escapes and rolls under the bed, the gold barrel disappearing into the dust bunnies. I crouch down to retrieve it, noticing something shiny has fallen behind the bedside drawers. Grimacing, I push my hand into the small gap to recover the tarnished silver frame, turning it over to study the photo inside. The glass is covered in what appear to be fingerprints, but when I look again I can see they are actually lipstick kisses, one on top of another, greasy imprints of my mother's spidery lips, almost concealing the grinning faces of the twins. Tony and Mick must be about fifteen, much too old to be splashing about in a paddling pool wearing matching red bathing trunks. Will is beside them, chubbier back then, his ten-year-old face bright red, as it always is in the heat. I rub the edge of my sleeve over the smeared glass, and spot Mum's skinny legs behind the paddling pool, tanned and bare, the tops of her denim shorts just visible. There's another pair of legs beside her, overalls, a man's boots, lace-up. I drop the photo, missing the edge of the cabinet so it lands face-down on the carpeted floor.

'Hello? Mrs Tidy?'

I grab the phone, pressing my socked foot hard down on to the back of the frame, a satisfying crunch beneath my grinding toes. '*Miss* Tidy, and as I said to the last *three* people I've spoken to, I'm ringing about my mum's house, she just died, and I need to notify someone, anyone, regarding the tenancy.'

'I'm so sorry to hear that,' says a softly spoken man at the other end, and I burst into tears.

Two more conversations and I finally have the contact details of Mum's landlord. He sounds pleasant enough, his voice croaky, an elderly gentleman, I think. I try to warn him about the state of the place, but I don't think he takes it in, or maybe he doesn't hear me properly; he says 'pardon me' a lot.

As soon as I end the call my phone lights up again, a woman's voice informing me she's from the undertakers, ringing to finalise arrangements. She gives me a lot of information very quickly, and I realise it's the *way* she says things, rather than *what* she's saying that draws my attention. My foot continues to grind the frame into the carpet as I listen, something very familiar about her voice, although I can't place the accent. I concentrate, certain I know her.

'The thing is, there's quite a big bill coming, and Will said you'd be able to contribute, with your new job and—'

The mention of Will's name recalls me to the content of the conversation. 'I'm sorry? Will said *what?*'

'He's suggested half,' she drops her voice to barely a whisper, 'but more would be great if you can manage it.' The affected enunciation is slipping, a 'telephone voice' as Mum would have called it.

'Becky, is that you?'

There's a long pause, but I know it's her. She was my best friend for years, we used to talk on the phone for hours, our cheap handsets hidden under the bedclothes, a hotline from her house to mine at all hours, running up bills that were probably never paid. We were so close, but that bond was severed over ten years ago – the night of the prom – and we haven't spoken since.

'Yes, hi,' she replies, the certainty in her voice replaced by hesitance. 'How are you, Jess? Been a long time.'

'I'm fine, Becky. You?'

'Yeah, good, thanks. Must arrange for you to meet Jackson, your nephew.'

'Yeah, I'd like that.' I wait for her to say something. When she doesn't, I start to speak, but so does she.

'Sorry, you go ahead,' she says.

'I was just saying there's no way I can afford to—'

'I'm sorry, Jess, I have to go. We'll talk soon, arrange a meeting.'

After Becky's gone I wonder if she'd meant a meeting about the funeral, or to introduce me to Jackson as she also suggested. I do want to meet my nephew, but the prospect of seeing the best friend who deserted me when I needed her most is unappealing. I look at the broken photo frame, the glass driven into the filthy carpet, then across to the wardrobe I still have to clear, Mum's clothes tumbling out. I should throw away the acid-wash jeans and tight tops, bagging anything decent up for a charity shop – there's one in the High Street, I think – but instead I close the door on the mess and go back downstairs.

Outside, school kids wander past the house as I watch from

the front room. One is lighting a cigarette in the alley opposite, another kicking a water bottle ahead of him. There's a pinkish sky, the light starting to fade, cars muddied as they drive to the end of our road and turn left to the village, their lights bouncing around the shadowy room. I close the curtains and turn on the light, but the room still feels empty and cold.

On an impulse, I call my supervisor. She answers straight away, but I don't know what to say, every potential opening sounding wrong.

'How are you coping, Jess?' she asks, apparently unfazed by my silence. 'It must be hard for you. I know you had little contact with your mother in recent years. I'm guessing there are a lot of conflicting emotions for you, being back home after so long, and in such difficult circumstances. Would you like to talk?'

'This was never a home.' I walk through to the kitchen where I pick at a solidified stain on the worktop.

I set the phone to speaker and prop it up against the cold metal of the kettle, opening the fridge to pour myself a glass of wine. I didn't have one with lunch, if you can call a Pot Noodle lunch, so I reckon I'm owed one now, especially after the shitty day I've had. I pour quietly, setting the bottle down on the worktop away from my phone.

'This was always going to be a tough time for you, Jess,' she says, 'for so many reasons.'

I'm grateful for my supervisor's presence, her voice filling the kitchen, but her kindness seems to spark something in me that so far I've managed to contain, or maybe it's the wine, it certainly seems to have woken me up.

'I'm alone in this house, and it's filthy,' I rant, pacing up and down the chessboard lino, the lighter squares grey with dirt, the floor tacky under my bare feet. 'I spent yesterday evening cleaning the sodding bathroom, my hand down the toilet for ages, scrubbing at other people's filth, fucking disgusting it was . . . I should be at work, helping people. I do an important job!' I stop talking, worried I've overshared, but she says it must feel good to have at least one room sorted, reassuring me what I'm doing here is equally important. Then she asks why I'm having to deal with it on my own, don't I have a brother nearby, can't he help? I explain that Will has his gardening business. 'He's very busy,' I say, downing my wine, the excuse sounding as pathetic to me as I expect it does to her. 'He says he'll try to see me tomorrow, but . . .'

'What is it, Jess?'

'You remember I told you how I'd pushed him away, even changed my number so he couldn't contact me? I guess he might be pissed off at me for that. But he asked me here, so I thought that . . . oh, I don't know.'

'I imagine you must feel quite abandoned. Left alone to cope with the aftermath of your mother's death. Maybe you could speak to Will, explain how you feel?'

'Of course I feel abandoned.' I pause to look at the phone as if my supervisor were there, looking back, then I start pacing the kitchen again, pouring more wine as I ask, 'Wouldn't you?'

'Yes, I think I would, but maybe your anger isn't only directed at your brother?'

'*Who then?*' I ask, slamming the fridge door.

'There are other ghosts in your past, Jess.'

My attention is caught by my reflection, distorted by the curve of the metallic kettle. I lean in a little closer, gasping and jumping back, almost dropping my glass, my mother's eyes staring at me in the smudged reflection.

'Jess? Are you OK?'

'Yes, sorry, just surprised by how bloody awful I'm looking, and so old.' I set down my wine and pull back the skin at my temples, my mother's wrinkles temporarily gone.

'You're not old,' she assures me, her voice slow and deliberate. 'You're tired and angry and upset, which is unsurprising. Is it likely you'll bump into Mark Winter, whilst you're home? Does he still live locally?'

'I should go,' I tell her, 'I've taken up enough of your time.'

'I have plenty of time if you do?'

I look at the almost empty glass, and tell her no, it's fine, raising it to toast her then picking up the phone to make sure she can't see me, laughing at my paranoia. All my emotions are jumbled up.

'You're grieving, you need to be kind to yourself. Nourishing food, good company, and not too much alcohol. OK?'

'Yeah, sure. I know the drill,' I say, her insight unnerving.

'I know you do. Now take care of yourself. I'll see you on the thirteenth, OK?'

'Oh yeah, I meant to say. I can't make it that day,' I pause to wait for an unexpected spike of tears to pass. 'It's the day of the funeral.'

'How about the day after, the fourteenth, same time? Will

you be home by then? It's important we catch up soon.'

'Yes, I will. I'll see you then.'

I hang up and realise I need to get out of this bloody house. This stinking, fucking house. That's what's doing my head in. Not Mum, not Will, it's this place. It's disgusting. I wipe my eyes and grab my coat and keys, slamming the door behind me, the letter box rattling as I march away.

Four Months Before . . .

Supervision Session #4 – Jessica Tidy – Tuesday, August 2nd, 2016

Full notes in client file ref: 718/16

Meeting taped, transcript of relevant section below (abridged)

Me: You seem agitated today, Jess. Would you agree?

Jess: My mum used to call it 'antsy', and yeah, I suppose I am a bit.

Me: Why is that?

Jess: I've got a new client, my first man, well, not my *first* man. My first male client, I mean.

Me: Is that problematic for you?

Jess: No! Of course not! *God, no!* Just wanted to talk to you about him. He hasn't said outright, but I think his partner is abusing him.

Me: What's given you that impression?

Jess: She sounds very controlling, possessive . . . and there's a child, an unplanned pregnancy as far as he's concerned. I've told him he doesn't have to stay with her just because of the baby.

Me: Why did he come to see you in the first place?

Jess: He's finding life very stressful. He blames his work, says he's ridiculously busy, and with the new baby he's losing sleep. I think there's more to it than he's admitting.

Me: Do you think he or the child are physically at risk?

Jess: No, not that I know of.

Me: Then who he chooses to spend his time with is his business. Concentrate on the presenting issues, the stress and its cause. I know it's difficult, but you must remain impartial. How have you been since our last meeting? I was a bit concerned how we left things. You mentioned a mentor, Mark Winter, and I got the impression—

Jess: I'm fine. It was a long time ago now.

Me: Have you talked to anyone about that time? Any counselling, other than for your training?

Jess: I tried, couple of times, but it never worked out.

Me: Have you thought about trying again?

Jess: Maybe . . . but I like to think I've rebuilt my life.

Me: You have, Jess, and it's important to recognise your achievements, revel in them in fact, but also to acknowledge any work still to be done. Have you considered contacting your brother? Explaining how much you miss him?

Jess: I think it's too late. I pushed him away, like I do everyone.

Me: It may not be, Jess. And you won't know unless you try.

Jess: You really don't understand, so—

Me: Then tell me, Jess. That's what I'm here for.

LYING TO YOU

Jess: I've said, it's fine, no longer an issue. I have my work and my flat, a social life. I'm good. Really good.

Me: It's OK not to be.

Jess

Tuesday, 6th December 2016 (Late Afternoon)

I turn away from the school kids and shoppers on the High
Street, towards the older part of the village, the same route
I often took as a child, except back then there were crops
covering the ground, by autumn taller than me, only an occasional cottage to break up the view. I walk faster now, as if
I'm outrunning someone, or maybe just the setting sun, the
fields I once knew replaced by unfamiliar roads taking me
deeper into new housing developments, along streets named
after flowers, then authors, a blur twisting this way and that.
Some of the homeowners have attached plaques with house
names by their front doors, or placed matching trees in planters
either side of their porch. It reminds me of the elegant bay
trees and topiary you see in the smarter areas of London,
where the expensive houses look like iced cakes. I like city
living, the contrasts in every street, how rich and poor co-exist,
the acceptance that requires. I glance inside the front windows

and see a television lit up, a child in a high chair, another jumping on a sofa. A mother looks out and draws the curtains on me, a baby on her hip.

When the roads and houses run out, I still need to walk, as far away from that stinking house as I can, so I continue across a bare field, mud beneath my trainers, my breaths short, almost painful as my lungs pull in the freezing air. I lean over my knees to catch my breath, the exercise at last helping, my anger less intense, although the pain is still there in my chest, a tightness I try to swallow down. Perhaps it's grief, but it feels physical, like I need to lash out.

As I straighten up I see him, on the horizon, silhouetted against an orange and pink sunset. A retreating figure. Alone, except for the dog circling his boots. He throws a ball and the dog runs, the man turning, a quick profile that startles me; too familiar, even after all this time. He looks straight at me, and the moment freezes. Then I'm running, back the way I came, the pain in my chest forgotten, my legs outrunning my fear, but only just.

When I reach the edge of the field I glance back and see he hasn't moved, his feet planted, no attempt to follow me. Perhaps it's that which changes my mind, or the realisation I came here to find him. Either way, I find I'm walking towards him, still wary, watching him for any movement, but each stride I take bringing him more into focus, defining features, filling in details of the changes since I last saw Mark Winter over ten years ago. I've imagined how this might feel, panic always accompanying the thought of being near him again, but a strange sense of calm urges me on. I stop a few paces away and grasp handfuls of my wind-blown hair to pull it inside the collar of my padded coat, the hood inflating like a wind sock.

'Tell your wife to keep away from me!' A fierce gust almost steals my words. 'Tell her not to talk to me again, or even look at me, or get in my way, or . . .' I look down at the bottoms of my jeans and trainers, caked in mud. 'Just tell her.'

'Karen was as shocked to see you as—'

'Is that what she told you?' I look up. 'She grabbed my trolley, I couldn't move, I was—'

'No, there must have been a misunderstanding, Karen was just shopping. It's our local supermarket and she's, well, she's not been—'

I stare straight at him, his arm reaching out to me, daring him to even *try* to touch me. I'll scream, we both know it.

'I was so sorry to hear about your mother,' he says, restraining the dog who lunges at me, although it looks friendly enough. Mark takes a step closer. 'If there's anything—'

'You keep away from me!' I tell him, backing up. 'Or I'll tell my brothers, OK? Just keep well away, Mark!'

I retreat, half-walking, half-running, the hedges distorting as I wipe the wind from my eyes, faster now, until there are no more hedges, no fields, just houses, and the prospect of home. I don't look back, not even a glance, the street lights coming on as I round the final corner, keys rattling in my shaky grasp, my breaths sharp as I fight the freezing air to sprint down the front path. I shove the key in the lock but it resists, always a knack to it after the door was broken down, and I'm clumsy in the semi-darkness, Mark's face all I can see.

'Come on!' I say as it demands more finesse. *'Come on, for fuck's sake!'* I keep checking behind me, but he's not there. He never was. *'Come on, Jess, stay calm, then it'll be easier.'* I take a deep breath and try again. *'Grrrr! Open up!'* Next-door-but-one step out and call over to ask if I'm OK, do I need any help? I shake my head and they shout, 'Suit yourself!' then slam their door shut. I'm close to tears, but also fighting a strong urge to smack the bottom of the door with my foot. It would go, it's been kicked in before, more than once. I jiggle the key again, offering up a silent prayer as I feel the latch click free.

The hall is dark, and silent except for the sound of my ragged breaths. It feels safe in here, just me and the mess, even the smell is less repulsive. It's Mum, and it's home. I can't believe I was so close to Mark Winter, only a few paces separating us. I could have easily stepped forward and touched him, or him me. I shudder, but I'm not afraid any more. I'm safe now. He looked older, of course, but smaller too, as if he'd shrunk into himself, a pathetic figure. Would I have banged on the cottage door if he hadn't been out with the dog, spoken to the Winters, warned them off? I might have. I made the choice to go back and face him, didn't I?

I straighten up, pulling back my shoulders as I walk through to the kitchen, switching on every light as I go, still shaky, but better. I should eat something, I haven't had anything all day apart from the Pot Noodle. I could throw a pizza in the greasy oven, or heat up the ready meal I bought yesterday, although I'll have to scrub the hell out of the food-spattered microwave first. I open the fridge, pretending I don't know what I'm looking for as I glance at the pizza box, but it's the opened bottle of wine I reach for. The chilled white slips down nicely, glass in hand as I wander from the kitchen to the front room. I close the curtains, then I double-check the lock on the front door, shoving it hard with my shoulder. I pour a second glass to finish the bottle, then I look at my phone, debating the call I'm about to make. I hadn't planned to contact James whilst I was home, but after seeing Karen, then Mark, it feels like I have no choice. His instructions had been explicit, and I imagine they still apply. I scroll through my limited contacts and tap on his name, still saved as 'James Facey (My Policeman)'.

He always answers quickly, or at least he used to, but it's been years. I lean against the counter and listen to the rings, trying to remember exactly when I last called his number. I Googled him last year, panicked that perhaps he'd died, or stopped being a detective, but he was still there, his face in the newspaper for an award he'd received, which made me smile.

I'm sure he had other cases, still does, many victims to look after, but it never felt like that with James. On the rare occasions he couldn't take my call, he would text me instead, asking if it was something urgent. He'd seemed imposing at first, using phrases like *'evidence capture'* and *'allegation management process'*, but he would always explain everything in ways even I could understand, persuading me to hold my nerve *'just a little longer'*, reassuring me I was doing the right thing, and telling me how brave I was. He never promised me anything, he knew the odds were stacked against a conviction – particularly as I'd refused a medical examination, horrified by the thought of being opened up like that by some stranger – but James kept me strong, said there was still a chance. All I had to do was tell the truth, that was my only job.

Afterwards, when Mark was in prison, and I was moving away, James asked if I'd like him to keep in touch. It wasn't for everyone, he said, but some victims found it reassuring. Entirely up to me. His calls were monthly at first, then only when he knew I might be struggling, like on the anniversary of the prom. The last time I saw him was when he turned up at my flat in London to break the news Mark was about to be released. The memory of that day convinces me James doesn't want to talk to me. Of course he doesn't. I'd told him to get lost, leave me alone. Which he did. He must have hoped he'd finally got rid of me, and now here I am, bothering him again after all these years. I imagine him looking at his phone and sighing, wondering what to do for the best. I'm about to hang up, save him the trouble, when I hear him say his name and ask who is calling. There's warmth in his voice when he repeats my name back to me, asks how I am, it's been too long. He didn't recognise the number, he says, but he's so pleased to hear from me.

'Of course, sorry, I changed it . . . doesn't matter. It's good to hear your voice too.' I'm smiling to myself as I take a seat in Mum's smelly old armchair, swinging my legs over the side so my cold feet dangle in mid-air.

'Where are you living these days?' he asks. 'Same place?'

'Yeah, but I'm back at Mum's for a few days.' I pause, wondering how to say it. 'She died,' I tell him. 'Her heart.'

'I'm sorry to hear that,' he says, offering his condolences, but he doesn't make a big thing of it, remarking how it must be difficult for me being back after all these years.

'Yeah, it's a bit weird after so long, but I'm coping.' I swig at my wine.

James was one of the few people who never tried to excuse or ignore the hideousness of my family. He knew what they were like, saw it for himself first-hand, forced several times to face the naked aggression his presence as a police officer provoked, fists batted away, threats ignored or returned in a calm, authoritative manner.

'Now listen, Jess. Mark mustn't approach you, and if he does—'

I interrupt him to explain I've already seen Mark Winter. 'He was walking his dog in the field. We spoke, only briefly, but—'

'OK, stay put, you're at home now, right? At your mum's house?' I detect the sound of a car engine, or at least I think that's what it is until I recognise the buzz of a printer, probably spitting out something important and formal.

'Yes, I'm home, but I'm fine, James. Honestly. I was a bit shaken up to have seen him, but really, I'm OK, there's no need to—'

'Hang on a sec, Jess.' James waits for the background noise to die down, then he asks me to repeat exactly what happened. He offers to send someone round to the Winters' house immediately, his voice louder now, as though he's stopped what he's doing to focus fully on our conversation. 'In fact, I'll go myself.' There's a pause, then he says it will have to be in a couple of hours, he's involved in a 'live case'.

'There's really no panic, I just wanted to check in, let you know I'm back, that's all. It was a shock seeing Mark, but like I said, it was me that went up to him, not the other way round.'

'It doesn't matter, Jess, I still need to—'

'Look, if you have to warn anyone off, then tell his wife to—'

'Karen?'

I explain how I'd bumped into Karen yesterday, quite literally. James listens, then sighs, asks me again to tell him exactly what happened, and this time I have the sense he's taking notes.

'OK, you need to keep away from them, Jess. It won't help matters, and you're putting yourself at risk. I'm going to have a word. Emphasise there's to be no contact of any kind. If they see you coming, they must walk the other way. Mark knows what will happen if not, but I'll remind them both anyway.'

James explains Mark is in breach of his licence, he could go back to prison, which I knew, but it's reassuring to hear it from a detective sergeant, making it more official. One word from me and I can have Mark Winter in custody again, the knowledge of that providing some security for the next few days, as well as the fact James is still only a phone call away.

'Hopefully a warning will do the trick,' he says, then he suggests we meet up, later this evening or tomorrow morning, depending on work, so he can update me.

"Thanks, I really appreciate it, James.'

I end the call feeling so much happier than before.

It only takes a second or two before a new worry creeps in. One I'd put to the back of my mind earlier, although I noticed it at the time, just hadn't registered its significance. Mark should have been intimidated by our meeting – even the simple act of talking to me could have serious consequences for him – but he hadn't seemed at all concerned. I'd been terrified, run away, locked the door with trembling hands, but he wasn't scared, or even nervous. Quite the opposite . . . he'd seemed happy to see me.

Karen

Tuesday, 6th December 2016 (Early Evening)

The kitchen window is dark, the sun now set and still no sign of my husband. He's been gone a long time, much longer than I needed to catch up on my reading.

The changes he made this afternoon were tracked in the document, and therefore easy to spot, annotations and notes in balloons in the margins, red jumping out from black where he'd deleted sections, or thought of a better word to use. It's clearly important to him that the words flow, but I wasn't interested in the improved phraseology he deployed, or the long descriptive passages added in, although his recall of that time is pin-sharp. Instead, I skipped ahead to the latest chapter.

Chapter Three – April 2006

'What do you think I should do after I leave school?' Jess asked me, another of her diversionary tactics, her attention span ridiculously short.

'I don't know, Jess,' I replied, with a sigh. 'Why don't you finish the practice paper, then we can have a chat about it, how's that?'

'I was thinking maybe I could be a nurse, or perhaps a counsellor, helping people,' she suggested, eyes wide as she waited for my reaction, her pencil in her mouth, the end gnawed away.

'I think you'd be really good at any kind of compassionate work,' I replied, drawing the pencil from her lips. 'Now concentrate!'

Jess smiled, looking down, then frowned at the next question. She always found maths the trickiest to master, and without a passing grade she stood no chance of securing a place on any of the courses she would need for those types of job. Realistically, Jess wasn't going to recover years of messing around in just a few short weeks, however much we both hoped it could be done. I imagined her working in a care home, wiping down the old folk, a plastic apron over her short skirts, but I knew that wasn't what she had in mind.

'I'd like to do what you do,' she said, looking up again. 'Not teaching, but maybe mentoring, helping people everyone else has given up on.'

'You know what, Jess, I think you can do anything you set your mind to, you just have to believe in yourself. Now, hand over that paper, and let's see how you're getting on so far.'

Perhaps it was an unkindness to offer her that hope – the maths paper certainly didn't echo my optimism; her answers scant and often wildly wrong – but Jess had begun to rely on me for so much more than academic input. And who was I to squash that spark of ambition?

'Mum says it's a waste of time,' she told me as I worked my way through the marking. 'Told me I should get a job at the supermarket, *stacking shelves, or in the café; minimum wage, which she reckons ain't . . . sorry, isn't so bad.'*

'Jess, you are a beautiful, kind, intelligent, caring girl . . . please don't waste all that.' I slid back the marked paper, now covered in red pen. 'Let's go through these corrections together, shall we?'

I'm filling a pan with water from the kitchen tap when I finally hear Mark come in through the back door, the clatter of the water covering his movements, although I know he'll be in the hall, unwinding his scarf then taking off his coat and unclipping Walter's lead. I busy myself dropping handfuls of chopped vegetables into the pot. Another vat of soup, food for the soul as Mum called it. When I turn to see Mark standing in the doorway, he's smiling, although when I look more closely I sense his unease, his eyes alive with something I can't define, or maybe it's the fuzziness of my maturing eyesight.

'I think I'll head back up,' he says, pointing above his head. 'Worked out what I want to do with it now.'

'With what?'

'I told you, a critical essay, Gatsby, Fitzgerald, blah, blah . . . it's probably rubbish.' He's animated, and verbose, which isn't like him at all.

'You didn't actually tell me what you're working on.'

'Oh, didn't I?' He looks back into the hall for Walter.

'No, you didn't, not before.'

'Well now you know,' he says. 'So, I'll get back to it, if that's OK with you?'

'Why wouldn't it be?' I look at the dog. 'Have you wiped his paws?'

Mark glances down, Walter's head pushed into the gap between him and the door. 'Of course.'

I take the muddied towel Mark's holding out, then I listen as he takes the stairs quickly, Walter at his side, both eager to be away from me it would seem.

'I'm off to my meeting soon,' I call up from the hallway. 'Back in a few hours. Shall I leave you some soup for later?'

Mark pauses, says he's not hungry, his voice coming from above me on the landing. I wait, imagining how he might lean over the bannister to say something, a challenge about the meeting perhaps, my time away often questioned, but then I hear the door to his study click shut.

The minutes spool by slowly, the kitchen clock above the table counting down each painful second until I can leave. I eat in silence, spooning in the soup without enthusiasm, the roll of Mark's chair across the floor above the only sign I'm not alone; an unwanted reminder of what he's doing. I tidy away my bowl, spoon and water glass, carefully washing the blade of the paring knife I was using.

I call up a goodbye as I leave, listening for a response, which does not come. I open my mouth to call louder, then change my mind, slamming the door behind me. I'm at the end of the path when I look back and see Mark at the landing window, watching me. A blink, and he's gone. The pool of torchlight my focus as I join the unlit lane.

The treacherous potholed terrain requires my full attention, the soles of my best knee-high boots slipping on the iced mud. *Shit!* I lose my footing, almost toppling over in the dark, cursing under my breath, a palm to my chest as I inhale deeply to compose myself. It wouldn't be the first time I've fallen in the street; not drunk like Lisa Tidy, but reality spinning away from me just the same as I hurtled towards the busy road. I smile as I recall a hand grabbing mine and pulling me back from the brink, the way he'd held it for a moment longer than he needed to; our first touch.

'*Did you mean to do it?*' Mark asked when I told him what had happened, irritation in his tone as he insisted on driving me to the surgery for a check-up. '*Of course I didn't,*' I said, repeating my assertion once more for the doctor, Mark beside me. '*Do you honestly think I was deliberately trying to throw myself under a car?*'

It was my husband who took my hand and led me away, a prescription I hadn't wanted clutched in my palm, but it was *his* touch I felt, *his* tight grip keeping me safe.

I adjust my pace, more cautious after my stumble, wondering if I should have brought the car, but I prefer to walk, and parking outside the village hall is always a nightmare. It's not far now, and the path will be much easier once I reach the lit section along the main road. No point rushing this last bit and breaking my ankle. I glance up for the moon, hoping it will appear from behind a cloud. A supermoon is predicted for the fourteenth, they were talking about it on the radio, but I'm not sure exactly what that is – certainly more than the thin, watery slice peeking out tonight. The idea of a time when the moon might transform the landscape is somehow comforting, a blueish light rinsing the monochrome landscape clean.

I turn the corner and switch off the torch, street lamps and passing cars taking over. A few minutes and I'll be there, although I've little interest in the meeting, just the bit that comes later, the thought injecting more urgency into my stride as I approach the slope leading up to the village hall.

I open the door to the heat of a packed room, standing room only behind the rows of plastic chairs. The usual suspects are all here, fellow committee members and do-gooders, but there are plenty I don't know so well, the importance of the matter finally drawing out those who had previously left the banner-waving to others. Although I'm a fine one to talk, my attendance is sporadic at best. I used to go to everything, a focus when I had nothing better to do, and was desperate to get away from the gloomy atmosphere at home, but now it's just a convenient excuse. Fortunately, Mark doesn't bother with the protest meetings, never has. He sees the fight against the developers as my domain. He'd hate it here, far too many people, and it suits me better this way. It's hard to come up with a plausible reason to leave the cottage on a dark winter's evening; tennis games and country walks lacking in credibility when the sun sets at four o'clock in the afternoon. I show my face just enough to keep abreast of the current situation, but the increasing sense of urgency as the developers snap up every parcel of land in and around the village has certainly worked to my advantage.

I scan up and down the rows of chairs and spot the back of his head, his distinctive red hair unmistakable. He's seated to the right-hand side of the crowded room, beside a notice-board with the developer's plans pinned to it, a leaflet in his left hand, raised as he tries to find the extra space he needs to sit back. Even from behind he has the power to flip over my stomach, but it's not love. I'm hardly a teenage girl. Although lust is a powerful and vastly underrated emotion, in my opinion. I particularly like his shoulders, broad to Mark's narrow frame, and the way he dresses, always unruly, his shirt trying to escape his trousers. I imagine squeezing in beside him, inhaling the musky scent generated by a day's labour, a heady mix of pheromones and testosterone. Beneath the check shirt his skin is white, sometimes freckled by the sun, but now, in the depths of December, deathly pale, except for the odd cut or graze from a bramble, livid red against the fine hairs on his forearms. He almost took an arm off with a chainsaw a few years back; when I only knew him as Jess's older brother, and long before our affair began. I've traced the scar with my tongue, the saltiness transferred from his skin to mine, swallowed down. *'I need you intact, Will Tidy,'* I warned him. *'Don't lop anything else off, will you?'*

He stands to allow someone through, and that's when I notice Becky is sitting beside him, their child balanced on her ample lap. I pause, my right hand curled into a fist, so tight my short nails dig in. I walk to the front of the room, pretending to search for a vacant chair, doubling-back and sneaking another quick glance in their direction. Becky is chatting with someone seated behind her, but the child looks straight at me, smiling. It strikes me how his face is a tiny replica of his daddy's, the same nose and mouth, and of course the trademark Tidy family red hair. We didn't discuss how he felt about the baby, Becky's pregnancy clearly a shock, but it was obvious he wanted it. I'd felt an odd sense of relief. A difficult decision I feared was coming, taken away from me. Not that he's ever offered me anything more than a purely sexual affair, and I've never dreamt of demanding it, but we'd grown closer over that first year together. It surprised me how much it hurt when he began distancing himself from me, his intention clearly to be a better partner to his pregnant girlfriend. He even agreed to move in with Becky and her terrible mother. For a while I was afraid I'd lose him and the escape our times together bring, but he doesn't love her, just the child, and so I soon got him back.

I look away from Jackson's grin, tempted to return it, and instead pick up a leaflet from the trestle table beside me. When I look up Will is staring straight at me, one sandy brow slightly raised then lowered. I smother my smile, relishing the connection we've established.

Will is fifteen years my junior, but when I'm with him, he's so in charge I often feel like I'm the immature one. In my more romantic moments, I think of us as star-crossed lovers, drawn to one another despite our families' feud, like the protagonists in one of Mark's dramatic texts. I'm not sure what conclusion there will be for our affair, but I do know I'd prefer there weren't one, rather a continuation of how we are. Perhaps that's unrealistic. Nothing remains the same, and I'm aware the illicit nature of our encounters makes them even more appealing, but the years we've maintained our liaisons have so far increased, not diminished, the clandestine thrill of it all. It may be wrong of me, both of us, but there's no denying how delicious it is to be with the one person you know you shouldn't, for oh so many reasons, and although the fear of losing him has returned along with his sister, her reappearance in our lives placing so much in jeopardy, the tiny ember that glows inside me burns on; sometimes the only part of me that feels alive.

I move nearer to where he's sitting, pushing my way through the tightly packed bodies, faces turned away from me, or weak smiles offered which I choose not to return. Awkwardness clings to me because of Mark, but today I barely notice it, my attention only on Will, although I force myself not to stare. I reach the makeshift bar beside him, two trestle tables pushed together, topped with plastic glasses and bottles of screw-top wine and cans of beer. He's whispering something to Becky as I help myself to a plastic glass of warm wine. She frowns and then thrusts Jackson into his open arms. I should probably back off before she notices me, but the bubble of rage has risen again. We made very careful arrangements. I don't understand why he's gone back on them without letting me know. I shove the leaflet I'd picked up into my coat pocket and retrieve my mobile. There's a message, received as I was walking the dark lane. I type a reply, then watch as he removes his phone from his jeans back pocket, Jackson giggling as he's bumped up and down in the process. Will frowns at the screen, then says something to Becky, handing over the chunky toddler as he gets up. I turn away, but feel the cold air rush in as he opens the side door. I sip my wine and count to a hundred in my head then I place the plastic beaker back on to the table and move back towards the door I came in by, pushing it open.

A hand reaches out for mine through the cold, taking it firmly, making me gasp, although I say nothing, allowing Will's strong grip to guide me between the parked cars until we're by the huge bins behind the hall. He manoeuvres me up against the wall, his face so close to mine I can almost taste him. I wait for that first kiss to press on my lips, the strength with which he will hold me, squeezing the air from my lungs, but instead Will says, 'Don't you ever do that again, Kar! Not in front of Becky, she doesn't deserve that.'

She does, if village gossip is to be believed, but I keep that thought to myself, my information about Becky based on nothing more than overheard conversations in the post office. I laugh and push him away, ask him why on earth he brought her to the meeting? We were supposed to show our faces then disappear. He doesn't reply, leaning in to kiss me determinedly on the mouth, his whole body against mine. I'm lost in the moment, unable to move, even if I wanted to, my hands held in his, the rough brick scraping against my coat as his lips move over my neck then down. When he releases me, I feel bereft, reaching out again for him, but he steps away.

'Half the bloody village is in there,' he says, his voice filled with anger, although it's barely raised to more than a whisper. 'It was a stupid plan to start with.'

'It was your plan!' I reply.

He grabs me again, his hand reaching inside my coat, seeking out skin beneath the layers.

'Not here,' I tell him, but I'm not sure I really mean it, especially when he takes me at my word and steps away, the chill air surrounding me instead. 'Can we meet where we planned, maybe in half an hour?'

'Not with Becky here.'

'Why didn't you tell her to stay at home?'

'I couldn't think what to say.' His voice is softer now, my disappointment no greater than his, apparently. 'She seemed suspicious.'

'Of what?'

'Dunno, maybe nothing.' He shrugs. 'I should get back soon, told her I needed a smoke.' He searches in his shirt pocket and pulls out a lighter and a roll-up, exhaling a plume of white smoke into the freezing air. 'You said you wanted to talk to me about something?'

My nerve fails me as before, the confession I'd rehearsed now feeling too much of a test. I don't know where his loyalties lie, although I suspect they may be with his sister, my actions in the supermarket indefensible in his eyes. All I manage to offer are my half-hearted condolences again, asking him how he's coping.

'It's no great loss, you know that.' He drags deeply on the cigarette as a car speeds by at the bottom of the slope, casting a second or two of bright light. We both turn away from the road, and Will says, 'You look nice,' touching my cheek. 'Smell good too.'

'Have you seen her?' I straighten my coat and pat down my hair.

'*Mum?*' He flicks the cigarette butt into the night.

'No,' I wait, breath held. 'I meant your sister. Is she home?'

'Yeah, till the funeral. Listen, Kar . . . you tell that husband of yours to keep away from her. No trouble, OK?'

I nod, but it's probably too dark out here for him to notice the small drop then lift of my chin.

'I won't have him bothering her, Kar.'

'He won't.' I hold on to Will's arm then nestle into his chest, my arms around his waist. 'I promise.'

'Are you sure?' He kisses the top of my head.

I tell him, yes, I'm sure, then he says he should get back, his voice receding as he walks towards the hall. 'I'll see you tomorrow instead,' he calls back to me. 'Properly, I promise.'

'Yes, tomorrow, but in the day, Frey's over for dinner in the evening.'

He pauses to turn and raise his hand, then there's an eruption of voices as he opens the side door before all is quiet again. I wait in the dark, the scent of exhaled smoke still hanging in the air. His kiss still imprinted on my frosty lips.

I guess Will's always been there, a quiet presence in the village, but I didn't take any notice of him for at least a year after Mark came home from prison. I'd started going to the shops each day, walking if the weather was good and I felt up to it, an hour away from the constant need to be the positive one, Mark's moods darker if anything, despite his reclaimed freedom. It was on those walks, no urgency to my pace, that I'd occasionally see Will cutting a front lawn, or chopping back overgrown shrubs, and for some reason his absorption in the tasks caught my attention. He always looked so content, his life undemanding, and I was drawn to his strength, the way he appeared to have moved on, despite what had happened. I assumed he hadn't noticed me, maybe never would, but then he started looking up, smiling at me, and although I rushed on, pretended I hadn't seen, sometimes I would smile back, just a little. It took us a long time to build up enough trust to exchange a few words, then a proper smile, even a joke, my laugh like a stranger's, so unfamiliar to me. Maybe it would have always been like that; the wife and the brother, caught in the glare of other people's lives, and through that finding a connection. Not that we ever discussed the past, but it was there, binding us, moments we'd both witnessed, some that still coloured my cheeks as I remembered my outburst in court, wondered if he'd been there to see it, comforted his sister after I'd been led away.

When I stumbled near the road, his hand instinctively reaching out to save me, his touch couldn't be ignored. It demanded more; lingered. He was wearing gardening gloves, had been cutting back brambles he told me, but he'd held my hand a moment longer than was needed, asked if I was OK, and it was so good to be held. So good to be asked how *I* felt, for once.

The first time Will kissed me, I'd begun to wonder if he ever would. I'd imagined him touching me, holding me, more . . . but it was a daydream, something to pass the lonely hours whilst Mark read, or slept, or walked the dog. Then it happened. We were at the far end of the village, beyond the school, a nice house with a sweeping drive, the crispness of the day causing me to shiver as we talked, the exertion of the long walk to find him wearing off. Will had looked up at me from the endless rake of the gravel and suggested we sit in the van to warm me up. I knew what I was doing as I climbed in, his hand guiding me. After that first time, he suggested we drive to a quieter place in future, and I agreed. He never mentioned Mark, or Jess, and I took my lead from him. It was a relief to be in a world where they weren't discussed, as if they were unimportant, and yet I knew that aspect of my life was understood and, within the boundaries we'd created, accepted. Will has been through everything I have, well mostly, and although we come from opposing sides, we both know better than anyone the pain that has been inflicted, and how far the ripples travel.

I walk towards the hall, pushing on the door that leads me closer to Will. It's an unsatisfactory compromise, but preferable to going home.

Jess

Wednesday, 7th December 2016 (Morning)

James Facey waits for me outside the house, leaning against his shiny black car, staring at his phone. It's like I've been zapped back to 2006, sneaking into Mum's room if my step-father wasn't home, and climbing on the bed to see if James had arrived, hoping to spot him before someone else beat me to the door. I half-expect to look behind me and see Mum's shrouded figure hunched under the covers, muttering under her breath that she needs her ciggies and a mug of tea. James looks up at the bedroom window and raises his free hand. He's exactly as I remember him, even his dark coat could be the same one from all those years ago, the collar turned up. I run downstairs and out through the front door, slowing my pace as I walk towards him. His face creases into a familiar smile and he pockets his mobile phone, his attention now turned entirely to me. 'Jess, how are you? You look very well.'

'You too, James. You haven't changed a bit.'

The last time we met was the day he came to London to tell me Mark Winter was due for release, his full sentence served as he continued to protest his innocence to the very end. I hadn't expected James at my door that day, or any day in fact, but I suppose it was easy enough for him to find me in his line of work. I was nineteen by then, still a kid, although I thought of myself as a grown-up. James's presence had felt strange in my tiny flat; he was too formal, too much of a reminder of the past. It had turned into an odd kind of reunion, and we parted on awkward terms. I think we both knew it would be a while before we saw one another again. The way he is today – the James I know best, smartly dressed, of course, but less ill at ease than last time – is exactly how I'd hoped he would be.

'Must have been . . . 2009 . . . over seven years,' James tells me, rubbing the third finger of his left hand as he always did, although I notice the wedding band he would constantly turn is now missing. 'I've thought about you a lot over the years, Jess. Wondered how you were doing.'

'I've been good,' I reply, looking down at my feet, the uncomfortable memory of our last meeting hanging over me. 'I expect you've been busy?'

He smiles, says yes, he has, a shrug to acknowledge he still dedicates himself almost entirely to his work.

We walk towards the park, even though it's started raining, and we sit side by side on the now crumbling bench, the same one where Becky and I cracked open a bottle of vodka before the prom. I trace a wet fingerprint across the names carved into the rotten wood, love hearts linking them, the steady drip-drip of the raindrops like a curtain around us. We're alone; the only ones mad enough to be out here in this weather.

'I was sorry to hear about your mother,' James says, offering me a cigarette, which I refuse. The memory of the last time I smoked, strangely in this very spot, feels like a lifetime ago. He clamps his lips around the filter and cups long fingers to protect the flame from the rain, then he undoes his coat and uses his lapels as a shield, drawing deep until it finally catches. 'She must have only been a few years older than me.'

'She was never going to live a long life.' I fan the smoke away with my hand. 'And neither will you at this rate,' I tell him, clearing my throat.

He drops the cigarette and stamps on it with the toe of his black lace-up, although the puddle at his feet had already extinguished the flame. He apologises under his breath, and I imagine his wife nagging him to give up too, then I remember the missing wedding ring, the finger an even colour, as if the band has been removed for some time. I never liked what it represented, a reminder of his connection to a stranger who was more important to him than I would ever be. In counselling they call it Transference, but my feelings for him had felt real when he'd arrived at my door with the news Mark Winter was days away from being a free man. The thought of what happened next passes through me, and I turn away from James, staring instead at the swings, water pooling beneath them.

'You're right, I should give up. My daughters tell me off all the time.' He pushes his hands deep into his pockets. 'So, what have you been up to, still waitressing?'

I tell him I'm retraining as a counsellor and he smiles, says he always knew I was a bright girl. We're getting soaked, but he doesn't suggest we move, knowing I prefer it out here, so much easier to talk. He once told me I was only myself when we were looking at the empty swings and slide. I must have been a nightmare back then, but he never lost patience with me.

'How's life treating you?' I ask, pulling the hood of my coat over my wet hair, tucking as much as I can inside. 'Sorry, don't mean to pry.'

'This job takes its toll on family life: crazy hours and too many cancelled plans.'

'Sorry to hear that,' I say, knowing how much he idolised his daughters. He never talked much about his wife.

'Yeah, well.' He looks away. 'One thing this job teaches you is life is rarely fair.'

I smile at him and nod, thinking of his family, wondering if he was to blame for the split, or just *life* as he says. James would often begin our time together by talking about his girls, tiny details like a film they'd taken them to see, or his youngest daughter's favourite restaurant where she always ordered *'pizza with pig on top'*, a peek into a world as alien to me as mine was to him. Although he must have come across other families like ours; people who constantly brought disaster on themselves.

'I'm afraid I haven't had a chance to visit the Winters yet,' he tells me, apologising. 'How do you want me to handle things? A quiet word first, or a formal caution? Mark knows the score, he shouldn't have approached you.'

'I told you, he didn't. *I* went up to *him*.' James opens his mouth, his brow furrowed, but I speak first. 'Don't tell me off, James. I know I shouldn't have, but I wanted to warn him and his wife to keep away. She frightened me . . . the look in her eyes . . .'

'Karen always worried me too,' James replies, nodding. 'She was fiercely loyal right from the start. You normally see them waver, the resentment leaks out, all those months waiting for the trial and the ignominy of it all, the questions, the repercussions, it would test anyone.' He stares straight ahead, caught up in his own thoughts. 'But Karen Winter was scarily tolerant. I never saw any doubt from her, not for a second. Even that time in court—' James turns to me. 'You OK, Jess? I'm sorry, I shouldn't have brought all that up. You want to get out of the rain? You're shivering.'

'No, it's not that, it's just, hearing you say that about Karen Winter, I don't know . . .' I look away, half-close my eyes to concentrate before I look back. 'There's definitely something strange about her, isn't there? Something, I don't know . . . almost . . . like she's looking right through you.'

'I think she's doped up to her eyeballs most of the time,' he replies, as if it were a relatively normal state. 'Antidepressants, or sleeping pills, maybe both.'

'Oh, I hadn't realised,' I say, wrong-footed. 'Poor cow.'

'Yeah, poor cow, but she still shouldn't have frightened you like that.'

He stands up, shakes some of the rainwater from his damp coat and tells me he should probably get over to the Winters now, before he's called away again. 'Been a bit of a mad morning so far, but I'm glad we managed to catch up.'

I stand too, looking down at my trainers as I tell him I'm sure he's got much more important stuff to do than chase around after me, my hands shoved deep in my pockets, my hood obscuring me from his view.

'Jess, listen,' he places a hand on my arm. 'It's my job. I'm here for you, OK?'

He removes his touch and slips back into formal mode, straightening his back as he explains how Mark is under licence, his freedom dependent on him sticking to the terms of his release, and he's still listed on the Sex Offenders' register, which means he will have to take notice of the warning he's about to get, or he's straight back inside. 'I can't ignore the fact they've both approached you, even if you want me to. Ready to go?'

I shake my head and watch him walk away, a lonely figure. It's sad to think he had to decide between his family and his career. People like James are special, they shouldn't have to choose. I imagine his wife issuing an ultimatum. How he'd been tortured by guilt as he wondered if he could really abandon the desperate cases he swept up and took care of, people like me who would have fallen off the edge if he hadn't been around to tell them they mattered, that they were believed. It may be selfish, but I'm glad he chose us instead of her.

Karen

Wednesday, 7th December 2016
(Late Morning)

A black car, shiny except for the splashes on the paint-work, drives towards me from the other end of the lane. Whoever it is must have been visiting the cottage; you certainly wouldn't venture up here otherwise, not in a nice clean car. I step back on to the grassy bank, mainly mud at this time of year, waiting for it to pass. It's a man driving, his face partially hidden behind his coat collar, and although I hope I'm wrong, I think I know who he is, the realisation making my stomach clench. He glances over to where I'm standing, and I see a flicker of recognition in his expression as the wipers clear his windscreen, confirming my fears. He doesn't stop, or even slow down, but in that shared moment I understand why he's here, his face filling in the blanks, as I'm sure mine must for him. I watch as the sleek car reaches the junction with the main road, red brake lights illuminating briefly, flashes of brightness against the greyness of a winter morning. Then the car is gone. I wrap my coat tightly around me, shielding myself with the broken umbrella as I step back on to the stony lane, my trainers avoiding the worst of the puddles. I was warm a few minutes ago, held safe, and now I'm wet and cold, and with each step, a little more afraid. I try hard to hold on to the time I've just spent with Will, but it slips away, washed down the lane and into the drains. December weather is unremittingly grim, no bright cushions of fallen snow, just this constant rain, and oppressive skies filled with slate-grey clouds.

The cottage should look welcoming on such a miserable day, perhaps it did at one time, but today I'm reluctant to go in, my fear of what awaits me holding me at the end of the path. Surely Jess can't have made a complaint about what I did? I only held her trolley for a moment or two. Unless Mark has approached her too? I retreat further back, stepping from the path on to the muddy lane, the rain and wind driving at my back. I'm waiting, but for what I'm uncertain. I can't stay out here all day, but still I hesitate, imagining what I might say to my husband, how to explain my moment of madness. Hopefully, he's upstairs in his study, returned to his writing. I need a cup of tea before I can face him, maybe another tablet to steady my nerves. More time to get my story straight. The rehearsed one about how my exercise class ran over now less important than my account of what really happened with Jess on Monday. I swallow and walk towards the front door.

The cottage is quiet, no clue to Mark's whereabouts, but he's not out with Walter, I can hear the dog whining behind the kitchen door. I shake out my mangled umbrella and prop it up by the front door to dry out, kicking off my trainers to walk softly towards the kitchen.

'In here,' Mark says, his voice dull and flat, coming from the sitting room.

He's standing by the window, his back to me, gazing out at the drenched view. He must have seen me standing outside, getting soaked. He would have been in shadow, the sitting room window shaded by the ancient apple tree, concealed from my view as I debated whether to come in.

'Did you enjoy your exercise class?' he asks, still staring out.

'Yes, sorry it ran over,' I tell him, but he says nothing in reply. 'It's horrible weather again, not too cold today, but the rain—'

He turns, his eyes lifted to me, but only slightly, his expression shocking, not something I've witnessed for many years. I know my husband; it's not anger that twists his face, but fear, the realisation sending me towards him, arms open, as though he might allow me to offer that comfort. He looks out the window, informing me we've just had a visitor, DS Facey, but he expects I know that already.

'Yes, his car passed me coming back down the lane.' I focus my attention on the curtains, forming knife pleats in the floral fabric with downwards movements of my hands. 'What on earth did he want after all these years?' My voice is light and too high. I can hear the falseness in it, but I maintain my breezy tone. 'If it's about *that girl*—'

'He said you accosted Jess.' Mark is still looking outside, although there's nothing to see but our forlorn car, rusting in the now torrential rain. 'She apparently said you'd frightened her.'

'That's ridiculous.' I drop the faded fabric. 'You know what she's like, always prone to the dramatic. I told you what happened.'

'*Prone to the dramatic?*' Mark finally looks at me, a long, hard stare, then he walks towards the door, glancing back to say, 'You know I'm this far away from being arrested?' He holds up his thumb and forefinger, so close I can see no gap between them. 'This far!'

'I may have put my hand on her trolley, but that was all. It was the shock of seeing her. You of all people can understand that, surely?' He says nothing, his fingers to his lips as if he doesn't trust his response. 'It could have been a lot worse,' I say. 'No one would have blamed me if—'

'You think no one would blame you?' He laughs without mirth, then he moves towards me and places his hand lightly on top of my damp coat sleeve. 'Was it like this?' he asks, then he squeezes harder. 'Or like this?'

'What is wrong with you?' I shake free of him. 'I told you I didn't touch her. Why are you—'

'I could go back to prison, Karen,' he says, his voice raised. 'Is that what you want?'

'Of course not. And thank you for believing her, not me. She's only been back a couple of days, and she's already causing trouble.'

I call after him to wait, but he ignores me, pulling his raincoat from the hook in the hallway to slip it over his jumper. He's clipping on Walter's lead as I try again to persuade him to stay, at least listen to my side of the story, but the dog is barking, and Mark chooses not to hear me above Walter's excitement.

'Don't leave like this,' I tell him. 'You're clearly upset. I'll jump in the shower, then we can talk about it. I could walk with you, if you like . . . when the rain eases.'

Mark looks up from the dog, his expression hard. 'I expect you're worn out after all that exercise?'

I say nothing, my breath caught in my mouth as I press my lips tightly together.

'One word from Jess and they'll haul me back in.' He's struggling to hold on to Walter who is pulling him towards the back door. 'And you could be prosecuted for witness intim-idation, do you know that?'

'Don't be ridiculous,' I reply, flustered now. 'I told you nothing happened.'

Mark sighs. 'You have to stay away from her, Karen. I can't go back to prison. I just can't.'

He rubs at his eyes and this time when I step forward he doesn't back away, allowing me to wrap my arms around his narrow shoulders. Walter looks up at us as Mark leans into me and I support my husband, his body shaking with the shock of what might be, but it's only a moment before he steps away, his free hand shielding his eyes. I tell him he won't have to go back to prison, it's over, or will be, just a few days and she'll be gone again. He nods, looking away.

I watch from the kitchen as he crosses the back garden, the dog pulling him along. Mark pauses, leaning down to unlatch the waist-high wooden gate, allowing Walter through first. I wait, thinking he might look back before he follows, raise a hand or smile, but he doesn't, closing the gate behind them. Only when he's out of sight do I release my tight grasp on the edge of the sink, my knuckles white. I run the tap, the cold water spraying me so for a moment I'm shocked back to life. Then I swallow three tablets, one after another.

Four Months Before . . .

Supervision Session #5 – Jessica Tidy – Tuesday, August 16th, 2016

Full notes in client file ref: 718/16

Meeting taped, transcript of relevant section below (abridged)

Me: I know you don't agree, Jess, but I still feel it would have been beneficial to explore the issues that prompted you to leave home at such a young age, preferably before you underwent the intense training needed to become a counsellor. Although that's obviously theoretical now.

Jess: As I said, I didn't feel it was needed.

Me: I sense your reluctance to discuss it further.

Jess: I'm not reluctant to discuss anything, it just annoys me that everyone assumes I'm incapable of making my own choices. You know the ironic thing is, if it hadn't been for Mark Winter telling me I could do anything, be anyone . . . God, this is ridiculous! I can't believe I'm still talking about what he said to me after all these years. I guess I'm proving your point.

Me: Even if you hadn't consciously thought about his words, those feelings are clearly still there, and I think that's completely understandable.

Jess: I suppose, but it's depressing to think I haven't moved on in the last decade.

Me: Is that why you're reluctant to consider personal counselling?

Jess: I'll think about it, OK?

Me: Good, and if you need a name of someone—

Jess: One thing I will say is I used to hear Mark a lot, in my head, the things he told me, the way he manipulated me, but not so much since I've been coming to see you.

Me: It's OK to look back, to remember. It can be very cathartic.

Jess: I don't think that's possible in my case.

Me: Perhaps we can try an exercise I sometimes use with my clients. I'd like you to jot down any positive influencers in your life. It's best not to think about who, or why, just follow your instincts. I'll get you something to write on.

Jess: I won't need that. There's only one name. James Facey. We haven't seen each other for years, but if I needed him, I know he'd be there.

Me: He sounds like one of the good guys.

Jess: He is one of the good guys, he really is. My family made me feel like it was my fault what happened with Mark, that I somehow brought it on myself. James never did that. He said right at the start he would help me through it, every step of the way, simple as that. It meant a lot.

Me: Yes, I'm sure that must have been immensely important
      to you.

Jess: Sometimes James's support was the only thing that kept
      me going.

Jess

Wednesday, 7th December 2016 (Lunchtime)

Still holding my phone to my ear, I pull back the frayed edges of the curtain, the cream lining stained nicotine-yellow where Mum's fingers must have done the same, the brown outer fabric disintegrating like desiccated moths' wings. I thought I'd heard an engine, throaty and loud, familiar.

'Jess, did you hear me?' James asks. 'I've told Mark it applies to them both, they must keep away from you.'

'Yes, sorry, I need to go.' I drop the curtain. 'My brother has just arrived, but thanks for updating me, really appreciate it.'

'Keep in touch, Jess. I want to know everything, OK?'

'Yeah, sure,' I say, anxious to be off the phone.

I watch from behind the curtain, anticipating Will's jog down the path, but instead he comes around to the passenger side of the van and slides open the door. He's blocking my view at first, but when he turns back I can see he's holding a child, legs dangling, a sturdy bundle in a bright red coat which

110

he sets down on the pavement, their tiny hand gripped tightly in his. Then Will reaches up to help someone else clamber down. Revealing chunky calves between the top of her boots and the hem of her short skirt, Becky wriggles the skin-tight denim back down as she looks across at the house. I step away from the window, but I can't help watching as the three of them approach, the first time I've seen Becky since the night of the prom. Her mouth is moving rapidly and she frowns at Will, but I can't see my brother's expression; he's looking down at his son, helping him toddle up the path. Becky notices me, her scowl replaced with a hurried smile. I force a smile too; irritated Will didn't think to warn me they were coming.

'Not dressed?' Will asks as I open the door. 'It's lunchtime, Jess.'

'I wasn't expecting you,' I reply, looking at Becky. 'Any of you.'

'I did say I'd try to call in,' Will says, missing my point. 'It's Becky's day off, so she suggested—'

'Not just my idea,' Becky tells him.

Will introduces me to Jackson, my nephew, a swaddled mass of crimson polyester. The child wriggles free of his father but Will grabs his son by the hood and halts him before he trips over the step. Jackson looks up at me, flashing a gummy smile as Will lifts him to eye level. I smile back, struck by the resemblance to Tony and Mick. 'Well you're here now, better come in.' I lean away from a moist, toddler-sized fist extended towards my face.

Will carries Jackson over the threshold, the boy's tiny but pudgy fingers unfurling to reveal a biscuit mashed into his palm. 'Say hello to Auntie Jess,' Becky tells him, closing the door behind her as Jackson screams loudly for no apparent reason.

I lead them towards the kitchen, kicking aside the pile of soiled bedding from Mum's room. 'Sorry about the mess. The skip is due today. I'll get rid of it all then.'

'You should have said,' Will tells me, setting Jackson down on the kitchen floor. I think my brother's finally about to offer some practical help, but then he says, 'I could have got you a good price. What you paying for it?'

'Hundred-and-twenty,' I tell him, holding up an out-of-date bag of sugar to Becky who nods and asks for two please. I notice she's still wearing the same shade of luminous pink lipstick she always did, her eyeshadow a familiar semicircle of mauve. I used to admire that bright arc of glittery purple, tried to emulate it as best I could, but now it amuses me as I spoon out the sugars. Becky's filled out a lot since I last saw her, her face rounder, her stomach providing a soft resting place for a fidgety Jackson as she heaves him up from the lino floor. He digs his feet into his mother's flesh and pushes himself away, his body rigid, his head almost colliding with mine as he swings away from her. Becky wrestles him back, but in the process her jacket has ridden up, exposing a rim of protruding flesh around her waist. Jackson's boots rest on it as he screams again. It's ear-splitting, but neither of his parents seem to notice. I screw my face up, my head pounding.

'Bloody hell, one-twenty for a skip, Jess,' Will says, lifting his voice to be heard above the increasingly loud protests of his son.

He holds out his hands and takes Jackson, crouching down with him and tickling his son's neck until the child's screams are replaced with giggles. 'I could have got it for half that if you'd asked. What size you gone for?' He sighs when I tell him it was the smallest they had. 'Who's charging you one-twenty for a mini skip?' He straightens up to take his mug of tea.

'I found them on Google, Speedy someone, I think.'

'Not Speedy Ken?' Will asks, sipping his tea. 'You'll wait all day for him to arrive.'

I shrug, holding out Becky's tea to her although she has her hands full with Jackson, bending down to take over from Will. 'I'll leave the big items for the clearance company, unless you want to—'

Jackson's screams obliterate the rest of my words. I place Becky's mug on the worktop and look at Will, waiting for him to offer to help with the house, or at least quieten his son, but he's watching Becky as she tries to pick up Jackson. She gives up, plonking him down on to the floor then grabbing his hood to steady him as he leans forwards and smears wet, biscuit-covered fingertips across the cupboard doors.

'Can you maybe ask him to stop doing that?' I suggest, looking down at the mess. 'I only just cleaned those.'

'Is it too late to cancel the skip?' Becky asks Will, ignoring me as she slurps her tea, smacking her lips as if that will reapply the lipstick now deposited on the mug. 'Will's right, Jess. He'll get you a much better price.'

'It's literally on its way,' I reply, gritting my teeth as I watch all my efforts undone by an unsupervised Jackson. 'So yes, far too late to cancel.' I look up to catch her eye, a cold glint in it before she looks away.

'Jackson!' Becky shouts, making me jump. 'Get your mitts off Nana's cupboards.'

Jackson continues his work, undeterred.

'He looks just like the twins,' I tell them, and both Will and Becky stare at me, completely horrified. 'I mean when they were little, he's really cute.'

Becky informs me what a clever boy he is, just started walking, which seems about right for his age, but apparently signifies some special talent. I wrinkle my nose at the trail of toddler saliva making its way from his fingers to every possible surface, nodding when required.

'Can you come in the office Friday afternoon?' Becky asks. 'Finalise everything for Tuesday. We're on the High Street, opposite the new café.'

I tell her I know where the undertakers are, then I look at Will. 'I'll be working,' he says, 'but Becky will keep me updated.'

Becky agrees, squeezing his arm as she tells me how Will has organised most things for the funeral. I shrug, say that should be OK, I guess, but I notice Will moves his arm away.

'Thanks, Jess,' he says, smiling at me. 'I really appreciate everything you're doing.'

I smile back, then Becky announces they should get going, and Jackson starts screaming again, resisting her attempts to scoop him up.

They leave before the dregs of tea are cold in their mugs, the noisy approach of a truck signalling the arrival of Speedy

Ken. I resist the urge to point out the obvious, but Will is already on his way out, raising his hand when Speedy Ken toots his horn and hangs out his window to call out, 'All right, mate?' Will hands Jackson up to Becky before climbing in the van himself, but then he jumps down again, his boots hitting our front path as he runs towards me.

'I know I should be doing more.' He's breathless, his hand to the doorframe. 'I will try, I promise. It's just . . . well I can't really explain, Jess. I'm juggling a lot of things right now, and I know I need to put you first, but . . . well, it's complicated. I'm sorry, I really am.'

'What things?' I ask, but he shakes his head.

'Look, if you need me, I will be there, I promise, Jess.'

I open my mouth to tell him everything that's happened, about seeing Karen then Mark, how frightened I'd been, both times, but he says he should get going, Becky's waiting, and I say of course, I can cope, my chin tilted up. Then he's off again, a cloud of fumes all that remains as he drives away.

'Where do you want it, love?' Ken shouts out of his truck window, startling me.

'On the road, I guess?'

'You'll need a permit for that, and lights. You got those, love?'

I'm tempted to grab the broken fairy lights from the box by the door, but I shake my head and point at the front lawn, then I run inside the house to find my purse. Ken was very specific about payment: 'Cash on delivery, or no can do.'

He's waiting for me on the path, his bulk stalling me as I rush out. I hand over six crisp twenty-pound notes, only withdrawn two days ago, and pretty much all I have. 'Is that right, we agreed one-twenty?'

Ken looks up and down the road, his beer belly spilling over his belt as he distractedly scratches the exposed hairy flesh, warning me I should be prepared for fly-tippers around here. 'Best get it filled and collected as soon as poss, love. I'll put it as close to the house as I can.' He scratches again. 'Text me when you want it picked up.'

He pauses for a moment, the money still in his hand, staring at it. I'm about to reassure him it's not fake, if that's what he's worried about, when he hands back one of the twenty-pound notes and says he's sorry for my loss, telling me to put it towards flowers 'or sommat'.

'I knew your mum pretty well.' He winks as if I hadn't already guessed what he'd meant. 'Top lady. You remind me of her,' he says, staring at me. 'A lot.'

I know that look, a distant recollection of it bouncing around the outer corners of my memory. 'I should get on,' I tell him, rushing inside and closing the door.

I change into my joggers and sweatshirt, checking Ken's deposited the skip and driven away before I go back outside. It's grubby work, my clothes soon covered in sticky stains and damp patches of God-knows-what, but it's satisfying hurling everything into the skip, like having a giant dustbin. I turn my attention to the kitchen once the hall is cleared, pushing the piled rubbish into the black refuse bags I bought at the supermarket, and emptying cardboard boxes so I can squash them down flat. I find cereal packets which are years old at the back of cupboards, and even tinned goods past their dates, everything tossed into the open mouth of the grimy skip. It's cold and almost dark by the time I'm done, three hours gone by according to the kitchen clock. Two dog walkers passed the time of day with me and a group of cheeky school kids threw in their emptied drink cans, but other than that I've been undisturbed. I run up to my room and change into jeans and a jumper, my last set of clean casual clothes, and then I start work again, manically spraying the fronts of the kitchen cabinets with antibacterial liquid as I wipe away tiny handprints.

I'm not normally a fan of kids, always spilling their drinks and throwing food, and Jackson did make a lot of mess, and noise, but he was quite cute, a mini version of Will, and it was sweet the way he smiled at me as they left, Will waving his son's chubby hand to say goodbye to 'Auntie Jess'. I've never been an auntie to anyone before.

The kitchen finally clean and tidy, I open the fridge and pull out a fresh bottle of wine, unscrewing the top to pour myself a well-deserved drink. I take my glass into the sitting room and fall into the chair, ignoring the unpleasant smell that puffs out with the dust. I'm dog-tired, but my mind is still buzzing.

It's Becky's cold stare that preoccupies me most, the unfairness of it, and the way she'd insisted she come around, but then been desperate to leave at the first opportunity. If it was her idea, why be like that? Had I annoyed her, said something wrong? I drain my wine and stand up to get another, talking to myself as I go. 'The thing is, Becky, I'm the one who should be annoyed, not you!' I slam the fridge door shut and swallow a couple of mouthfuls on the return journey, falling back into the chair. 'Some friend you turned out to be!'

She was drunk the night of the prom, and people say things they don't mean when they're that wasted, I know that, but not a word since, not even during the trial. Not even a message to ask how I was doing. *Nothing!* 'Well, cheers to you, Becky!' I raise my drink to the empty room, then knock it back in one go. 'Fucking cheers!'

It's much later, when I've had time to calm down, the wine doing its job, that I begin to imagine how she must have felt seeing me again after all this time. I did say some terrible things to her at the prom, we both did, our disagreement quickly degenerating into name-calling on both sides, but she'd slapped me, hard, her handprint burning my cheek. I lift my hand to my face, my palm cool from the wine glass, a shudder spasming down my spine. We were kids, Becky and I, we didn't mean it, any of it, but it had been painful, and not only the slap. *'I'm sooo fucking bored of you going on about Mark Winter all the time, just drop your knickers and get on with it! Or are you all talk?'* Then she'd kicked the cubicle door off its hinges, and left me there, sobbing on the toilet.

I never thought she and Will would stay together. It was disappointing how easily he'd been pulled in by her obvious, if limited, charms. Becky was pretty, but in a shallow way, big tits, and a fun attitude. I could see why guys would go for her, but she wasn't relationship material, or so I'd thought, and I'd never considered she might be Will's type. Clearly, I was wrong. I think of Jackson, waving goodbye to me, and wonder if that will be the one and only time I'll see my nephew. Becky had clearly regretted her decision to force Will into a surprise visit, realising her mistake once we stood toe-to-toe in my dead mother's kitchen. She'd wanted to parade her family in front of me, prove to me that I was wrong; that Will *had* wanted to be with her. She was showing off, simple as that, but Will hadn't wanted any part of it, his reluctance obvious as they argued their way down the front path, and when he'd pulled his arm away from her. She was left out again, and she didn't like it, never has. She always resented the fact I was the one with a big brother who looked out for me. She only had her needy mother, more of a liability than a support. My guess is Becky used Jackson to keep Will tied to her. *Selfish cow*. I throw their cold, half-drunk tea down the sink and rinse away the spatters of brown liquid and curdled milk. Mum never trusted Becky, said she was a bad influence, I should find someone new to hang out with. I thought she was jealous of the fun we had together, the attention we attracted, but perhaps she was right. I wonder what she thought of Becky bringing her grandson round to *'Nana's house'*, acting as if she was a part of the Tidy clan. Becky would have loved the idea of it, until she'd realised Mum was so far gone she frightened small children. I smile at the thought of Mum's disapproval, wonder what she would have said. I imagine her cackling at Becky's half-arsed posh accent. Mum was always one to speak her mind, at least where her sons were concerned. Then I remember Mum's gone, and my smile disappears.

Karen

Wednesday, 7th December 2016 (Evening)

Walter barks and rushes towards the front door, flying out as soon as I open it.

'Get inside, you daft mutt,' I tell him, stepping on to the damp path with my bare feet, eager to greet Frey.

'Hi, Mum,' she says, locking her car and laughing at the dog's antics. 'Dad not home?'

'He's upstairs, be down soon.'

Frey crouches down, reciprocating Walter's wild enthusiasm, then she straightens up to hug me, one hand fending off the frenzied dog. I turn back to the cottage and spot Mark at the landing window. Frey hasn't noticed, but Mark catches my eye, and for a second I imagine the scene as he must view it, an outsider. I link my arm through Frey's and walk her inside, closing the door.

'So, how's my girl?' I ask, our voices running over one another, both anxious to swap news, not that I have much I can share.

'Yeah, I'm good,' she replies, making me giggle as she tells me about a student who has a terrible crush on her, his adoration compared to Walter's as the besotted dog stares up at her.

It strikes me the only time there's laughter in the house is when Frey's here, then I hear Mark on the stairs and I tense a little, Frey too, the unsuitability of the joke immediately obvious now Mark is about to join us. He comes down quickly, Frey's expression clouding over although she rearranges it so fast I wonder if I only imagined her initial reaction. She asks her father, as she always does, how he is, her reticent tone so different from the easy way she'd greeted me.

'Oh, you know, not so bad,' he tells her, pausing on the bottom stair.

I go through to the kitchen to see to the food, but I can still hear them perfectly well, their stilted exchange continuing in the hallway.

'Good week so far?' he asks, as though he was passing the time of day with a stranger, not his precious only child.

'Yeah, fine; busy. I'm pretty tired. You know what it's like . . .' She trails off, turning to look at me through the open door as she hangs her coat on one of the overly full hooks.

'Takes it out of you that first year,' I hear Mark say, and I notice Frey's shoulders tightening. 'Once you've got your teaching plans in place, you can reuse them for the next year.'

'Yes, I know, I'm on top of it, Dad.' She raises an eyebrow to me, and I pretend not to notice.

'Good, yes, of course. Sorry, I didn't mean to—'

'Dinner!' I call to them.

They take their usual places at the kitchen table, Frey tucked into the corner, Mark opposite her, oblivious to her discomfort as he continues to vicariously live the professional life now denied him.

'The students still engaged, well behaved?' he asks. 'Sometimes this close to Christmas they can get a bit lively, it's always the toughest term.'

'All good,' she replies, lifting her hands to take the plate of lamb casserole I pass across the table to her. 'Thanks, Mum. This looks amazing.'

'Thank you, sweetheart. Don't just talk about work,' I tell Mark as I return to the steaming pot on the hob. 'What about that lovely young man of yours, Frey? I see you with him on Facebook.'

'*Facebook?* I didn't know you bothered with that, Mum.'

'I lurk occasionally.' I glance at Mark. 'Only on my phone.'

'Tris is good,' she replies, fanning her mouth as she tries to cool a mouthful of overly hot stew. 'Busy, like me, but at least with both of us doing the same thing—' Frey pauses as I pass Mark a filled plate.

'You can always bring him with you,' I tell her. 'He's very welcome. You know that. It would be nice to meet him again, get to know him a bit better.'

'Yes, you said. Let's see how it goes, OK?'

I place a bowl of peas on the table, spoon beside them, then I help myself to a small portion of stew, sitting down beside Mark, our elbows touching in the cramped space as I drape my napkin across my lap.

'You OK, Mum?' Frey is studying me. 'You look tired.'

'I'm fine, sweetheart. So, still going strong, you and Tristan?'

Frey sidesteps my question, spooning peas on to her plate as she tells us about a film they went to see last night, something arty with subtitles.

'We'd like that, wouldn't we, Mark? A nice trip to the cinema, next time they go. Sounds right up our street.'

He picks up his fork and fills his mouth with hot food.

'And how are you two, any news?' Frey adds a squirt of ketchup to her plate.

Mark glances at me, and Frey immediately picks up on the unspoken exchange, asking us what's happened. 'Mum? Dad?'

'Jess Tidy is back,' Mark tells her, placing his cutlery down. 'Her mother died at the weekend, so she's here for the funeral.'

'That shouldn't affect you, should it?' Frey's eyes travel from her father to me. 'Just make sure you keep away from her and . . .'

I look away, wiping my mouth with my napkin, then gulping down my water.

'*Mum?*'

'I bumped into her in the supermarket,' I reply, pushing a pea around my plate with my fork until it topples on to the tablecloth. 'She contacted that pet policemen of hers straight away, said I'd assaulted her, which of course is completely ridiculous.' I pick up the pea and squash it flat between my thumb and finger, wiping the mess into my napkin.

'Facey's been round?' Frey allows her fork to land noisily on her plate. 'I thought we'd finally got rid of him.'

'He called by this morning,' Mark tells her.

'For fuck's sake! This never stops, does it?' She gets up quickly, her chair scraping the floor. 'We need to make a complaint, do something. This is harassment.' She strikes a palm on the table in front of Mark and leans in. 'Are you going to say anything? *Do anything?* She's accused Mum of God knows what—'

'This isn't helping, Freya,' he replies, sitting back. 'We have to remain calm, accept that—'

'Accept that whatever that bloody girl says is believed immediately?' Frey is still on her feet. 'Mum wouldn't hurt her, it's ridiculous to even suggest it. You were just in the supermarket.' She looks at me. '*Your* supermarket, in the village where you've lived your whole life!'

Mark asks Frey to please sit down. I'm staring at my napkin, but I spot their concerned looks as they both focus on me, Frey sighing as she re-takes her seat.

Mark answers Frey's questions one by one, explaining what DS Facey said, emphasising that yes, the detective is perfectly within his rights to warn us off. 'I'm out of prison on licence, remember.' Frey closes her eyes. 'I need to be very careful, or—'

She shakes her head in protest, picking up her fork and looking down at her food with disinterest. We eat in silence, my jaw set as I gather up the plates and scrape the leftovers into the bin.

'This has gone on long enough, Dad,' Frey whispers to Mark whilst my back is turned. 'There must be something we can do? Mum looks terrible, is she still on those tablets?'

I don't catch Mark's reply, Frey insisting we need to make a complaint about Jess or Facey, it's tantamount to harassment, surely? Mark says nothing, at least nothing I can hear above the hot blast of air released as I open the oven door.

'There!' I'm holding up the bubbling pudding to show them, the kitchen now perfumed with sugar and apples. 'Doesn't that look nice?'

Frey grins at me. 'Amazing, Mum.'

It's the reaction I'd anticipated as I peeled and cored, rubbing butter through flour, but my pleasure is short-lived, for I can see the flashes of anger behind her eyes. I open my mouth to remind her resistance is only a waste of emotional energy, a destructive path that leads nowhere, but I say nothing, returning her smile instead. How can I begin to explain I'd have lost my mind if I railed against every injustice that I've been forced to endure, the pills the only thing propping me up at times?

For Frey it's still so raw, resentments never voiced, at least not to me, despite the humiliation of the court case, and the ultimate shame of having a father in prison. Her protest against the education system that had unceremoniously spat out her father came much later, after university, when she decided she no longer wanted to be a teacher, a career she'd seemed destined for from a young age. Now, if I'm honest, I wish she'd stuck to the shop-work which she seemed to enjoy. It was certainly much easier to discuss around the dinner table.

'Who wants apple crumble?' I say as brightly as I can, the dish cradled in my oven-gloved hands. 'And don't think I haven't heard what you're saying behind my back.' I set the dessert down between them. 'Your dad is right, Frey. There's nothing any of us can do, we all need to accept the situation, or the next few days will be unbearable.'

Walter, lying at Frey's feet, sighs and grumbles, wriggling as he tries to get up, our hands flying out instinctively to steady the rocking table. 'Did you walk him?' I ask Mark, complaining under my breath about how he's shut himself away all day. Mark retaliates, something about me being the one who's always out, how else is he supposed to fill his time?

'Only for a couple of hours this morning,' I reply. 'You've been writing all day.'

'You're writing again?' Frey asks, nodding when I point at the dessert.

'A bit,' Mark tells her, settling Walter with a promise he'll take him out after we've eaten.

'*A bit?*' I say loudly, poking the point of a serving spoon into the steaming apple crumble. 'You've barely done anything else since *that girl*—'

Mark looks up at me, but I refuse to return his stare, dropping the spoon to push my hair back from my face.

'I wasn't aware it was a problem,' he remarks, still looking directly at me.

'See!' Frey glances at me then her father. 'Jess Tidy is back and already you two are sniping at one another.'

Our daughter leaves soon afterwards, her visit cut short by our disagreement, although she assures us that's not the case, she's just got loads of marking to do. Mark follows her out, a head torch strapped around his woollen hat, Walter at his side. I watch them from the front door, Frey addressing her father in a petulant manner, telling him he looks ridiculous, her tone frosty rather than teasing, like a teenager collected too early from a party, the teenager she was before she was forced to grow up overnight. She pauses by her car, stroking Walter who is sniffing at the foil-wrapped leftovers in her hand.

Frey whispers something to Mark, then she opens her car door and climbs in.

I step on to the freezing path to wave her off, Walter barking after her car as it slowly makes its way along the pitch-black lane, the headlights bouncing off the trees and hedges; bright for a moment, then all too quickly gone. Mark walks away too, the beam from his head torch jumping along ahead of him, reflecting off the iced puddles as he turns towards the back of the cottage and the path that leads to the fields. It's bitterly cold, a crazy time to take the dog for a walk, but it was me that insisted. I go inside, running hot water over the dirty dishes in the sink, my disappointment hard to shift, although I do my best to take it out on the bits of burnt-on food still clinging to the casserole dish, scrubbing at it with little result. I allow the encrusted dish to submerge in the brown water and rinse my hands, glancing at the kitchen clock. Only five minutes since they left, maybe less. I don't suppose Mark's in any rush to get back.

Upstairs, I pause on the landing, pulling back the curtain. The lane is in darkness, but when I look out from the study window I can see a single pool of light making its way across the fields towards the new houses at the far corner. I drop the curtain and sit down, a deep breath before I begin.

Chapter Four – May 2006

As we entered May, the exams loomed larger, the weeks speeding by. Maybe it was the reality of that which rattled Jess, her insouciance replaced with excuses and procrastination. She told me she didn't have the time to study, things were difficult at home, and she had a prom outfit to buy, although I got the impression no money would exchange hands.

'Don't know why I'm bothering with a new dress,' she said, working hard on her gum as we sat in the corner of the Exclusion Unit. 'Don't even have a date. Bex and I are going to split a bottle of vodka and arrive together like a couple of losers.'

'Jess, you need to concentrate,' I told her, pointing out the question she'd been working on. 'This is important. It's the rest of your—'

'I'm never gonna pass my exams, anyway.'

'What makes you say that?' I held out an empty palm for her gum. 'Your grades are good enough, I promise. Not top marks in every subject, that would be unrealistic, but to say you won't pass any . . .'

She shrugged, but she got back to work, another strip of gum inserted as I dropped the first moist piece in the waste-paper basket by my feet.

'You're the only one who believes in me,' she said, her hand to my arm.

I removed myself from her touch, as I always did, checking around the Exclusion Unit in case anyone had seen. 'Jess, you mustn't do that.'

I'd noticed a few raised eyebrows in the previous weeks, even the odd snide comment, which I dismissed as jealous and petty-minded. I'd done nothing wrong, and it certainly wasn't Jess's fault. She was a vulnerable girl, with no adequate role model. If at times she pushed things a little further than she should, then who were my colleagues to judge her? Or me, for that matter? They should try living Jess's life for a day, just one day, and see how it made them feel. How could I tell her to back off when she was confiding in me about the guy at the greengrocer's who offered to take her out for a drink, but only if she promised sexual favours at the end of the evening? Or the 'step-father', not married to her mother but apparently insistent that title be adopted, who constantly asked if she were interested in him in the same way her mother was.

'I can handle myself,' she always told me, a casual levity belying what I believed to be her true feelings.

With each new horror story, I came to understand how damaged she was, how hurt. I tried to follow the correct protocol, to tease out as much information as I could, particularly about her mother's boyfriend who concerned me the most, but Jess always backed away from her previous statements when any mention was made of 'alerting the authorities', making me promise I wouldn't share the scant evidence of abuse she'd given me in confidence.

'I haven't told anyone else,' she said. 'Not even my brother, Will.'

'OK, but remember, Jess, it's my job to protect you, make sure you're safe,' I told her, and that at least, seemed to reassure her.

Other than that, all I could do was listen, almost impassively, and the information would trickle out. Heart-breaking accounts delivered with understated ease, as if everyone had spent the previous night collecting their comatose mother from the pub and sitting by her bed to make sure she didn't choke on her own vomit, whilst her brothers had a fist fight in the hall with her step-father. Exams seemed less important when it was a small miracle Jess had even made it into school, but I still hoped I might educate her away from the carnage of her life. It was all I had to offer.

'Listen, Jess,' I said, gently removing her persistent touch. 'We need to have another chat about respecting boundaries.' I dropped my voice to an almost-whisper, ever conscious of the proximity of my colleagues, and the other students in the Exclusion Unit. 'For a start, this constant messaging has to stop. I only gave you my mobile number as a convenient method of arranging our meetings. It was never my intention to trigger a regular out-of-hours communication.'

'You said I could contact you if I ever felt unsafe,' she replied, parroting back my own words, a little too loudly for my liking.

'Yes, I did,' I agreed, glancing behind me. 'But literally only in an emergency, Jess. You've sent me a message every day, sometimes several, and it's not appropriate. We could both end up in a lot of trouble.'

'I'm already in trouble,' she told me, a harshness to her tone I didn't like one bit, a dismissal of my very real concerns. 'You shouldn't reply if you don't want me to message you back.' Her expression was defiant, followed by a quick smile for the benefit of anyone looking over. 'And you shouldn't say you care if you don't.'

It was then I first saw another side to Jess, one I had chosen to ignore, but one I would come to know all too well. It was only a glimpse, but it scared me.

Four Months Before . . .

Supervision Session #6 – Jessica Tidy – Tuesday, August 30th, 2016

Full notes in client file ref: 718/16

Meeting taped, transcript of relevant section below (abridged)

Me: We talked last time about positive influencers, and you
       mentioned a James Facey as the only one you could think
       of.

Jess: Yes, DS Facey.

Me: Oh, he was a detective. I hadn't realised. Anyway, I wanted
       to ask if you were in love with him?

Jess: *In love? With James?* No, of course not! Why would you
       ask that?

Me: It seems the obvious question.

Jess: I respect James immensely and value his friendship, but
       no, not love. It was a professional relationship.

Me: Thank you for clarifying that, Jess. Have you given any more thought to our discussion about seeing a trauma therapist?

Jess: Yes, and I've decided you're right, I do need to address what happened with Mark, but I'd rather discuss it with you, if that's OK? I know it's not exactly supervision, but as it's clearly affecting my work.

Me: Yes, true . . . I tell you what, why don't you give me a bit more of an idea about Mark Winter, what kind of man he was when you first knew him. You said you trusted him, at first.

Jess: Yes, I did, completely. He was a great teacher. I'd never really been interested in school stuff before, but he opened my eyes to lots of things, made me feel special, like I mattered. As if . . . as if I could be something in life. Anything I wanted to be, in fact. I was having a lot of trouble at home; Mark said he'd be there, protect me if I needed him to, keep me safe. It was a lifeline, to be honest.

Me: So you liked him?

Jess: I did. He seemed genuine. Just shows what a terrible judge of character I am.

Me: When did you realise you were wrong about him?

Jess: Not until the night of the prom.

Me: The prom?

Jess: It was a final celebration before exams. We arrived late, me and my best friend, Becky, and we had a massive row in the toilets. Mark was there, he was one of the chaperones, so I went to look for him. He was always so kind to me, you see. Even outside school, lifts home and stuff. He got me out of the hall, away from everyone, they were

132

laughing at me, I was in such a state, really drunk. But once we were alone, I ran away from him.

Me: You were afraid of him?

Jess: No, I wasn't afraid, it was more of a game. I wanted him to follow me into the Exclusion Unit. It was our place, where we'd spent a lot of time together. Sounds bad, doesn't it? But it was just a game. Then he, he—

Me: Do you want to stop, Jess?

Jess: You get used to hearing yourself say those terrible things again and again, deadens the impact, but now, it's like . . .

Me: Like what?

Jess: It's like it's not real any more. Like it never was.

Karen

Wednesday, 7th December 2016 (Evening)

I take a moment to gather my thoughts before I stand up from the desk. The field is dark, no sign of the torchlight that will soon be guiding my husband home, but I'm not ready for any more of his 'book' quite yet.

I knew about the text messages, of course, but reading how Mark had the opportunity to stop them, and had for some reason chosen not to, has stirred up past resentments, ones which at the time I forced myself to absorb without retaliation. Mark was so beleaguered, so determined justice would prevail. He needed his strength to fight his case, not me, but perhaps I should have questioned him more, demanded an explanation. He admitted in court he'd been a fool replying to Jess's messages – giving out his contact details to a student in the first place was a stupid mistake – but he told the jury that didn't make him a rapist. I saw the look in their eyes, not all of them perhaps, but at least half clearly didn't believe him. I knew

then he'd be convicted, although I kept up my cheery plati-
tudes, right up to the moment the guilty verdict was delivered,
denying the obvious to myself, as well as Mark and Frey. Why
did I choose that route, ignoring my gut feeling that something
was off to blithely play the loyal wife? For my husband, of
course, and to protect our daughter as much as possible, but
was it also so I could avoid the truth, too awful to face?

I sit back down, opening the next chapter with a heavy
heart. He's written a lot today, and he'll be back soon. I need
to be pragmatic, fight my emotions and read on whilst I still
have the chance.

Chapter Five – May 2006

By the second week of May Jess's results were once again steadily
improving, back on track despite the diversion of the upcoming prom,
her history grades particularly encouraging. Maths and English
percentages were also slowly increasing, although there was still a
long way to go. It seemed my rigorous study plan was finally paying
off, passing grades looking much more likely in core subjects, a real
possibility in fact, three percentage points in each—

I scan down a page of similarly dry statistics, growing tired of
Mark's self-congratulatory tone. I'm not interested in Jess's
grades. I need to know what happened the night of the prom,
and anything leading up to it that might lend me more insight.
As reassuring as Mark's preoccupation with Jess's academic
achievements might be, that's of less concern to me right now.
I quickly move on to the next chapter.

Chapter Six – May 2006

I remember feeling only annoyance when the headmistress asked to see me after school that day in mid-May. No alarms had rung inside my head, at least not loudly, and there were certainly no premonitions of impending calamity as she ushered me aside in the busy corridor, insisting it was a matter of great urgency.

'I'd really rather not cancel my planned session with Jess,' I told her as we were jostled by the students pushing past us. 'I'm sure I don't need to remind you this is a crucial time.'

'I really must insist,' the officious woman replied, taking little notice. 'I'll see you at the end of the day, Mark.'

Perhaps I should have felt some immediate concern, a prickle of portent, but I didn't. Before that meeting, I had little idea how my relationship with Jess was being viewed. Granted, I'd noted a degree of disapproval from my colleagues, but the wide extent of their censure had not been impressed upon me at all. I was soon to discover another teacher had taken it upon himself to report their collective concerns, a damning indictment.

Barry Johnson had taught at the school his whole teaching life and was, in my opinion and that of most of my colleagues, a poor teacher, and an unpleasant human being. Borderline abusive, he passed off his inappropriate comments as 'banter', boasting how he'd thrown board rubbers in the 'good old days', and ruminating on the satisfaction of landing the hefty thwack of a ruler across a thigh, or even better the back of a head. 'I'm old school,' he would often pronounce in the staffroom, pipe in hand. 'Can't change, won't change.' He clearly hated his job, his colleagues and the students. But most of all, Barry Johnson hated the Tidy family. Rumour had it he'd taught

Lisa Tidy, Jess's mother. That may or may not have been true, but he'd certainly had the misfortune to teach the notorious Tidy twins. I largely escaped their exploits, but Johnson had borne the brunt of their jokes for years, his tweed jacket held at arm's-length with exaggerated retching sounds as he begged for its return in front of a pack of baying students. It must have been horrendous for the poor bugger, but it's hard to feel sorry for a grown man who could be so petty. Jess wasn't even at the school at the same time as her disruptive siblings, but Johnson clearly hoped to extract his retribution from the final Tidy in his care, and if he took me down with her, then so be it; revenge, not only for Jess's false allegation, but also for everything that had gone before. Barry Johnson was an outsider, a man looking for a reason to belong, and Jess and I unwittingly provided it.

I left the headmistress's office that day with a stern warning and an unequivocal edict: I was no longer to act as a mentor for Jessica Tidy. Of course, I protested vehemently, explaining, at length and as calmly as I could, that Johnson was wrong; Jess and I worked well together, that was all, nothing untoward was going on. I had already made a huge difference to her grades, I could show the headmistress the stats, if she liked. Jess's work was really improving. To jeopardise everything we'd achieved thus far, so close to exams, based on gossip and hearsay – well, it was madness.

Alternative arrangements had already been made, she advised me coldly. Jess would be assigned a new mentor, a female member of staff this time. 'To avoid any further difficulties.'

I should have been shocked, worried, angry, and possibly grateful that no further disciplinary action was being taken, but all I could think was, how am I going to help Jess now? What can I engineer to make sure I'm still there for her? And that, to me, was much more *of a revelation than Johnson's perverted assertions that Jess and I were 'unnaturally close'. Was I really prepared to risk my profession for the sake of one girl? A girl so provocative, so needy, that our relationship had attracted the unwanted attention of 'several of my colleagues', sufficiently troubled by what they had supposedly witnessed that they felt 'compelled' to take their worries directly to the top.*

I was barely in my car by the time I decided yes, Jess was much more important to me than their petty accusations, and with that epiphany came a great sense of calm, for it didn't matter what the personal cost was, as long as I could still be there for her. Nothing else was as imperative as—

I force myself to stop reading, tears blurring my vision, obliterating the rest of my husband's damning words. What is he saying? That she was the only thing that mattered to him, and Frey and I were what . . . *nothing?* He was prepared to risk his profession for *that girl*, but not only that, he was happy to sacrifice us too – his wife and child? It didn't matter what he lost – his career, his marriage, his reputation at the very least – if he could still be there for *her*.

I push the chair back so forcibly the wheels catch on the rug and I almost topple over, my outstretched fingers reaching forwards to steady myself on the edge of Mark's desk. I stand and wipe my eyes with flattened palms, pausing to cover my tracks before I leave the room; the chair and rug neatly placed, the computer in sleep mode as he'd left it. Closing the door behind me.

I go downstairs, but it's not enough to be away from the

study. I need to leave the house, clear my head for an hour or two, somewhere I can vent the anger which grows within me, begging for release.

I grab my keys from the kitchen table, then stop, staring at the empty chair where Frey had been seated earlier this evening. She was a sixteen-year-old girl, still a child when she'd looked up from her place at the table and asked if I believed her father – a whispered question across the toast and cereal. Mark was on bail, the months to the trial stretching out before us, a hideous limbo in which we were expected to eat, sleep, and Frey still attend school. I told my daughter that yes, of course I believed her father, an automatic response which came without much thought, and mindful of the fact Mark was across the hall in the sitting room. She nodded, seemed relieved. Her world was crumbling, who could blame her for seeking that assurance? She was my baby, and I needed to protect her. What else could I do but choose to believe him when he told me nothing had happened?

I message Will, then slam the front door behind me, anxious to be gone before Mark returns with Walter. Even if Will can't get away at such short notice, I need to get out, to walk in the cold and the dark, away from the cottage, and my husband's imminent return. I need to *do* something.

Jess

Wednesday, 7th December 2016 (Evening)

A loud sound jolts me awake. I sit up, my eyes adjusting to the darkness as I wipe the drool from the side of my mouth, my bare feet like ice blocks. Beside them, a wine glass is on its side on the carpet, but it isn't smashed, so I don't understand why there's so much broken glass, the scattered diamonds catching the light from the street lamps as the curtains flutter towards me. I stand, one hand to the arm of the sofa, woozy as I catch my breath. I must have dozed off, exhausted after Becky and Will's visit, then the exertion of filling the skip. I pick my way across the room to close the window, and something sharp embeds itself in my bare foot, slicing into the calloused skin. *Fuck!* I flick the light on and see my own blood as I lift my heel to pull out the pointed sliver of glass. The curtain flaps again and I shiver, wondering why I opened the window, and that's when I notice there's a bundle lying on the carpet. The parcel is wrapped in lined paper, an elastic hairband securing the note which covers three sides of the muddy brick. I hop towards it, turning it in my hands to feel the weight of it, then I reach for my phone.

'Will? Can you hear me? Are you at home?' I fall back on to the sofa and lift my bleeding foot in the air. 'No, I can, just about, but it's a terrible line. Listen, you need to come over. Yes, now! Someone's thrown a brick through the window. Just like before. Who would do that after all these years, Will? Who?'

'Thank goodness you're here.' I step aside to allow Will inside. 'You were quick!'

'Lucky I had this on the van,' he says, showing me the large sheet of plywood wedged under his arm, his metal toolbox in the other hand. I follow him into the front room and flop down on the sofa, a collection of bloodied tissues surrounding me.

'You sure you're OK?' he asks, looking around at the mess.

'Just a cut foot.' I wave it in his direction as he moves closer. 'I'm OK, honestly.'

He pushes my foot away in mock disgust, and crouches down to open the toolbox. 'Stick it under the tap while I get started, and put some shoes on!'

'Lucky it didn't hit you,' Will says when I come back, my damp foot now pushed into a trainer, although there's a stab of pain when I try to walk on it. 'Did you see anyone outside?'

I shake my head, kicking the trainer off. 'I was asleep on the sofa.'

'Quite a party,' he remarks, glancing up from the broken pieces of glass he's gathering into his open palm.

He's looking at the emptied bottle of wine, now placed on the table next to the muddied parcel. I hop over to inspect the wrapped honey-coloured brick, completely different from the red bricks used round here.

'Reconstituted stone,' Will informs me as he concludes his fingertip search of the carpet, emptying his hands into a piece of rag he's spread out at his knees. 'It's what they're using for the new developments.' He stands up and takes the brick, balancing it across the palm of his right hand. 'The ones near the Winters' cottage.'

'Probably kids, mucking around like before,' I reply, watching as Will peels back a corner of the paper to rub his thumb across the angles of the stone beneath.

Will shakes his head. 'And they walked over the fields to bring back this one brick specially to smash our window?' He points to the broken pane of glass. 'I didn't believe the "kids mucking about" theory last time, and it seems even less likely now.'

'You're probably right.' I hug myself as the wind lifts the curtain and blows the used tissues around the room, spattered with blood as though I'd cleared up after a major incident, not just a small cut to my foot. 'But you know what the gossip is like round here, anyone could have heard the rumours and thought it would be funny to—'

Will raises an eyebrow as he pulls the elasticated hairband free of the brick, then he turns over the mud-streaked sheet of A4. 'Let's take a look, shall we?'

'What does it say?' I snatch it from his hand, the corner ripping off between his thick thumb and forefinger as he tries to hold on to it.

'Don't read it, Jess!'

The words are scrawled in thick black felt pen, the mud from the brick merging with the writing to form smudges and runs, although the simple message remains clear.

You're a lying bitch, Jess Tidy!

'Same as last time,' I say. 'I assumed it would be.'

'Ignore it, sis.' He holds out his hand for the note. 'Two sugars for me, and better put some in yours too.' He's smiling, although I can tell he's worried.

'Yeah, sure.' I close my hand around the sheet of lined paper, scrunching it into a tight ball. 'I'll get rid of this.'

Will gets to work as soon as he's downed his scalding tea. I watch from the sofa, my heel wrapped in a tea towel, the bleeding slowed by the cold water I plunged it in, but the throbbing pain remains. He retrieves the plywood from by the front door and nails it over the broken window, pin-tacks in his mouth as he tells me through gritted teeth it will have to do for tonight. It's too late to get the new glass now, the suppliers will all be closed. He doesn't suggest involving the police, not a surprise as it's not something we were raised to do, but when he turns to go I panic at the thought of being alone, limping along the hall behind him. 'Can't you stay a bit, Will?'

He opens the door and cold air rushes into the hallway. 'I would if I could, but things are a bit tricky at home right now.'

'Trouble in paradise?' I ask, regretting my comment immediately. Will doesn't smile, just shakes his head. He looks so tired, dark circles under his eyes as he looks down at my foot, asking again if I'm OK. My toes are creased as if I'm wearing an imaginary high heel, and I'm hobbling, but I say it's nothing really, grinning to reassure him.

'Where is she tonight?' I ask.

'*Who?*'

'Becky, of course.'

'Oh, right. She's at home, with Jackson. Why do you ask?'

'No reason,' I reply, wondering if he's worked out what it is I'm trying to say.

I watch from the hallway as he carries the heavy toolbox towards his van, calling over his right shoulder, 'Lock the door and go to bed. I'll pick up the new glass and see you first thing in the morning!' He stops. 'You sure you're gonna be OK?'

'I'll have to be,' I reply, but when he says he can call Becky, let her know he's staying a bit longer, I shake my head and close the door, pushing hard with my shoulder to make sure it's shut tight. Then I hop into the kitchen and open a fresh bottle of wine.

The alcohol exhausts me, the adrenalin emptying me out as it leaves my limp body. I climb the stairs slowly, my hand to the bannister, hauling myself up, a jabbing pain in my heel when I try to put my foot down. I pause, balancing a full glass of wine on the tread above me as I take my phone from my jeans pocket.

A car speeds past, startling me, the headlights tracking across the hallway through the etched glass in the door, the curtains closed in the front room to cover the makeshift repair. My thumb hovers over James's number as I decide if that's what I want. He would come straight over, I know that; reassure me, make sure the Winters are properly warned off this time, but what if it's not them? I'm sure there are plenty of people in this village who still think Mark is a good man and I'm the liar. And then there's Becky, a cold glint in her eyes when she'd looked at me. She could have left Jackson with her mum, come over, they're not that far away.

Head down, phone tucked back in my pocket, I pick up my wine and climb the rest of the stairs. I just need to get through the next few days, then I can put all of this behind me.

Karen

Wednesday, 7th December 2016 (Late Evening)

The front door is thrown open as I walk up the path to the cottage, Mark flying out. 'Where have you been all this time, Karen? I was worried sick.'

'I was walking it off,' I tell him, pushing past to go inside.

'Walking off what?' He follows me along the hallway into the kitchen. 'Karen, stop! You owe me an explanation, you've been out for ages. Where did you go?'

'I owe *you* an explanation?' I turn to look at him. 'You've got to be joking!' I take off my coat and throw it on the kitchen floor between us. It's soaked and streaked with mud along the hem.

'Look at the state of you!' He points at my shoes and tights. They're caked in sticky brown clods of earth, footprints trailing behind me. 'I came back with Walter and you weren't home. Why didn't you answer my calls?'

'I didn't hear my phone,' I lie.

'For God's sake, Karen. It's difficult enough at the moment, without you—'

'*Without me what?*' I kick my shoes off so violently mud and water spray up the fronts of the kitchen cupboards and on to Mark's trousers.

Mark stares back at me, his mouth set. 'What is the matter with you? Has something happened? Where have you been?'

I want to scream at him that I know how he felt about Jess, that I've read it all in his own words. But what do I know? That he was a fool? That he was flattered by the attention of an infatuated tart of a girl who played him for everything she could? I try hard to say nothing, to internalise my emotions as I've done before, but this time something inside me gives. 'Don't you dare blame me for all this! Don't you bloody dare!'

'For what?' Mark asks. 'You're not making any sense.'

'You're the one who brought all this on us, not me! You're the one who's made me—'

'Be careful, Karen.' Mark's face is white with shock, his hand held up as though I might run at him with fists raised. 'Be careful what you say!'

'Frey and I did nothing wrong.' I'm no longer shouting, although the urge to hurt him is still strong, not physically, but to wound him with words, as he has me. 'It's just as much our punishment as yours, this . . . *life.*'

'You think I deliberately ruined your life, and Freya's? That this was all my fault? Is that what you're saying?'

'No, of course not,' I concede, falling back on familiar ground. Mark looks so shaken. 'I don't know what I'm saying.

I'm exhausted. Exhausted by the whole thing. It's been ten years. When will it ever stop? Tell me that!'

'Maybe it won't,' he says, turning away.

'Don't you dare go back up there!' I scream after him as he walks out of the kitchen. 'Don't you dare!'

I follow him into the hallway where he's stopped, his hand to the bannister. The blackness is there, waiting to engulf us both, the fear of it almost as terrifying as my panic this nightmare will haunt our whole lives. I've hung on, just about, but what if I really let go, tell him I've had enough? What if I say I don't know whether I still believe him?

'I don't know what you want,' he says, as he turns back. 'I can't fight you or the system any more, Karen. I'm done.'

'You know what, Mark? Doing nothing is a decision too,' I tell him, although the words could just as easily apply to me. 'Sometimes you have to fight for the things that matter.' I stare at him, unblinking, waiting for his reply. 'Stand up and fight back!'

'What does that mean?'

'Nothing, Mark. There's nothing more to say, is there?'

I watch as he climbs the stairs, knowing he will return to her. To Jess. To a time when she was his obsession, perhaps still is. I don't know what I wanted from him, but something other than a retreat to the past. I scream under my breath, but if Mark hears me, it makes no difference, the door to his study closing behind him.

The study is empty when I finally follow Mark upstairs. I undress beside our bed, my husband's slight form unmoving beneath the duvet, his face turned to his pillow, my bedside light left on so I can find my way. He's so still I wonder if he's pretending to be asleep, but I say nothing as I slide in beside him, hoping the sleeping tablets I took downstairs will soon work. An hour later I'm still wide awake, staring at the clock as Mark's proximity crowds in on me, the bed too small tonight.

He doesn't stir as I get up, his breathing deep. I close the bedroom door behind me, then cross the landing, feeling my way through the darkness. In the study, I draw back the curtain just enough to let in the moonlight. The screen casts a blueish glow as it slowly comes to life. I type in the familiar passcode, then listen for Mark next door, hearing only my own breaths, in and out.

I start by opening a department store website, one I've visited before, clicking on the dress I recently ordered, the one I had to return. Then I roll the chair a little closer, as slowly and quietly as I can, although the sound of the wheels on the uneven wooden floorboards still alarms me enough to pause again, listening to the silence before I begin to read.

Chapter Seven – May 2006

Following my frank exchange of views with the headmistress, it was difficult to maintain regular contact with Jess, our mentoring sessions now banned, but somehow we managed to meet between my other lessons, falling into step with one another as we pushed our way through the crowds funnelling along the corridors. I'd been told with no equivocation that I must relinquish my mentoring duties, but there was no explicit instruction to keep away from Jess completely; and certainly nothing that stopped me from speaking to her should our paths accidentally cross. Besides, Jess had little else to occupy her at school, her new mentor already abandoned, or so I deduced, for Jess was only interested in discussing the imminent 'prom', an awful Americanism I refused to adopt, although in the end it was a word I would be forced to use again and again, a jocular note to it that always jarred.

'I'm going to get sooo drunk,' she told me as we walked the length of an empty corridor together one bright mid-May morning.

'Jess, I really think—'

'What do you think, Mark?' she asked, looking up at me with those big eyes, flicking her mass of curls, such a startling shade of flaming red, like a Titian Venus.

'You mustn't call me that, Jess,' I told her. 'It's Mr Winter to you. And don't plan to get drunk, in fact maybe don't go to the prom at all.'

'But that would be such a waste of my sexy new dress,' she replied, telling me about the strapless bra she needed to borrow from Becky, although 'Bex's tits' were apparently much bigger than hers, which might be a problem. She knew she was pushing me too far, but she seemed to enjoy my embarrassment, an amusement to her, especially as we were forced to meet in the most public areas of the school, the threat of another warning from the headmistress, or worse, ever present.

'What do you think, Mr Winter?' she coaxed. 'Should I try a tiny lace thong, or not bother with knickers at all, shave everything off just in case?'

She was reckless, pushing for something to happen between us, or if not, ready for when it did. It was an amusement to her, something to fill those long, final few days at school, but it was my professional reputation she was risking.

'You need to be careful, Jess,' I told her, my patience running out. 'I might get tired of your silly games.'

She said nothing, but her expression was enough.

'Jess, wait! I'm sorry!'

I had to pick up my pace to keep up, both of us startled to find ourselves surrounded by a curious group of Year Sevens as we rounded the corner too fast, thirty or so pairs of wide eyes staring at us as their form tutor shepherded them away. Jess used the confusion of that moment to disappear, knowing I was trapped, unable to call after her this time.

I spotted her the next day walking across the playing fields, towards the hall. She was alone, head down, phone in hand. She didn't notice me wave through the window, or perhaps she was still annoyed at my comment, her lack of response a schoolgirl sulk. I chased after her, leaving my Year Eight class to 'silent reading', the ignominy of my breathlessness a great delight to her, a peal of giggles erupting from her open mouth as I approached. At least I'd made her smile again. And I smiled too.

'Do you have a date for the prom yet?' I asked, as we circled the empty hall side by side, our meanderings taking us back inside. I was whispering to avoid anyone overhearing our less than appropriate conversation, although we were thankfully quite alone. I hoped that by engaging her in conversation that interested her, we could then move on to more academic matters, but her plans for the prom were also troubling me.

'No, and I won't do now,' she replied. 'Why do you ask, Mr Winter?'

When she used my full name, she always pronounced it as if it were the filthiest swear word she could think of, an upwards inflection on the second syllable.

'Because . . . if you found someone reliable, someone who cared about you, then you wouldn't need to get drunk, and I wouldn't have to worry what might happen to you at the prom.'

'You worry about me?' she asked, looking up at me and smiling. 'No one worries about me except sometimes my brother, Will.'

I looked across the hall then, past Jess, towards the woman who'd wandered in from the other side, a peripatetic music teacher who always wore a scowl, her sanctimonious gaze finding me across the expanse of parquet as she lifted the lid on the piano and struck a deep chord. Oddly, her disapproval made my position clearer. Why should I bow to the pressure and prejudices of others? I was Jess's mentor, or at least I had been until recently. The frustrating thing was, her grades had been improving; it had already started to make a difference. It seemed to me that I was the only member of staff likely to provide Jess with the kind of positive adult role model she so desperately needed, and yet my efforts were constantly thwarted.

'Of course I worry about you,' I told Jess, loud enough to be certain the hard-faced woman would hear me too. 'And if there's ever anything you need, you only have to ask. I'll always be there for you, Jess. Always. I want you to know that you're my absolute priority, OK?'

If the woman looked over again, shook her head or glared, then I chose to ignore her, for she knew nothing of my motivations. It was no one's business but ours, or so I thought, but of course I was entirely wrong.

I close the document with a heavy heart, but what else had I expected? A vindication of my loyalty as a spouse? A justification for all the years I may have wasted in unquestioning faith, believing my husband was as much a victim of *that girl* as I was? The thing I find hardest to stomach is that Mark clearly feels he has done nothing wrong. Nothing at all. The anger rises in me and I suppress the urge to march into our bedroom and pull my husband from his sleep, demanding answers.

I glance at my phone again, checking for a new message or missed call, and finding neither. I'd been so desperate to see Will when I left the cottage earlier this evening, but now I'm less certain. Panic rises at the thought I might have already lost Will; an answer of sorts, but it's more complicated than that. I have no idea how I'll cope without those moments of escape, the only respite I have, but so much was said that cannot be taken back. I pick up my phone to send him a message, but despite my fears, pride stops me. It was such a breach of trust, and one I know cuts deep for us both, accusations and recriminations on both sides. The moment that brick was thrown, our elaborate but fragile negotiation of the past was shattered. And now, in this loneliest of hours, I'm afraid there may be no way back for us. Any of us.

Three Months Before . . .

Supervision Session #7 – Jessica Tidy – Tuesday, September 20th, 2016

Full notes in client file ref: 718/16

Meeting taped, transcript of relevant section below (abridged)

Jess: Yes, it was tough talking about it, but good too. I've resisted it for years, locked it away in a box inside me, pretended it wasn't there, but now I've opened the box it's like I can't shut the lid back down.

Me: I'm pleased you feel it's helping. There was one thing I wanted to clarify with you from last time. You said you were upset when Becky told you she fancied your brother, that you didn't think she was good enough for him, but you also said she was your best friend?

Jess: I suppose I didn't like the thought she might take him away from me, which she kind of did in the end, but it was mainly because she slept around, loads of different boys, and she was trouble. Even Mum warned me about her, and Mum was the worst judge of character.

Me: You don't approve of Becky, even though she and your brother have stayed together and now have a child?

Jess: None of my business.

Me: Do you feel excluded?

Jess: Not really. I haven't heard from Becky since the night of the prom, but I don't think we'd have stayed friends anyway. It was one of those friendships you make because it suits at the time. We never had much in common, other than a bad reputation. And she showed her true colours afterwards, dropping me like that.

Me: So you turned to Mark, after you'd argued with Becky?

Jess: I knew he'd look after me. He said I was his number one priority.

Me: It sounds very much like he was grooming you.

Jess: *Grooming me?* I don't know. I guess. But I thought he was genuine, some of the time at least. He risked a lot too, to be there for me.

Me: Why do you think that was?

Jess: Because he cared? I don't know. Maybe it was just a sexual thing.

Me: You said that once you were alone you ran away from him, towards the Exclusion Unit. You called it 'a stupid game'.

Jess: Yes, and it was stupid, but I had no idea I was leading him on . . . well, not exactly leading him on, but if I gave him any wrong signals that night, or before . . . I know I was flirty—

Me: Jess, I'm sorry to interrupt, but you mustn't legitimise his behaviour. It wasn't your fault for *'leading him on'* or *'giving out the wrong signals'*. And in any case, there was never an issue of consent. You were his student, under eighteen, it was incumbent on him to behave appropriately. To put it bluntly, even if you initiated a sexual liaison, or any kind of physical contact, in the eyes of the law the onus was on him to stop it.

Karen

Thursday, 8th December 2016 (Late Morning)

The washing machine turns my muddied clothes from last night, the kitchen floor mopped clean, my coat on a hanger over the bath to finish drying out after I sponged it down. The morning has come and almost gone, and in that time I've gathered enough strength to clear up the physical damage from last night, although my thoughts are still a mess. I contemplate the glint of the sharp knife as I chop carrots for soup, our frugal lunch, pausing to run the blade lightly across the pad of my thumb, the indentation satisfying. In the soft dent of skin is a trace of carrot juice, a line of deep orange, although a crimson bloom of blood would be better.

Frey befriended a girl at school who self-harmed. A mousy thing who barely spoke the one time she came here. I'd been pleased at first, Frey seemed to have so few friends, but then I'd noticed the silvery lines criss-crossing the girl's skinny forearms. I couldn't understand, didn't get the point of hacking into your own skin repeatedly, or see how it could possibly alleviate any suffering. I told Frey to keep her distance after the girl had finally gone home, and fortunately the friendship soon fizzled out, but I worried Frey would do something stupid like that. She was always such a sensitive child, especially after Mark was arrested. I watched her for a reaction, against me perhaps, the parent left behind to take the flak, but she remained a compliant, caring, devoted daughter. I raise the knife and strike the chopping board with it again and again, the hefty whacks doing nothing to assuage my frustration. *Everything comes back to Jessica fucking Tidy! Bitch!*

'*Karen?*' I turn to see Mark behind me, his brow furrowed in irritation. 'What are you doing?'

'Nothing.' I drop the knife into the sink, the sound echoing around the kitchen. 'Just making soup for our lunch.'

'Soup again,' he comments. 'We have a lot of soup.'

He returns to his study, the sound of his chair rolling back and forth overhead grating on my nerves.

I resist my natural inclination to leave the house, allowing my imagination to take me out the door instead, visualising how I would turn left at the end of the lane, towards the village to find Will, my boots tapping hard on the pavement until he was there, the sheer force of him overtaking everything else. But he's not there; at least, not for me.

I stir the soup and try to follow my daughter's advice to hold my nerve, just for the next few days, her messages this morning full of touching concern. As her father so often tells us, we can never retaliate, any of us. We have no rights, no recall, no power. We are the guilty and we must pay. All of us, not just Mark.

But surely it would be understandable if I were to falter? I'm only flesh and blood. There's a limit to how much I can take. We thought that good sense would prevail once before, but it never did, and now I know it never will, and the pain of that, and the loss of contact with Will, is too much.

'How could you, Kar? How could you?' he'd asked, and the embers inside me had died. 'She was on her own in the house. She was terrified. It could have hit her. Did you think of that?'

I pick up the knife and slice a carrot in half, from green fronds to root. Then I hold the blade up to the window, twisting the wedge-shaped sliver of metal to catch the low rays of winter sun, smiling to myself as I imagine it cutting into flesh, the ease with which it would all be over; so easy.

It's quick, hardly any discomfort, just a moment of hurt, hot and heady. I look down at my hands in the sink, covered in blood, the knife in my palm, the blade slicked deepest red. The water gushes from the cold tap and I force myself to shove my upturned hand beneath it, grimacing at first, the cut soon cleaned, only shallow after all. The pain had taken away every other thought, and I immediately miss that moment. Almost as much as I miss Will.

'Karen, what the—?' Mark grabs my hand and holds it in his, the blood oozing again, this time over his palm too.

He plunges our linked hands under the cold tap, his face contorted with anger, his words shouted, the passion I tried to invoke in him last night as we'd argued finally here, and then I'm laughing, and I don't even know why.

He shoves me away, swears and walks out, shrugging his coat on as he crosses the back garden with the dog, the gate opened so roughly I think it might fall down as it swings shut behind them.

Jess

Thursday, 8th December 2016 (Afternoon)

It's cold standing in the front garden, the drizzle soaking my hair and shoulders. My curls start to sag, the dampness leaching into the fabric of my cheap polyester coat, but I don't go inside. I like watching Will work, always have. The way he pokes the tip of his tongue out without even realising it, and the concentration in his face. He's so good at this kind of thing, and he never makes a big deal of it, just gets on with whatever needs doing, shrugging off any praise as if everyone is as skilful as he is.

'Where were you this morning?' I ask. 'You said first thing.'

Will looks up from the replacement pane he's holding to the frame and frowns. 'I couldn't pick up the glass till now.'

I watch him for a while without further interruption, but then I'm reminded of something I can't help sharing. 'Do you remember that dolls' house you built for my eighth birthday, tiled paper on the roof, and carpet in each of the four rooms?'

'It was only a few bits of ply screwed together.' He asks me to pass him the tub of fresh putty he's brought with him. 'No big deal.'

'That's what you said at the time.' I hold up a tub and he nods. 'But I loved it. What happened to it, do you think?'

Will shrugs. 'No idea, Mum probably burnt it for firewood.'

'We don't have a fire,' I point out, and he raises his eyebrows.

Mum had been so jealous, said he never made anything like that for her, wouldn't even cut the grass when she asked. It wasn't true, Will had often tidied up the garden, or taken a strimmer to the front path, but never again after that comment.

I lean against the skip, already full, and pull my hood over my soggy hair, watching whilst Will carefully fits the new pane of glass to the opening, pressing the soft putty around the edges to hold it in place. He squints with concentration as he draws a flat rounded knife across the tacky edges to form a neat line around the window, then he wipes the excess putty on his shirt, streaking the checks with beige as he passes me the knife to hold.

'Have to wait a week or so to paint it,' he tells me, standing back to survey the window. 'Needs to harden off, and this weather won't help.'

'It looks a lot neater for the inspection,' I say, admiring his handiwork. 'Well done.'

'*Inspection?*' Will asks, spitting on his hands, then wiping them down the front of his trousers. 'What inspection?'

'The landlord's coming over later, make sure the house is OK for the next tenants.'

'He's in for a nasty shock.' Will takes a printed business

card out of his shirt pocket, asks me to pass it on. 'Something I'm trying to get into, expand the business.'

'Impressive,' I say, reading the card. A raindrop lands on his name, the *i* in Tidy spreading to look like an *o*. 'Landscaping and General House Maintenance,' I read aloud. 'I had no idea.'

Will smiles. 'Hidden depths, me.'

I follow him back inside, waiting in the hall as he rinses his hands under the kitchen tap. He joins me when he's done, pressing the toe of his boot into the swirls that charge their way between us. 'Carpets will have to go,' he says, screwing up his nose. 'They stink.'

'I'll get them all professionally cleaned,' I reply, asking if he wants a cup of tea, or maybe something stronger?

'Nah, I should probably get going.'

He picks up the brick one-handed from the console table, the note too, which I'd straightened out then folded and tucked beneath it. He catches my eye and says I shouldn't worry, it was probably just a sick joke from some idiot in the village who heard I was back. Nothing personal.

'You don't believe that any more than I do,' I reply, noticing something change in his expression. 'Will, do you know something?'

'No, course not.' He tucks the brick under his left arm and holds the note up to me, now sandwiched between his middle and index finger. 'I'll get rid of this for you, shall I?' He slips the folded sheet in his shirt pocket. 'Seeing as you haven't.'

He steps out the door, then looks back at me, the light fading on what must be one of the shortest days of the year.

'I wouldn't have given it to James, I was just—'

'You told me you were throwing it away, Jess.'

I try to think of an excuse, but Will knows me too well. 'I wanted to know who sent it, that's all. James is a friend. He's on our side.' Will opens his mouth to speak, then seems to think better of it and shakes his head instead.

'Who do you think it was?' I ask.

'Doesn't matter now, does it?' Will is looking at the brick as if it will offer up a name.

'Thanks a lot!'

'No, I don't mean it like that, Jess. Who do you think it was?'

I shrug, waiting to see if he pushes me for a name, but I've no evidence it was Becky, or anyone else for that matter. If he's protecting her, I won't draw him out with a half-hearted accusation.

'You call me if you need anything, OK?' Will says, turning away.

He walks to his van and tosses the brick into the back, a loud thud when it lands. I watch him drive off, then turn on my heel and close the door quickly behind me, my hands shaky as I double-check the lock.

Karen

Thursday, 8th December 2016 (Afternoon)

I wait a long time after Jess has closed the door, maybe five, ten minutes. It's raining hard now, although as Mum used to say, *'Once you're wet, you're wet.'* What would she say if she could see me now, skulking in the alley opposite Lisa Tidy's house? She certainly wouldn't be impressed. It wasn't like I planned it this way, but I was trapped once Will's van drew up, the pair of them outside for ages. Although, there was some comfort in seeing him, even if he was with *her*. He made a good job of the repair as far as I could see. No one would know a brick was hurled through the window last night.

I cross the road, a drip running down the back of my neck as I glance back to make sure she's not watching me. Then I pick up my pace; I'm late for my appointment.

I don't even know why I wanted to see the damage in the first place, perhaps in the hopes it wouldn't be real, but of course it was, and to compound my despair I'd then been forced to witness the bond between Jess and Will, still so evident, despite the years they've spent apart.

I take my vibrating phone from my coat pocket and reject the call before I can change my mind. I don't want to talk to Will, not now. Not until I'm sure what I want. Besides, I'm running late, and despite everything, I still have some self-respect.

The surgery is packed with damp coats and phlegmy coughs, the air polluted with germs, multiplying and spreading further illness. I take a seat in the corner, away from the sniffers and hackers, and pick up a magazine. I'm halfway through an article on the menopause when my name is called, a youngish woman, short skirt and jaunty Mary-Jane shoes, repeating my name, 'Mrs Winter?'

'Yes, sorry.'

I follow the heels through the door she holds open for me and then into her office. Her tone is clipped, a mask of friendliness that doesn't make eye contact. She consults her screen, and takes my blood pressure, higher than it should be.

'I rushed here,' I tell her. 'I was running late.'

'Everyone's BP is a little raised in the surgery, we do take that into account. Are you under any stress, Mrs Winter?'

'No, not really.'

'But you're here for more medication, for your anxiety?'

I tell her I've been on the same tablets for years, ever since . . . She looks at me to elaborate. Her eyebrows are prominent, pencilled in and neatly plucked. I wonder if she goes to the lady in the supermarket who has a chair like a dentist and a price list taped to the wall beside it. I tried it once, but my eyebrows were on fire as I pushed my trolley around the fruit and veg aisles. The thought reminds me of my encounter with Jess, and I must make a sound, a sigh perhaps, for the doctor raises both darkened brows at me, her eyes wide, waiting for an explanation. Maybe she doesn't know about Mark, the one person in the village who hasn't heard the tawdry tale; a newcomer, a professional and therefore not prone to gossip in her line of work. You can't be too careful, I guess, so easy to lose your job, one mistake—

'Karen?' She's looking at the plaster across my palm, a brown stain at its centre, the wound still weeping, although it's dried up a little. 'Have you cut your hand? Would you like me to take a look, whilst you're here?'

I jump when she touches my arm and asks me to explain what's been going on, says I should take my time, there's no rush. Which I know is a lie because there's a waiting room full of disgruntled pensioners out there. I tell her she's very kind, but really, I'm fine, just an accident, making soup. *Silly me.* A tear runs down my cheek and she offers me a tissue, which I use then tuck in my palm to conceal the plaster.

'Our family went through some very difficult times,' I tell her. 'It was a few years ago now, but . . .' I readjust my sleeve, still pushed up to my armpit where the blood pressure cuff was fitted. 'I'd just like a repeat prescription, please.' I look up at her and sniff. 'The receptionist told me I had to have a review, but I know what I need. My sleeping pills too.'

'The thing is,' she's tapping on her keyboard now, 'these tablets are meant to be a short-term aid to recovery. You've only recently had a renewal, and they should have lasted you a lot longer than this.'

'Sometimes I take an extra one, if I need it.'

'Have you thought about counselling?' She swivels back to face me, her high heels wrapped around the base of her chair. 'There's a long wait I'm afraid, but—'

'No!' I stand up.

'Mrs Winter—'

'I just want more of my usual tablets, and if you won't give them to me then I'd like to see someone else. The other doctor always gave them to me. Is he still here? I'd like to see him instead, please.'

'I'm not saying you need to come straight off them, but if we can talk—'

'I don't want to talk, I just want my tablets!'

She gets up from her chair and steps towards me, placing a hand on my arm, asking to see my cut palm. I don't mean to, but I instinctively recoil from her touch, and maybe I push her hand away, or perhaps I'm more forceful than that, batting her arm with mine. Her eyebrows knit together, and she picks up the phone on her desk, asks for someone to join us as soon as possible, tells them there's a *situation*, enunciating the word to reinforce its significance. I'm apologising to the doctor when the receptionist arrives, a nurse at her side, the latter dressed in a navy uniform and wearing a much more sympathetic expression than the hard-faced receptionist, or the doctor, who now looks upset, although I have no idea why. The harder I try to convince them, the more it seems to have the opposite effect, the three women inflaming the situation by telling me loudly to calm down, or they'll have to call the police. *The police?* It's the threat of that which cuts through everything else. I shout at them to get out of my way. Then I'm outside again, the cold air sobering me up, as if I'd emerged from a party, my thoughts muddled by the warm fuzz of alcohol rather than the white heat of frustration, and I'm so confused, so disconnected from what just occurred, that I'm left wondering if any of it really happened, except when I check in my bag there's still no prescription slip. I think about going back inside, but when I walk up the ramp to the door I see them all there, looking out at me, and I turn and run.

I'm almost home when I see a figure approaching, familiar, a dog at his side, although I can't be certain it's Mark until we are almost upon one another, the sheet of rain and my tears fogging my view.

'You OK? You're soaked again,' Mark says, but I walk straight past him and turn into the lane. 'Karen, wait! The surgery called.'

I stop, halted by his words, the incident I left behind running through me again as I wait for him to catch up with me, Walter beside him. 'What did they tell you?'

'Not much,' he replies, breathless. 'Can you explain?'

'I only wanted my prescription. They wouldn't give it to me.'

'It's waiting for you, at the surgery,' he says, linking his arm around my wet sleeve and turning me around. 'Only a few days' worth apparently, you'll have to make another appointment for a proper review, but it's enough to tide you over. Come on, let's go together.'

I don't go inside the surgery with my husband, standing on the pavement with the dog until Mark joins us again. I hand him Walter's lead in return for the prescription and an appointment card, then they wait in the rain as I take the dispensing note into the chemist and collect my tablets. It's all strangely amicable, as if we were on a pleasant outing together, a bubble of unreality surrounding us.

'All set?' Mark asks, looking up as I emerge.

I nod, linking my arm through his again as we walk home, Walter sniffing the damp air.

'What happened?' Mark asks more than once, but I shake my head and he eventually changes tack, asking, 'How's your hand?'

I stop, removing my arm from his. 'I don't want to talk about it, Mark. That's what we do, us two. We carry on, pretend everything's OK – why change now?'

I walk on ahead and they follow, Walter's claws tapping on the pavement, Mark's boots slapping in the puddles, the cottage dark as we approach from the lane. By the time we're inside, flicking on lights and drawing curtains, I'm almost back to normal, or close to, removing my wet coat and boots and telling Mark how it was all a misunderstanding, good to have it sorted now. I sense Mark's relief, and mine, but then he says he better get back to his work, he's left his manuscript mid-sentence. He laughs, and the air crackles between us.

'No,' I say, pulling at his sweater, 'I'd like us to spend some time together. We can cook, like we used to.'

'Karen, I—'

'Please, I'm asking you to do this for me. *For us.*'

Mark hesitates a moment too long, and I feel the anger surge inside me, then he says of course he'll stay, he just needs to pop up to his study first.

We work together to produce the meal, but instead of cheering me up, as I'd hoped it might, it only makes me feel worse. I ache for Will, checking my phone for messages or any other missed calls, regretting my earlier pride, and when I watch Mark I can see the pretence in him too, how he's trying to convince himself as much as me that so much damage can be fixed in a single act of reconciliation. But for now, we set aside the outside world, and Jess Tidy, the incident at the surgery, a broken window, even Will, and instead we hole up in our moated cottage, a normal married couple and their dog, enjoying a companionable meal in our cosy kitchen. Appearances, as they so often are, entirely deceptive.

It only lasts an hour before Mark is back in his study, door closed, and I'm returning Will's call.

Two Months Before . . .

Supervision Session #8 – Jessica Tidy – Tuesday, October 4th, 2016

Full notes in client file ref: 718/16

Meeting taped, transcript of relevant section below (abridged)

Me: I promise you, Jess, there is no problem as far as I'm concerned.

Jess: That's good. I was worried you might, I don't know, consider me unprofessional for only wanting to talk about my issues, not my clients. I went over and over it in my head, convinced you wouldn't want to see me again.

Me: Why are you so concerned with my opinion, Jess?

Jess: No, it's not that. I'm not looking for your approval, or anyone else's, but I'd hate to lose you as my supervisor, and after last time, I thought maybe I'd turned it into a kind of therapy thing too much. Do you know what I mean?

Me: It hadn't crossed my mind, and anyway, we agreed it was a relevant part of your supervision. I wish you'd called me, if you were worried?

Jess: No, that's fine. Thanks for putting my mind at rest.

Me: I meant to ask you about the sixteen-year-old client you mentioned before. Have you heard from her at all?

Jess: No. I did try to find her, but she didn't return any of my calls or emails.

Me: Such a shame, but you mustn't dwell on it. She's not your responsibility.

Jess: Easy to say that; dismiss people.

Me: No, not really, but it's important to remember clients leave therapy for many different reasons. I imagine you must have been disappointed to have lost her as a client?

Jess: Yeah, I'd have liked to see her again.

Me: What would you have said to her, if you did?

Jess: That she's still so young, nothing is set in stone. She can change, reinvent herself. Not that she would have believed me – you don't at that age, do you?

Me: Anything else?

Jess: I don't know . . . maybe reinforce the fact that just because someone older tells you something, it doesn't always make it right. You can challenge authority; respect should be earned, not demanded. And to rely on yourself, your own instincts, because no one else has your interests as their main concern. Only you.

Me: Do you think she would have listened?

Jess: I think she probably already knew.

Me: So she didn't need you to tell her, it was inside her all along?

Jess: I guess so. It's hard to tell, isn't it, what you sense in someone, whether it's real or imagined? Maybe I wanted to see something that wasn't there or perhaps she told me what she thought I wanted to hear. People say things because they want to please someone, it's as simple as that.

Jess

Friday, 9th December 2016 (Afternoon)

Becky looks completely different today, the plastered on make-up toned right down, her knee-length dress covering most of the lumps and bumps. I look hard but can't find any trace of awkwardness or embarrassment in her greeting, her right hand outstretched as she gets up from behind her desk, her expression sympathetic, thanking me for finding the time to come in. I almost laugh, but it feels inappropriate here, and Becky doesn't crack a smile, her mask of professionalism maintained. I'd like to rap my knuckles on the side of her skull and say, *'Hello?! Is the real Becky Lorimer in there?!'*

'Will's seen to most of the funeral arrangements,' Becky advises me again, sliding her chair in as far as it will go and gesturing for me to sit down.

'You said I needed to come in to finalise things?'

I fiddle with the folder of paperwork she's handed me. There's a picture of a family grouped around a desk like this one on the front cover. They look suitably sombre, but also oddly content, as though the process were comforting, which I guess is the idea.

'Just a few loose ends to tie up,' she replies, clicking on the mouse as she squints at her computer screen, screwing up her face and leaning closer as she talks me through the details. Her name plate, displayed prominently on her desk, advises me she's *Rebecca Lorimer, Manager.*

'Ah yes, cars. Will wasn't sure . . . they are expensive. He suggested you two might come in the van, but clearly that's not . . .' She starts typing on her keyboard at speed. 'Obviously, you'll need the hearse, and a mourners' car. Perhaps leave it at that?'

I nod, not really knowing what I'm agreeing to, but she's typing again, only pausing when a male colleague hovers at her shoulder. I watch their exchange, the discussion of little interest to me, although Becky's business-like persona is endlessly fascinating. It's crazy to think this is the same Becky Lorimer who would spit on the polished black cars parked out back, landing expertly aimed flying gobs of spittle on mirror-shine bonnets before shouting, 'Run, Jess! Run!' It's also hard to imagine her lobbing a brick through my window last night, then sitting here with no hint of discomfort. If she has something to hide, she's doing a great job.

'Sorry about that,' she says to me, dismissing her colleague with a quick-smart smile, but he comes straight back, apologising as he forgot to tell her that her mother has called again. Apparently, Jackson is being particularly—

'I'm with a client,' Becky snaps at him, staring at her screen.

'Now let's see, we've agreed on flowers, order of service, and although it's not strictly my remit, I've also organised a modest buffet at the pub opposite the church. Any idea on numbers?'

I shake my head, adjusting my opinion yet again. Is this really the same girl who sat beside me in Johnson's classes and called him every swear word under the sun – including some I'd never heard of before or since – and now uses words like 'remit'?

'I can't imagine many will come,' I reply.

From the phone calls I've made so far, leafing through Mum's ancient address book for any familiar names, our extended family are either impossible to track down, or uninterested.

'You'd be surprised . . .' Becky tells me, still typing, 'Lisa knew a lot of people.'

I don't believe many from the village will mourn Mum's passing, and Becky's presumed knowledge of my mother is hard to swallow without comment, but perhaps I'm underestimating the attraction of a free buffet. I decide to let it go.

'So, the vicar is aware of the burial request, and he'll pop round to see you at the house some time before Tuesday.' Becky looks up from her screen.

'Please ask him not to.'

She looks up at me, then clicks on the mouse. 'OK, let's see what this adds up to.' She clicks again, then winces. 'You'll need to settle your part of the bill soon, Jess. I can't make any exceptions for family, and burials are always more expensive. Will and I are happy to pay our share, of course, but—'

'Yes, about that—'

'And, Jess, as we're on our own . . .' Becky glances behind

her to the empty desk of her colleague then she leans closer towards me and lowers her voice to barely more than a whisper. 'I just want to say I'm sorry about that night at the prom, you know . . . slapping you. I was so drunk. God knows why. I could handle my drink back then, not that it's an excuse, but I was off my head that night. Anyway, we both said things we shouldn't have and—' She looks around her again, then carries on. 'I should have stayed with you and, well, I've thought about it a lot over the years, and I just wanted to say I'm sorry. I mean, you and I go way back, and I'd like it if we could be friends, now we're related.' She clears her throat and sits back in her chair, typing rapidly. 'Now, let's work out this bill.'

I rewind her words in my head, trying to catch up with the sudden shift in our conversation. She's right, she should apologise, but not only for that night. Compared with the hurt her lack of contact has caused me over the years, a drunken argument and a slap is nothing.

'OK,' she says, a little louder. 'That's four thousand and seventy-three so far. Shall we call it a flat four for cash? So that's two grand each.'

'*How much?!*' My shock echoes around the small office, attracting the attention of her colleague, who looks over. 'I don't have that kind of money, Bex.'

Her face falls, the professional veneer finally slipping. 'But you've got a job in London, Jess. I don't understand.'

'Not every job in London pays a fortune.'

'But Will said you're a qualified therapist, surely . . . ?' She trails off, and I can tell she's losing patience with me, although she does her best to control her temper. 'Surely you have some savings?'

'No, I don't. Do you?'

'We live with my mum, what do you think?'

'At least there's two of you working.' I pick up her name plate from the desk and turn it round to show her. 'And you are the manager.'

She frowns and takes it from me, placing it back down. 'I'm *acting* manager, if you must know. You're putting me in a very difficult position here.'

'Well sometimes people *are* difficult, aren't they? They do bad things, cruel things, hurtful things.'

'Is there something you want to say to me, Jess?'

'No, Bex. Is there anything else you'd like to tell me?'

Becky asks me not to call her Bex and I take that as my cue to leave, allowing the door to slam behind me. I'm annoyed at Will too, but mainly it's Becky who's got under my skin. I don't know why we were ever friends, but I guess we had no one else. We were the bad girls, the troublemakers, the slags. Although it was only Becky who slept around. I just pretended I did. I even told Mark Winter I'd lost my virginity when I hadn't, not until . . . I take a deep breath and look up at the Christmas lights strung across the road from shop to shop. It feels wrong, as if Christmas, never my favourite time of year, should be cancelled this year. Mum would have laughed, told me off for being daft, *'Once you're gone you're gone, Jess'*, but she'd left instructions for a burial not a cremation, and asked for her favourite music, even a hymn. It seems it *did* matter. Mum made detailed plans for her send-off, despite her usual policy of ignoring everything, even things that should never have been tolerated, like a boyfriend with an eye for her daughter. Behind me, Becky taps on the glass, beckoning to me to come back in, but I pretend not to notice, crossing the road towards the café on the other side. I need somewhere warm, a place crammed with life.

It's certainly busy inside, the tables occupied by construction workers wearing high-vis jackets and muddy boots. I wait, impatient at the lack of service – not the way to earn a tip – then I spot a free table in the corner. I decide to take it before anyone else walks in, squeezing past the builders, mugs of tea and doorstep sandwiches in front of them. I pretend not to hear their comments and catcalls, glancing over to a woman about my age at the next table, also on her own, although she doesn't seem to be receiving the same level of unwanted attention. Her body language is defensive, leant over her book, head down, but she looks up as I take my seat. I'm struggling to place her, except . . . of course, it's Karen Winter I'm reminded of, the same thin mouth, narrowed eyes and hard, unblinking stare.

'Freya, isn't it?' I smile, unsure of my next move. We've never had much to do with one another, even when we were in the same class, our friendship groups entirely different, although Freya seemed to mostly be on her own. She stands up fast, her book falling to the floor. 'There's no need to leave, Freya. I'll go.'

She picks up the book and shoves it roughly into a large tote bag, a marker pen falling out on to the floor. It rolls towards me and I pick it up. She looks at me, then the pen, snatching it back. The room has gone quiet around us. I step back, and Freya swings her overloaded bag past the table, her unfinished coffee knocked on to its side, brown liquid pooling, then running on to the floor. She ignores the mess and pushes past me, almost slipping on the spillage, but when I instinctively reach out to steady her, she throws off my outstretched hand and tells me under her breath to 'fuck off!'

'I just came in for a coffee,' I call after her. 'Is that too much to ask?'

She looks across at the woman behind the counter, and says, 'It's the Tidy girl, do you understand?'

'Don't worry, Freya, love. You go. I'll sort this out.' The woman is wiping her hands on her apron, then she locks eyes with me, staring until Freya has yanked open the door and stalked out. 'Wait there five minutes,' the woman tells me, 'then you can get out!'

'Do you know me?' I ask, shaking now, the tremble in my voice causing me to cough. *Do you?*

One of the builders comes over, asks if I'm OK. He has a shaved head and tattoos, but his expression isn't menacing, quite the opposite. 'No, I'm not OK, I'm being told to leave.'

'Don't go feeling sorry for her,' the woman instructs him, coming out from behind the counter. 'What she put that family through—'

'It's fine,' I say, looking up at him. 'I don't want a coffee any more.' I raise my voice and address the meaty-armed woman, 'I don't want your fucking coffee!'

'All right, love,' the builder tells me. 'That's enough!'

The darkness covers my burning cheeks as I push the door

181

open with force. I don't even know who the woman serving was, but she knew me, or at least *of* me, and her opinion clearly hasn't changed over the last ten years. I glance up and down the street looking for Freya – the Christmas lights now a blur, the cold a shock after the steamy fug inside the café – but there's no sign of her.

Karen

Friday, 9th December 2016 (Late Afternoon)

I watch, fascinated, my breath curling from my lips in the icy air as Will pulls at the filled teat of the condom, a final stretch of slippery rubber before it slides free. He knots the open end, then wraps the offending article in its crumpled foil packet and tucks it into his shirt pocket. The darkness covers his movements to a certain extent, but my eyes have adjusted to the gloom since we arrived, the space no longer an inky blur. Our accommodation isn't much more than a glorified shed, although it's spacious, recently constructed by the cricket or tennis club; I forget which. The announcement was made at one of the meetings I missed; Will and I otherwise engaged.

'Isn't there anywhere else we can go?' I'd asked when he suggested this venue; the days growing shorter, and colder.

'The hut or the van, take your pick!' he'd said. *'I don't have money for a hotel, do you?'*

The overpowering smell of freshly cut wood is cloying, but

Will has warned me not to open a window in case we forget to close it before we leave. I've told him we wouldn't, but he takes his key holder responsibilities very seriously, and besides, it's freezing. He was so proud the day he was awarded the contract by the parish council, his excitement infectious as he grabbed me and swung me round before I even knew why, both of us laughing like teenagers. Tending the common paths and cutting the grass on the playing field provides a good chunk of his income, but more than that, it's a validation of him as a trustworthy professional. So we shiver, afraid to switch on a light, or the heater, the sweat on our skin chilling.

I sit up and adjust my clothing, the floor hard beneath me, the sleeping bag Will spread out across the dusty floor providing only a scant amount of padding. He keeps the bedding hidden at the back of the corner cupboard, retrieving it in almost total darkness from amongst the stacked chairs and cleaning equipment. The polyester fabric is cold beneath my bare thighs, possibly slightly damp too, the smell of mildew synonymous with our affair, although we've only resorted to this venue a handful of times so far. The mildew also reminds me of past camping trips with Mark and Frey, when she was a toddler, finances dictating the modest nature of our holidays. I look at Will, still fiddling with the condom, taking it out of his pocket to wrap it in another layer, his handkerchief this time, and a particularly painful pang of doubt stabs at my insides. 'For God's sake, Will, just put the horrible thing away.'

'Do we really need to bother with these?' He's holding up the empty packet to the window for me to see what he means, although the park is unlit, and the moon nowhere in sight.

'Of course we do. I might be forty-six, but I'm not a dried-up old prune quite yet.' I laugh, struck by a thought I unwisely decide to share. 'Oh my God, can you imagine a Winter-Tidy baby? Red hair, and a super-complicated family tree.'

'You have a very strange sense of humour at times,' Will replies, zipping his fly before he jumps up, then he surprises me by crouching back down to look me straight in the eye, his breath close enough to be mine. 'What are we doing here, Kar?' He steadies himself with a hand to the floor.

'You want me to answer that?' I rise on to my knees, the moonlight making an unwanted appearance as I struggle with rolled down knickers and tights. 'Pass me my boots, will you?' I say, pointing behind him.

Will feels around in the gloom and I quickly get dressed whilst he's preoccupied, then I take the boots he's holding out and stand up.

'What I meant was,' he says, getting up too, 'you and me. *This*. It's not right, is it?'

'Be more specific,' I tell him, zipping the first boot up to my knee and reaching down for the other one. 'What isn't right?'

Will grabs me and pulls me to him, kissing me on the lips, his muscular arms wrapped tight around my waist. I tell him I need to get home, Mark will be wondering where I am, although I'm tempted, but we must have been here well over an hour already, the time unravelling at an alarming rate now we're back together. He releases me and asks again, 'I mean it, Kar, what *are* we doing? It's been three years, on and off. You must know how I feel about you.'

'How you *feel* about me?' I repeat, taken aback by his statement. 'I thought—'

'I care about you, Kar.' He steadies me as I stumble in the darkness, one boot on, the other still in my hand. 'You know that.'

I wince as he squeezes my hand. 'What's wrong?' he asks, feeling the plaster in my palm. 'You hurt yourself?'

'It was an accident,' I tell him, shrugging him off as I slip on the second boot and zip it up.

'I love you, Kar.' He reaches out to me, his grasp firm and protective.

'*Love?*'

'Is that so hard to believe?' He laughs, just a little, comments that it's not quite the reaction he was hoping for when he declared his undying love for me, but I can tell the joke is to mask the emotion in his voice, a slight crack when he says the word *undying*. He turns away to stow the sleeping bag back in the cupboard.

'Yesterday you were accusing me of throwing a brick through your sister's window,' I tell his back. 'And now—'

'I said I was sorry about that, Kar.' He closes the cupboard door with a slam. 'But I had to ask, you can understand that, can't you?'

'*Can I?* I mean if you love me, Will, why would you think I could do something like that?'

'I thought we'd sorted this.' He sighs as he turns and walks towards me.

'It doesn't even make sense,' I tell him. 'I was on my way here, to meet you.'

'Kar, I believe you. I don't think it was you. I really don't. What else can I say to convince you?' He lifts my hand from my side and raises it to his lips. 'Can we get going now?'

'I couldn't be at home.' I pull my hand away from him. 'I was so upset, I needed to see you, and when I couldn't . . .' I point in the direction of the hills. 'It was dark, I fell in the mud.'

'Yes, I know. You told me. Look, like I said, it was almost certainly kids, messing around, like they do. I know it wasn't you, Kar. I wish I'd never asked, but I can't go back and change what happened yesterday, so let's just leave it now. We both said things we shouldn't have, and we really need to get going.'

'*Kids?* That's what you think?'

'Don't push it, Kar,' he warns me, and I take the hint, afraid he might change his mind.

He locks the door behind us and reaches for my hand, careful not to take the injured one, then he guides me along the cinder path that edges the playing field. I lean into him, kiss his cheek, catch the scent of his aftershave, inhaling it deep into my lungs. We walk towards the road, instinctively letting go of one another as we approach the street lamps and passing cars. Normally we rush away, me walking home, Will to his van parked around the corner, but this time we pause at the end of the path, neither of us keen to go.

'Do you care about me, Kar?' he asks, lighting a cigarette, his eyes downcast to the match, his hand cupped to protect the flicker. He shakes the match to extinguish the flame and looks directly at me. 'I mean . . . It's got to be about more than a quick shag every few days.' He jerks his head in the direction of the park. 'Or it's a bit pathetic, isn't it? We're not kids. We've both *got* kids. We're risking a lot, so I think that says something, doesn't it?' A car passes and we both shrink back from the road. 'I don't want to be a bad father, an unfaithful partner, if it's just for that,' he jerks his head towards the dark hut. 'And I don't want to needlessly hurt Becky. She's already suspicious, and when I look at Jackson, I feel like the worst kind of dad.'

I turn away from the funnel of cigarette smoke, although he'd looked up at the cloudy sky before he exhaled. It hurts to think of him weighing me up against the guilt he feels when he looks at his son, but I know exactly what he means. I feel the same when I'm lying to Frey.

'I hadn't realised you felt that way,' I say.

'Leave Mark!' Will grabs my arm to turn me towards him. 'Leave Mark, and I'll leave Becky. You and I can go away, not far, but somewhere new where we can start again. Still see Freya and Jackson, but get away from this bloody place, and everything that's happened here. All the crap that gets in the way. We'll be good on our own, we always are. What do you think?'

'What's brought all this on?'

'Mum's death, I guess.' He drags on the cigarette. 'Life's too bloody short to piss it all into the wind.'

'Very romantic,' I say, although he doesn't return my smile, and when the silence stretches out between us I tell him I should get back.

'Why d'you stay with him all these years?' Will asks, closing in again. 'You're not happy, I can see it. All those bloody pills, Kar. They're not good for you, you know that.'

'I don't want to talk about it,' I say, ignoring his stare. 'Look, Will, there's no point dreaming up some alternative life where we're happy ever after. It would be a bloody mess, and you know it. Can you imagine what everyone would say, how Frey would react? And Jess?' I wait, breath held, but he doesn't respond, just draws deeply on his cigarette. 'You have Becky and Jackson, I have Mark and Frey. It's not perfect, and given different circumstances who knows what might be, but we can't be together full-time. You know that. Doesn't mean we can't still see each other, though,' I look up him. 'That's OK, isn't it? It's always worked in the past. Like you said, we're good together.'

'A quick shag in a shed or a van, the odd night at a hotel, or a grubby fuck under a tree?' He draws deeply before he flicks the dog-end on to the path at his feet.

'That's not fair, Will. We're more than that.'

'Not sure it's working for me any more.' He turns and walks away, raising a hand in the air when I call after him.

'Will, wait! We only just made up.' I look around me, afraid to call out again, watching until he turns the corner, hoping he'll look back, or at least glance over his shoulder, but he does neither.

Mark is waiting for me in the kitchen when I arrive home, his face an accusation before he's said a word.

'Everything OK?' I ask, taking off my coat.

'No, Karen. It's not.' He gets up from the table and stands in the doorway so I can't get into the kitchen. 'Where have you been?'

'I told you, emergency meeting. I wasn't that long, was I?'

'Frey's been here,' he replies, pushing past me to run up the stairs.

'Mark, wait! Is she OK?'

'No, not really.' He pauses, one foot above the other. 'You might want to give her a call. She waited a while, but then she gave up.'

'What's happened? Mark, tell me!'

He stops on the landing, looking down at me from his vantage point, his hands gripping the bannister. 'Our daughter needed her mum and you weren't here, that's what happened. Oh, and she bumped into Jess.'

Jess? Where? I'm running up the stairs now, chasing after him, but he's already in his study, Walter cowering behind him. I throw myself at the door as Mark slams it in my face. 'I'm here now!' I shout through. 'Why can't you get along with her, help her when I'm not around?'

The door opens, and Mark looks out. 'I tried, Karen. Of course I did.'

'I'm sorry that I wasn't here, but what else can I say?' I tip my face up to meet his angry expression. 'None of us are perfect, are we?'

'What's that supposed to mean?'

I don't respond, other than to shake my head. He looks pale, and for a moment his anger seems to abate, then he says, 'Just ring your daughter, OK?'

'Tell me what happened first. Please, Mark.'

'Ask her yourself,' he says, then he closes the door on me.

I try Frey's mobile several times, pacing the kitchen as her voicemail cuts in again and again. I message her too, tell her I'm home now, free to talk, but when there's still no response, I decide I can't wait any longer to find out what's happened. Mark clearly isn't going to help me out. I can hear him upstairs, moving around, the dog too, but I don't call out goodbye.

He doesn't deserve such courtesies.

Two Months Before . . .

Supervision Session #9 – Jessica Tidy – Tuesday, October 18th, 2016

Full notes in client file ref: 718/16

Meeting taped, transcript of relevant section below (abridged)

Jess: It's an ethical requirement of practice.

Me: That's the technical definition, Jess. I asked what supervision *means* to you.

Jess: I don't understand.

Me: Let me explain . . . I have a supervisor too, and last time I saw him I discussed our sessions, talked about how things have been going. I said that, at times, you seem to find it difficult to separate the personal from the professional, which is a very common issue for newly qualified counsellors, but is still a concern to me.

Jess: Wow! You're certainly honest.

Me: Have I offended you? That wasn't my intention. We're both
        professionals, Jess.

Jess: Yes, we are.

Me: And you've been very open with me so far. I wanted to
        return that favour. I'm sure your clients respond well to that
        honesty.

Jess: Yes, I think they do. In fact, do you remember the client I
        told you about, the woman who turned up drunk? She
        came back, sober this time, and it went well, she completely
        opened up to me, we had a great chat.

Me: That's wonderful, Jess. Well done.

Jess: I think I'm beginning to separate out the professional and
        personal. You're right, the edges were a bit blurred.

Me: It's not just an overlap of issues, or personal triggers, but
        the fact we must understand the nature of the relationship
        we build with our clients. We're not friends with them. It
        wouldn't work if we were. As counsellors, we must be impar-
        tial, dispassionate observers. We can say things loved ones
        can't, and sometimes it's our duty to do just that. As I have
        with you on occasion. But I recognise that's not always
        easy to hear. I agree, it's my job as your supervisor to
        safeguard you, and your clients, but more than that, I want
        to equip you with the personal insight you need. We both
        know we've strayed in difficult areas, which is fine, but it
        should be acknowledged, don't you think?

Jess: Yes, and I understand we're not friends. If you think I've
        overstepped the mark—

Me: No, I'm not saying . . . sorry, Jess, let me try again. I really
        want to impress on you that as long as you're honest with

me I can help you develop, and it would be a privilege. I think you're going to be an amazing counsellor, already are one in fact. And we're both learning, every day. It's when we're not we need to worry. If I get it wrong, then do tell me, it's a two-way thing. A matter of trust. That comes with time, but we're getting there now, we really are.

Jess: A matter of trust. Yes, I agree. There haven't been many people I could trust, but when you find someone, someone with integrity, like yourself, it's so important. It makes you realise that the world isn't full of Mark Winters, or Barry Johnsons, or the type of guys my mum always chooses, losers who knock her about and only want one thing. There are people like you, and James. People who actually care. Who genuinely want to make a difference. That's what I want to do. I want to help people like me. Does that sound stupid?

Me: No, not at all. I think it sounds wonderful.

Jess

Friday, 9th December 2016 (Early Evening)

I try to convince myself it's because I'm tired, and still feeling emotional after seeing Freya in the café earlier, but I *know* what I heard. I open the kitchen door and look out at the dark strip of concrete which leads to the back garden, heavy rain hitting the path. I can't see much, but there doesn't appear to be anyone out there, no shadowy figure with another brick in their hand. I debate going outside to investigate further, a quick tour of the back garden to satisfy myself it was definitely my imagination, but I lock the door instead. It's freezing, and my feet are bare. Besides, it's probably kids messing about, like Will said. But I can't shake the feeling I'm being watched. I check round the house, walking into the front room and peering out at the blackness behind the drawn curtains, searching for signs of a retreating intruder, before spinning back, half-expecting someone to be standing behind me.

It definitely sounded like someone running fast, trainers or boots splashing in puddles the other side of the kitchen window, but it was probably just a leaky gutter, or a huge rat. I end up back in the kitchen, pouring myself another glass of wine, then I listen again, but there's only the sound of the rain. When I've drained my glass I pour another, the cold acidity of it calming me a little, but I can't help thinking anyone could be out there, the sense of threat closing in on me, although when I try to put a face to it, there are too many possibilities, each one only heightening my unease. To prove myself wrong, I pull on the cord of the venetian blind, the wooden slats puffing out dust as I raise them to halfway up the wide window.

At first, it's just darkness and rain, an image of my face staring back at me as I lean towards my reflection, caught in a scowl. Then I catch a flash of something moving, fast. Someone is running from the back of the house to the front, along the side path. I hear my voice shout, 'Oi!', then I'm throwing the bolt to the kitchen door and turning the key with unsteady fingers. I run full pelt along the path and into the front garden, the long grass soaking my bare feet and the bottoms of my jeans as I call out, 'Wait! I see you!'

Ahead of me is a figure, hooded, not tall, almost certainly a woman, or maybe a teenager, hard to tell as they're wearing a long coat which billows out behind them as they run. They're ahead of me, sprinting across the road. I see them release something from their right hand, like a baton dropped in a relay race. The metal object bounces across the pavement, landing in the gutter as they disappear into the alleyway.

By the time I've caught up, the alley is empty, the other end leading out on to the warren of houses that back on to the school. I jog its full length, but the path is slick with rain and there's broken glass. I'm slow, afraid of cutting the soles of my bare feet. I turn back, towards the glint of the metal paint can in the gutter, bending to retrieve it but it slips from my grasp and sploshes back into a puddle. I grip it more tightly and straighten up, and that's when I see what they've done to the house.

The words daubed across the door and along the front of the brickwork are identical to the ones in the note, and the same message that was painted across our house just before the court case. Mum had gone crazy, screaming at the twins to get it off, but I'm the only one here to witness the vandalism this time. The rain, heavier if anything, isn't washing away the graffiti at all, the red spray repelling the water which runs over its surfaces. I look down at my feet, spattered with rain and smutted with grease marks from the road, my toes so numb I can't tell if they're cut from broken glass, or simply stinging with cold. Who would do this? Why would they be so cruel when I'm here to grieve for my dead mother?

A car drives by and the driver blares their horn, shouting at me to get out of the road. 'Do you want to get yourself killed, love?' he says through his opened window. I shiver and go inside, the paint can slippy in my wet hands, my chest heaving with the effort of holding in my sobs.

I try Will's mobile number first, several times, but he doesn't answer. I curse under my breath, sick of hearing his voicemail message. My feet are now blue, and they really hurt, but I still slap them down hard on the lino. 'Where the fuck are you, Will? Grrrrr!!!' I throw my phone on the floor, then panic I might have smashed it. It's fine, but I'm not, far from it. I gulp down more wine, then I try another number, someone I know will come over. Someone who bloody cares.

James arrives as I step out of the shower, a brown towelling robe, an old one of Will's, doubling as a towel as I rush to answer the door. I've never known where James lives; *'nearby'* the closest he's come to telling me, but he was probably at work, the head office where he's based only fifteen minutes' drive away in town.

'I didn't know who else to call,' I tell him.

'You did the right thing.' He's stood on the path, rainwater falling on his face as he looks up at the house. 'I know someone who can clean it all off, you'll never know it was there. By tomorrow. I promise. You OK?'

I nod, but he frowns back, tells me to go inside, he'll take some pictures on his phone first, be with me in a minute. 'Get some warm clothes on,' he says when I don't move, calling after me, 'And pop the kettle on, think we could both do with a coffee.'

I leave the door on the latch, then watch from Mum's bedroom as James walks to the other side of the road by the alleyway, taking photo after photo of the looping foot-high letters. He puts the phone to his ear and talks, the rain still falling, although he seems not to notice. My head is tipped down to dry the fine hair at the nape of my neck when James touches me lightly on the shoulder. I stand up straight, flicking my curls back and switching off the dryer.

'I'm trying to arrange for someone to come over first thing.' He steps back on to the landing and pushes his wet hair out of his eyes. 'Don't tell anyone I organised the cleaning, I should really leave it up there for testing, but I know you'll want it gone as soon as possible.' He's constantly tapping on his phone, but he pauses to glance up at me. 'You sure you're OK? You should put something warmer on.'

'I will, just drying my hair.' I shake out the damp ends. 'Is it round the back of the house too?'

He nods, staring at his phone. 'Ah great, the cleaning company can come first thing.' He quickly types a reply. 'You mentioned you found the paint can?'

'Yes, it's downstairs, on the hall table, but it was wet, and I dropped it in a puddle. *Sorry*.'

He says it's still worth a try, he can submit it for chemical treatment for fingerprints and possibly DNA profiling to identify potential suspects. 'We still have Mark Winter's sample on file, so if it's a match—'

'James,' I interrupt him, my hand briefly glancing his coat sleeve as I brush past him to walk out on to the landing. 'I know I called you, but is there any way we can keep this between us?'

'Why?' He looks up from his phone.

'This wasn't Mark,' I reply, pausing at the top of the stairs. 'I saw a woman. I think. I don't know for sure. And there was a note through the door, couple of days ago, the same message as the one tonight.' I decide not to mention it was attached to a brick, especially when James frowns at me, his lips tightening when I tell him Will took the note away with him.

'Why didn't you say anything before?' He takes a step towards me.

I place a palm to the wall, my back to the stairs, blocking his exit. 'The truth is, James, I don't want you to start another investigation; I just want to feel safe, here and now. You can understand that, can't you?'

He persists, asking if there's any chance I can get the note back. 'Although it's been through so many hands now . . . Jess, can I come by, please?'

'No, James, you're not listening. I don't want forensics, or colleagues running checks.' I run my fingers through my wild hair, the curls electrified by the heat of the hairdryer.

I know he's annoyed. I called him out and now I'm frustrating his attempts to gather the evidence he needs, and I'm barring his way. He's always been lenient where I'm concerned, but I guess there's a limit.

'Jess, you need to move, this isn't—'

'It's stupid, I know, but I don't want any more trouble.' I smile at him. 'You can understand that, can't you?'

'No, not really. Why involve me if you don't want us to catch whoever is intimidating you?'

'I'm sorry, I know I rely on you.' I move nearer to him. 'I just feel safer when you're around.'

I look up, searching for something in his eyes that might encourage me, as it did all those years ago when he'd held me close, our bodies warm despite the chill I'd felt knowing Mark was about to be a free man. I was glad James was there, in my tiny flat, the only person I would have wanted to break the horrible news. He'd consoled me, his arms around me as I wept. I hadn't imagined the affection I saw in him that day, had I? It was real, he cared for me, still does.

He resisted my advances back then, told me he didn't think of me in that way, and even if he did, it wouldn't be ethical. I can understand that now, although I struggled with it at the time. I was so young, mixed up, vulnerable. And he was married, and too close to the case, but I'm older now and he's separated from his wife. Those reasons have gone away. I reach up to brush the hair from his forehead, still damp from the rain and sticking to his eyes, the feel of his skin a shock.

'No, Jess!' He takes my hand and places it at my side. 'Please don't.'

Karen

Friday, 9th December 2016 (Evening)

I throw my mobile on the passenger seat and restart the car, pulling out of the bus stop and back into the flow of traffic. I've wasted enough time; better to get there now. I'm probably overreacting, but Mark's comments have stirred up something primal in me. Our daughter was upset, desperate to see me, and I hadn't been there for her; and now she's not answering her phone. With each minute that passes my panic increases. It wouldn't be so bad if I hadn't been with Will, fucking in the shed. I shudder, turning up the heating in the car, but there's something daring about the phrase as it rolls around my head, not as altogether distasteful as I expected. It was meant to be an admonishment, but now it feels like a boast. *Fucking in the shed*. Yes, it has an element of the congratulatory to it. Dread rises in my throat again, but this time it's Will's declaration of love and my reaction to it that panics me. I hadn't handled it well, but things are moving so fast, shifting everything around until I can't keep all the pieces in place, not any of them. I think of Frey, looking for me, needing me, and guilt floods my system again, my imagination taking me to ridiculous places, none of them good. Why did Jess have to come home? Bloody Lisa Tidy, drinking herself to death.

The town centre, rain-drenched and deserted, has the forlorn appearance of a ghost town, the inclement weather driving everyone indoors. I wait impatiently at traffic lights by an estate agent's window, my fingers drumming on the steering wheel as I glance across at the photos of sleek apartment blocks and modern new-builds. I used to daydream about selling up and buying a smaller place in town, somewhere for Frey and me to start again, a degree of anonymity the reward for giving up my childhood home, countering at least some of the inevitable remorse selling Mum's cottage would bring. Mark never figured in my plans, the practicalities glossed over, but when he finally came home from prison it felt as though I'd missed my chance. He was so mired in the past, barely leaving the cottage other than to walk Walter. Any enthusiasm for the move would have needed to come entirely from me, and I didn't have the strength for it, or the heart. Some days I secretly wished he was back inside, both of us slaves to a routine that we'd somehow grown used to, but of course Mark never did, the horror of prison staying with him, although he rarely spoke of it.

I pull into the courtyard where Frey lives and reverse into a visitor's space. I'll be fine once I see her, a chance to smooth things over, feel useful for once. I run across the forecourt, sploshes of rainwater dripping on to the top of my head as I press the intercom and wait for Frey to answer. I should have grabbed my umbrella from the boot, or a pill from my bag; that would have been even better. I press the button for a second time and look up at her window on the first floor. A raindrop lands in my right eye, making me blink. Frey comes to the window and looks down, raising a hand, then the entrance door releases with a loud buzz.

Frey is wrapped in a thick robe, a towel twirled turban-like around her head. 'You didn't have to come over on a night like this.'

'Hello to you too,' I say, following her in. I remove my coat and fold the wet side in, draping it over the back of a dining chair. 'I've been calling you for at least half an hour.'

'Sorry, I was in the bath,' Frey replies. 'I put a conditioning treatment on my hair. It's so soft afterwards, but you have to leave it in for ages, then it takes forever to rinse out.'

'Your father made it sound like a disaster, but you're obviously feeling better now.'

'I'm getting there.' She pulls the towel from her head and shakes out her damp hair. 'But it was a nasty shock bumping into Jess like that.'

'Yes, it must—' I pause as Frey walks out, coming back a moment later, her hair combed out, the towel gone. 'Are you going out?'

'Tris is coming over, but I've got time for a cup of tea.'

I sit on the sofa, watching my daughter in the kitchenette. In profile, she has a straight nose like Mark's, but her lips, a tad too thin although still plumper than mine, are just like

204

Mum's, as are her dark eyes. She fills two mugs with hot water from the kettle and shares a tea bag between them, dunking and lifting.

'I'm sorry I wasn't home when you called round, where was it you saw Jess?'

'Dad didn't tell you?' Frey glances over. 'I was in the café in the village.'

'I didn't know you ever went in there,' I say, recalling the clientele I've seen going in and out, and the formidable reputation of the woman who runs it. Not a place I'd choose to spend my time.

'I haven't before,' Frey replies, still dunking the tea bag up and down. 'But the one at the supermarket is so grim.'

'Why were you in the village anyway? It's miles out of your way.'

'I needed a few bits at the supermarket, for tonight. I can't go to the one near work as I see every child I teach, you know how it is?' I nod. 'I thought it would be nice to go for a coffee afterwards, a chance to read something other than a school book, Friday treat and all that. It was such a shock when I saw her come in, as if she had nothing to be ashamed of, as if—' Freya looks at me for approval.

'Yes, quite!'

'She wandered up to me, as if . . . I don't know. As if she'd done nothing wrong.' Frey meets my eye. 'I think she was hoping to join me.'

'No shame,' I say, clicking my tongue. 'Even now.'

'That's the point, isn't it?' Frey replies, stirring in clouds of powdery sweetener. 'She can do whatever she likes, whereas

205

you . . . and me to a certain extent . . .' She sighs. 'It's like we're all being punished.'

I tell her that's not true, but she shakes her head. 'Dad said you were at a meeting?'

Unable to meet her eye, I spin another lie about verbose planners and irate residents. It's much harder with Frey than Mark. I hate deceiving her, and she's always been able to spot a lie, even as a child.

'*It's fine,*' she replies, indicating I should stop explaining.

'Well, I'm here now.'

'You won't win,' Frey tells me, throwing the squeezed tea bag into the bin.

'*Sorry?*'

'You can have as many meetings as you like, won't make any difference. They'll build where they want to; where the money is.'

I tell her it's still worth a try, but she pauses, a teaspoon in her hand. 'It was just such a shock.' She hands me my tea, her face set as she recalls Jess's intrusion into her world. 'I had no idea she'd be there.'

'You knew she was back in the village, Frey.'

She pulls a chair out from the dining table and sits down, facing me, her bare feet pushed into slippers, her legs shiny with moisturiser. 'You think I wanted to see her? I was already there, Mum. She came in after me.'

'No, sorry, of course. It must have been horrible, darling. Did you speak to her?'

'I don't remember.' She looks up from her mug. 'I think I just stood up and left.'

'So, you're OK now? Dad said you'd seemed agitated.'

'That's what he said, *agitated*?' She laughs, a derisory sound, dismissive. 'God, he really doesn't do empathy, does he? Sometimes I think he literally has no idea where I'm concerned.'

'He tries his best, Frey. You could make more of an effort too.'

'*You think so?*' She fixes me with one of her stares. 'I should probably get on.' She stands up, taking my half-drunk tea from my hand.

'Oh right.' I get up too. 'Have I annoyed you?'

'No, it's just I haven't started dinner yet, spent too long in the bath. Tris will be here soon.'

I assume it's an excuse, but as I walk to my car I see Tristan's BMW pull into the allocated space next to Frey's car. His teeth are as white as his car as he flashes me a smile and waves cheerily. I don't know if he recognises me, or is just being polite, but I wave back. He seemed nice when we met him, a PE teacher, runs a Youth Club on a Saturday night, coaches a local kids' football team on Sunday mornings. His life is devoted to the next generation, much as Mark's once was. He has everything my husband covets, including our daughter's admiration. I notice his smile slipping as he looks away, already dismissing me, and I realise I don't actually like him that much. If at all. There's a veneer of something outwardly attractive, but veneers are thin, too easily scraped away.

I drive off, watching in my mirror as Frey runs out to greet him, no delay in answering the door this time.

Jess

Saturday, 10th December 2016 (Early Hours)

Two a.m. The time on a Saturday night when I'm usually knocking back shots in a club, or staggering home on my own, another new friend made, then lost. There's a guy at work, he's always asking me out, but I prefer my own company.

I sit up and put my phone back on the bedside cabinet, wrapping the duvet around me. I desperately need some rest, but James's words from last night are rattling around my head in an endless loop. *Anything else you need, anything else at all, but not that, Jess.*

I throw the duvet back and pad downstairs to the front room, breath held in case I wake him up. James looks different without his huge coat, his shirt unbuttoned at the collar, his shoes removed. Like a plucked bird, vulnerable and almost unrecognisable. I miss the familiar. I miss the old James. I wish I hadn't disgraced myself, *again*, just as I did when he turned up at my flat all those years ago. He stirs and I step back a pace or two as he adjusts himself to the lumpy upholstery, then his breathing settles, soft and steady. I watch him sleep for a while, his body twisted into Mum's chair. It's a strangely intimate experience, as though I'm stealing something from him. When it starts to feel too weird, I leave him alone, climbing back into bed. Not in my room this time, but Will's. It feels safer somehow.

An hour later I'm still wide awake. I imagine the red paint soaking through the brick and transferring itself to the dirty cream walls, the words lit up before me: *You're a lying bitch, Jess Tidy!*

I don't know why it's upset me so much, there's nothing in it that I haven't seen or heard before, many times. Karen Winter called me a lying bitch in court, shouting it out over and over as she was led away. It was the only time I saw her anything other than impassive. It was almost a relief that she'd finally lashed out, a bit of humanity at last. '*Stepford Wife*' the press called her, photos of her standing dead-eyed at Mark's side to prove their point. I looked the reference up, found an old film about robot wives, which was spiteful I felt, especially as most people seemed to have a lot of sympathy for her. I remember so clearly the way she looked at me as she screamed those words, the hate finally exploding out of her. It scared the hell out of me, but now the fight seems to have all but left her. She looks vacant. I guess too many pills can do that to you.

I try again to sleep; only a few hours until the cleaning company are due to arrive. James said they'll be quick and thorough. It will all be gone by lunchtime at the latest, and I don't need to be involved, but lots of people will pass by before then, the message hard to miss. Soon everyone will know, the gossip linking up in chains across the village, person to person, until there's no one who hasn't repeated the words daubed on Lisa Tidy's house.

I hear James coming up the stairs, his tread light, but I'm alert to every sound, every movement. He opens the door, peers in, asks if I'm awake, am I OK? I tell him I'm fine, but I can't sleep. He doesn't come into the room, and when I sit up in bed he steps back even further, so he has to raise his voice a little to tell me he'll be in touch, make sure the contractors do a good job.

'You're leaving?'

'Yes. Bye, Jess.'

I jump out of bed and follow him downstairs, adjusting the huge pyjamas I'm wearing, a pair of my brother's I found folded into the bottom of a drawer. James is already at the door, his coat on.

'Go back up, get some rest,' he says. 'I'll make sure there's no one hanging about before I leave.'

'Thanks for staying. I'm sorry I—'

'Forget it.' He smiles, closing the door behind him.

I crawl back into Will's bed, hitching the duvet up to my chin as I listen for James checking outside the house. The side gate is opened and closed, then he starts his car and drives away.

I turn my head to the pillow, wishing Will was still living at home. I'd be in the room next door, tapping on the thin divide between us to call out goodnight, and he'd call back, reassuring me. I could never bring myself to tell him what happened when he wasn't here, when it was just me and our step-father. Will had no idea why I was always wandering the streets or hanging out at the park, waiting for someone to come and find me, drag me home. Mum stayed with that man for seven more years after I left, nursed him for the last two, devoted to him to the bitter end. If she knew what was going on behind her back, she never said.

I close my eyes, shutting out the world, but somewhere outside, not too far away, someone hates me enough to throw bricks and daub messages, and although I'm exhausted, I still can't sleep. James was right when he said life is rarely fair, but that doesn't make it any easier to accept.

Karen

Saturday, 10th December 2016 (Early Hours)

The commotion wakes me before Mark, Walter's barks quickly turning to howls, escalating his wild efforts to escape from behind the kitchen door. Mark must hear the noise downstairs, it would be difficult not to, but it takes him longer to surface, his sleep deeper than mine. He sits up eventually, but even then I have to shake him by the shoulders and tell him to get up for God's sake, there's someone banging on the front door. We lock eyes, and finally he moves, running downstairs in his boxer shorts. I follow close behind, tying a robe over my nightdress.

As we reach the hall, I spot the outline of a dark coat the other side of the front door, a face close to the frosted glass, a pixelated oval of beige, punctuated by heavy eyebrows and a high hairline where he's pushed back his fringe. I shout through the kitchen door and Walter whimpers and falls silent, then Mark and I both jump as Facey says, 'Mark, Karen, let me in! It's bloody freezing out here.'

The rain has stopped, replaced by a biting wind which rushes into the hall. I shelter behind Mark, my hand resting on my husband's narrow waist, the pose unnatural, my fingers cold against his warm skin. Facey steps inside and the three of us shuffle around, crammed into the narrow hallway.

'Much colder,' Facey observes, as if he'd called at a reasonable time instead of this unearthly hour. I squeeze the skin at Mark's waist, prompting him to do or say something, but he just nods.

'Couldn't this have waited until morning?' I make eye contact with Facey. 'We were asleep, unsurprisingly.'

Facey smiles, a few more crease lines on his face than I recall, but he hasn't changed much over the years, his expression as implacable as ever. Mark remains mute.

'I'm sorry,' the detective says. 'But no, it couldn't wait.'

'I'll get dressed,' Mark announces, unwinding my arm from his waist. 'Karen, can you make some tea?'

Facey waits in the hall as I usher Walter from the kitchen to the sitting room, the detective looking up from his phone to let us through, apologising when he realises he's in the way. I fill the kettle and Facey stands in the small space between the wall and the kitchen table, still concentrating on his phone.

'How have you been, Karen?' he asks, glancing up as I open a cupboard and take out three mugs.

'How do you think?' I reply, banging them down.

'I have a job to do, you know that.'

I turn to face him, a teaspoon in my hand, jabbing it towards him. 'All I know is my husband has paid for whatever you think he did, and still, *still*—'

Mark walks in, wearing jeans and a tee shirt.

'OK, what can I do for you?' he asks, his tone brighter than feels appropriate.

I narrow my eyes at my husband as I pass Facey a black coffee. He remains standing whilst Mark sits down, my husband's deference an irritant to me which escapes as a heavy sigh. I turn my back to them both, making myself a hot lemon, but every fibre of me remains tuned to their conversation.

'I had a call from Jess Tidy this evening,' Facey tells Mark. 'To report an incident at her mother's home.'

'An incident?' Mark repeats, shaking his head at me when I hold up a mug.

'Can you confirm where you were between five-thirty and six-thirty yesterday evening?' Facey asks, sipping his coffee, then he glances across at me and says, 'Both of you.'

'I was here, at home. In my study, writing.' He points need-lessly to the ceiling.

'*Writing?*' Facey asks, a maddening incredulity in his tone. 'Can anyone vouch for you?'

Mark begins to speak, but I step forwards, talking over him.

'We were here, together. Mark was in his study, writing a very important critical essay on Gatsby. Have you read it, the book I mean?' I don't wait for the detective to answer. 'I was down here, preparing our evening meal; cod.' I flip the lid of the bin open to expel a scent of fish bones, thus, it would seem, proving my point.

'So, you two were together for the whole of that hour?' he asks Mark, who glances at me then nods.

'If Jess reported this *incident* yesterday evening,' I ask Facey, 'why has it taken you until now to come here?'

My question seems to faze him, and he mutters something about being tied up elsewhere. He places his mug next to the sink, then he looks at Mark, still seated at the kitchen table, and explains it was a serious attack on Lisa Tidy's home, unsavoury messages daubed on the front and back walls, very much like before. Do we recall the previous attacks that took place just before the trial?'

'Yes, of course, but they had nothing to do with either of us,' Mark tells him. 'And neither does this.'

'There's evidence of an intruder, they were spotted running away, and there's the can of paint which they dropped, which will be tested. I can assure you we *will* identify the culprit this time.'

'Good,' Mark replies. 'Then you'll know it wasn't anything to do with us.'

'It's far too similar to be considered a coincidence, Mark. If either of you,' Facey glances at me, 'have any other thoughts, let me know. The fact you are one another's alibi could prove problematic for you both.'

Flustered, I drop my mug into the sink where it breaks clean in two, one piece in each hand as I retrieve them. 'Well we were *not* involved, either of us.' I look at the detective. 'It was probably kids; rough lot round there. If there's nothing else?'

Facey apologises for disturbing us and leaves, closing the front door behind him.

'Why did you lie to him?' Mark asks in a whisper, glancing from the kitchen door into the hallway. 'You weren't even here at half-five, were you? And we ate late, after you got back from Freya's, must have been—'

'Why do you think?' I demand, interrupting him. 'Facey clearly thinks you did this, Mark. Don't you see?' I throw the broken bits of mug into the bin and slam the lid shut. 'You need an alibi, and I'm all you've got.'

'You think he means it, about catching the culprit?' Mark walks to the sink to run the tap, pouring and draining a glass of water in greedy gulps. He wipes the back of his hand across his mouth and stares at me. 'He means me, doesn't he? You're right.'

I shrug and walk out, but he follows me into the hallway. 'What about you?'

'What do you mean?' I stop halfway up the stairs, looking back.

'Do *you* think I did this?' Mark's tone is frosty. 'In theory I suppose I could have—'

'Can we please try and get some sleep?' I sink down to stair beneath me. 'I'm exhausted.'

Mark opens the sitting room door and releases Walter who has been oddly silent. 'I'll be up in a minute, you go ahead.'

'No,' I tell him, stroking the dog who has run up to sit beside me on the stairs, his tail between his legs, his head down. I rarely make a fuss of him, but he knew I would this time, his tail wagging.

'Karen, I don't want a row. Just go up to bed, get some rest.'

'I didn't mean that,' I reply, getting up as Walter trips back

216

down to Mark. 'What I meant was . . . No, I don't think it was you who daubed those messages.'

Mark's face creases into a half-smile, a mix of tiredness and relief, then he closes his eyes and mouths, 'Thank you.'

Karen

Saturday, 10th December 2016 (Morning)

I must have slept for four, possibly five hours, but it feels like I've only just closed my eyes when I'm woken again by my phone. The screen is lit up, a low thrum as it vibrates. I glance at the message, then across at Mark, sleeping soundly as I type, *Just coming, don't knock on the door!* xx

'I didn't wake Dad, did I?' Frey whispers.

'No, it's OK, he's still fast asleep.' I usher her in. 'We had a bit of a disturbed night. Facey was here.'

'Oh,' she replies, her head down.

I wait for a stronger reaction, but she says nothing more, kicking off her trainers on the mat. She's wearing a hoodie over pyjamas, and her feet are bare.

'So, why are you here so early on a Saturday morning? Not that I'm not pleased to see you of course, but—'

She looks up at me, and I notice her eyes are red, then her

face crumples as she blurts out, 'He's left me, Mum. Tris has finished with me.'

'Oh, darling, no. I'm so sorry.'

Mark walks into the kitchen half an hour later, bleary-eyed, still in his boxers and tee shirt. Frey glances up at him from her place opposite me at the table, then back to the tissue scrunched in her fist. I shake my head to warn Mark it's not a good time, but he chooses not to notice.

'Freya, whatever's happened?' He moves closer to her, but she shrinks away.

'Just give us a moment, Mark.' I get up from the table to place a hand on my husband's chest, not pushing him back with any force, but stopping him before he reaches Frey. 'Why don't you go upstairs, get showered and changed then we can—'

He ignores me, asking Frey, 'Are you OK, sweetheart?'

'Mark,' I'm holding on to his arm, but his focus is on our daughter, in obvious distress again, the tissue pressed to her eyes. 'I'm asking you to please give us a moment.'

'Freya?' he persists. 'What is it?'

'She's had a bit of a shock,' I tell him. 'Last night, some bad news. I'll explain it all if you can just—'

Frey looks up at her father with such disdain that any chance I had of persuading Mark to leave is now lost. He shakes free of me and sits down, reaching across to Frey who pushes his hand aside. Mark glances back at me, his brow knotted. 'Is anyone going to explain to me what's happened?'

'It's Tris,' I reply, 'but can you please let me handle this?'

He ignores my request, reaching out again to try and comfort Frey.

'Leave me alone!' she tells him. 'Haven't you done enough damage?'

'I don't understand,' Mark says, looking round at me. 'What have I done?'

'They broke up last night,' I reply, taking the seat beside him.

'Oh no, I'm so sorry, Frey. But I don't see what I—'

'Do you want to know why?' she asks, her face blotchy from crying. '*Do you?*'

'Of course I do. To be honest, I was never that sure about—'

'Don't you dare!' Frey tells her father. 'Don't you dare say you didn't like him!'

'Sorry, that was tactless of me.' I wince as he's forced to retract his hand, met with that same cold stare. 'I'm just shocked,' Mark blusters. 'You seemed so happy together.'

I take over, trying my best to pass on the gist of the previous evening's events whilst glossing over the more painful details to spare Frey's feelings, but it becomes more difficult as the story goes on. Frey's sighs and tears make it almost impossible to keep Mark's attention until I say, 'After seeing Jess yesterday, she felt she needed to explain a few things to Tris.'

'You told him what happened?' Mark looks at Frey. '*Everything?*'

'She would have had to tell him at some point,' I say when Frey ignores him. 'She thought it was the right moment, that he'd be more understanding, less—'

'He left me because of you,' Frey blurts out, her words a

mass of snot and tears. 'He said . . .' She drops the tissue and rubs her flattened fingers under her red eyes. 'He said that if he'd known from the start, he might never have . . . he probably wouldn't have asked me out at all.'

'I don't understand,' Mark replies, but of course he must.

Frey drops her head back as she inhales. 'He said,' she tells him, her voice steadier now, but full of cold rage, 'he said that his life is all about helping kids, teaching, coaching, everything he does is connected to young people. He couldn't be tainted with anything like that, any kind of association with a man convicted of something so awful, so . . . fucked up.'

I look at my husband and witness the awful moment of acceptance, self-hatred taking over, turning inwards, like an assailant, a haunted look in his eyes. He says nothing, listening to our daughter without further protest, her loathing undisguised as she vents her frustration.

'I told him I'd choose him instead of you. We wouldn't ever have to see you, but—'

I hold up a hand to Frey and she stops talking, her outrage immediately replaced with distress as once again she's consumed with emotion, her shoulders shaking as she sobs.

Mark watches her, helpless, then I see the film of tears coating each eye as he looks away. I tell Frey if that's what Tristan thinks then he's not worth her tears, but every word is kindling to the fury still burning inside her, her hostility towards Mark so real it's as if it were a weight piling on his shoulders, ounce by ounce pushing him down in the chair as he bends beneath the pressure, his breathing hard and fast. I help him up and he somehow stands and walks away on his own, his hand to the bannister. I watch him drag himself up each stair and across the landing, making his way instinctively towards his study.

'You should leave now,' I tell Frey as I walk back into the kitchen.

'*What?*' Frey stands up. 'I came here for some comfort, because of him!' She points above us. 'You're my mum. I need you.'

'I mean it, Frey. Time to go.'

She leaves silently; a heavy silence, filled with recriminations. I resist the urge to call her back – wrap my arms around her, tell her it will be all right – because she was cruel, and I won't tolerate that, not even from her, although as soon as I close the door my rage echoes her own. I go back to the kitchen, leaving Mark to his own private hell.

He deserves it.

Jess

Saturday, 10th December 2016 (Late Morning)

I sit up, head aching, mouth dry, forcing my feet from the rucked sheet on Will's bed to the brown carpet, the same sticky polyester fibres I felt under my toes every time I walked into this room looking for my big brother. I open the curtains, blinking in the brightness of a new day. Will not only got the bigger bed, but a nicer outlook too. All I could see from my room was the side path and a bit of overgrown lawn, but from here there's an uninterrupted view of everyone's back gardens. Next door's is as messy as ours, but it's unoccupied, so that's not surprising. We have no such excuse, although soon this house will be empty too. Will says next door has been for sale for so long the sign fell over, then it promptly disappeared, no doubt thrown in a hedge by bored teens.

It's a lovely morning, last night's heavy rain replaced by an almost spring-like warmth which bathes my face through the glass, lifting my spirits, although when I open the window the air is icy-cold. There's a child being pushed on a swing two doors down, squealing as it goes higher and higher, that heady mix of fear and thrill expelled as a piercing cry which hits the back of my skull. I close my eyes, breathing deeply. Only three days until the funeral, then I can get back to normal life: London, work and my studies. *Shit!* I left a pint of milk in the fridge. It'll stink the place out. The thought curdles the anticipation of my return, but there's nothing I can do about it. I lean out further and look down, inspecting the back wall of the house, relieved to see the spray-painted messages have disappeared. The cleaners James organised must have worked very quietly, or I was a lot drunker last night than I'd thought.

I found it hard to settle after James left, although I must have dozed off eventually, my bladder waking me around four. I never usually touch spirits, maybe the odd shot. Wine is my drink of choice. The trouble was, the wine was all gone. I found the vodka under the kitchen sink, behind the U-bend, where Mum always kept her not-so-secret stash. I drank it as she would have, neat, from the bottle, raising it to her memory, not that the memories are good. Mum plus vodka was never a pretty combination.

After a particularly heavy session, she would often curl up outside the bathroom, her head touching her knees. Once I found her balanced precariously at the top of the stairs, a clawed hand welded to the bannister. Tony or Mick would scoop her up as if she were the child, not me, tucking her into bed and closing her door. If they caught me peeking out from my room, they'd shout at me to stop gawping and go back to bed. I was never a good sleeper, lying awake for hours listening to Mum singing or crying, relieved she wasn't dead like Becky's mum once told me she soon would be if she didn't stop drinking. If it was quiet, too quiet, I'd console myself with daydreams of what it would be like to live with another family, or in a children's home, a Jaqueline Wilson world where dysfunctional relationships were replaced with happy endings. I even asked Becky if I could stay with her, after my step-dad had moved in and things got even worse, but apparently her mum had been adamant. I remember laughing at first, not sure what she meant, then realising it was a firm 'no'.

I lean out as far as I dare so I can see the mother's smiling face, the sun in my eyes as the swing moves back and forth, hands reaching out to push and catch the little girl, her childish shrieks filled with delight.

I don't remember many occasions when it was just Mum and me, but there was one time when we were on the sofa together, watching kids' TV. Both of us were shovelling in cheese crackers straight from the red box, Mum's fingers running through my hair, teasing out the knots. I must have been quite young, maybe nine or ten, the nicotine stains on her fingers fascinating me as her yellow nails pulled apart my matted curls. I can still feel the drag against my scalp, the pleasurable tingle, until her smoker's cough took hold and she ran into the kitchen to throw up, spluttering over the previous night's dirty dishes. She'd started drinking again that day, the stench of the regurgitated crackers lasting longer than the promises she'd made.

I close the window and walk downstairs, holding up Will's pyjama bottoms by the waist. There's a letter on the mat, the effort of bending over to pick it up making my headache even worse, as though I've tipped the contents of my stomach into my brain. It reminds me of a very particular kind of hangover that only half a bottle of vodka can inflict; the reason, well one of them, why I swore I'd never touch the stuff again. The last time was a few months after I left home, a solitary night in London doused with neat alcohol to chase away the memories. It didn't work then either. I close one eye to study the envelope, addressed to Mum, then I place it on the kitchen counter with the others, letters from months ago squirrelled away in the most unlikely of places. Her life was unravelling, but she didn't seem to care, or maybe she knew it was already too late.

The empty vodka bottle is by the sink. I drop it into the mouth of the bin, the echo bouncing back. It had been almost full, vodka on top of wine . . . *slippery slope.* Maybe I emptied some of it down the sink, but it seems unlikely. I need tea, that will help, and paracetamol. The kettle boils as I hunt in my handbag for some painkillers, then I drop one of Mum's tea bags into a mug and watch as the hot water turns instantly dark brown. Mum used to light up her first ciggie as soon as she got up, hacking coughs as she made a *'brew'*, the tannin in the liquid cutting through the phlegm in her voice. She'd tell me to get out of her way, shouting at me to leave her alone, especially as I got older. *'You look like I used to,'* she said to me not long before I left home. She'd seemed so sad, her skin grey, her hair dirty-blonde, but red at the roots. I had no sympathy for her, she'd let me down too many times for that, and besides, she was letting him kick me out. She hadn't comforted me when I tried to explain what happened with Mark Winter, quite the reverse. She said it was my own silly fault, and he'd chipped in too. Taking her side when she was there, then running his hands over me when she wasn't. Insisting he was my step-father and I should show him some 'fucking respect'.

In the months before her death, Will said she talked about me a lot, how she missed her baby girl, and how we used to get along so well, *'girls together'*. Funny how the mind plays tricks. She was on her own by then, my step-father long-dead, and surprisingly never replaced.

I wait for the tea to brew, picking up my phone to check for messages, but there's nothing new to see, no one desperate to get hold of me, make sure I'm fine, not even my supervisor checking in to see how I am.

Karen

Sunday, 11th December 2016 (Late Morning)

I'm in the shower when the thought strikes me cold, the scouring heat of the jetted water obliterated by the fear that prickles all over me. I jump out and wrap towels around my hair and body, telling myself not to panic. Even if I have left my phone on the kitchen counter, and Mark's noticed, which I doubt, it's PIN-protected, and Will and I have made our arrangements for later, so he's unlikely to have contacted me again. I rush out the bathroom and see the study door is now open, the room empty as I check inside. Mark's probably out with Walter, walking off his despondency after yesterday's terrible argument with Frey, but I still rush downstairs, almost slipping in my haste, my feet slick with bubbles.

Mark's seated at the kitchen table, his back to me, his head buried in a book, a mug of tea in front of him. I pause, wandering in as casually as I can whilst only wearing a towel and dripping wet.

'Ah, here it is,' I tell him, grabbing my phone from by the kettle.

'You had a message,' Mark says without turning around. 'Few minutes ago. There's tea in the pot if you want one.'

I glance down at the notification on the screen, and feel the colour rise in my cheeks, pressing the phone to my chest. Mark looks over his shoulder at me, and I'm certain there's a penetration to his stare, a lingering moment that stabs at my conscience, my heart bouncing around my chest as he remarks, 'Something important?'

I shake my head, not trusting myself to respond.

'I'll take the dog out now.' He gets up and puts his mug in the sink, then he pauses and looks at my exposed legs. 'You're still covered in lather.'

I climb the stairs and step back into the icy water, the hot tank drained, doing my best to rinse myself clean. Then I run the damp towel over my body and get dressed, all the time convincing myself Mark can't have been suspicious, or he'd have said something, *wouldn't he?* I hang over the bannister, listening, but all is now silent. He must still be out with the dog.

More out of habit than desire, I go into his study to read his latest offering, but it's hard to concentrate, my thoughts elsewhere as I tap in the passcode. The text had been explicit, if Mark had somehow opened it there would have been little I could say in my defence. It was sloppy of me, and thought-less of Will to send it. I consider replying to him, a retaliation for his negligence, but he wasn't to know, and I don't want to fall out with him again now we've resolved our differences. I take a calming breath and begin reading.

Chapter Eight – May 2006

It was after five when we left school, waiting for the end-of-day rush to die down. There were a few stragglers wandering around the bus bay, most in rugby or hockey kit, waiting for lifts home after matches, but I doubt any of them noticed the girl standing in the shadows behind Mr Winter's car. It was the only time we were truly alone, the drive to the end of Jess's road all too short, although sometimes we chatted for a while in the car, and occasionally I took a detour to lengthen our route, using those precious extra minutes to catch up as much as we could.

'Oh come on, Mark,' Jess begged, her sing-song voice swaying with the movement of the car as we rounded the corner by the park. 'I need you at the prom, you can protect me from myself. You know what I'm like. It's bound to get messy.'

'That's true,' I replied, glancing across at her in the passenger seat, her curls bouncing around her face as she smiled back. It was only a few days until the prom, our time together fast running out.

'You can look after me, make sure I behave myself. I don't want to get excluded again, not just before exams, do I? Not after we've worked so hard together.'

'I'm not acting as a chaperone at the prom,' I told her for the third time, pulling in to park a few doors down from her house. 'We've been over this, Jess.'

'OK, how about I promise to try really, really, really hard with all my revision between now and then?' She fluttered her eyelashes and grinned at me. 'Pleeease.'

'How hard?' I asked, and she squealed, jumping out the car straight away, presumably before I could change my mind.

Opening the window, I called out, 'No promises, I'll have to ask the headmistress first.'

But the headmistress almost bit my hand off when I offered. They were so short of volunteers, almost at the point where they'd have to cancel, which would cause a huge furore, apparently. 'Although . . .' she said as I got up to leave her office. 'You must stay well away from the Tidy girl, I can't emphasise that enough, Mark.'

In the days leading up to the prom, I maintained my clandestine mentoring of Jess as best I could, but she barely paid lip service to our quid pro quo arrangement, our snatched corridor conversations confirming my suspicion that she'd already abandoned not only her new mentor, but also her studies. All those weeks of quiet but hopeful anticipation, lost. She was a bright girl so there was still potential for some success, but she was so lacking in academic purpose I began to wonder if she would even bother to turn up for her exams. Nevertheless, I clung to the idea that maybe I could still change her mind, inspire her once more, and it was on that basis I continued to seek her out, tracking her down during my free periods as she wandered the empty corridors alone.

'Are you studying at all?' I asked, holding out my hand for the gum she refused to relinquish. 'Any revision last night, the night before?'

'Looking forward to our date at the prom?' she asked, avoiding my questions.

'Jess, this isn't a game. This is your future!' I dropped my voice, and exchanged a nod with a colleague who wandered past. 'And I think you know that, or you wouldn't keep coming into school.'

'You know why I come into school,' she replied, looking up at me, although her demeanour was sulky that day. 'To see you.'

'Then study, Jess! Make me proud! You're behaving like a silly little girl. Jess, wait!'

Visibly upset, Jess stormed off along the deserted corridor. I thought it best to let her calm down, so I didn't follow, but I couldn't find her for the rest of the day, and I looked extremely hard, even missing a lesson to do so. She also ignored my messages, and then all my calls, made in desperation from the end of the garden whilst my wife and daughter watched television. I told myself it was a teenage sulk, Jess would be fine the next day, but she missed that day too, and the day after, my messages still unanswered, as was every call. I could see only one course of action.

I was awash with guilt before I left home that warm spring evening, a ridiculously convoluted story about a forgotten laptop and important marking forming my garbled excuse. My wife suggested I should take the car, it would be quicker, but I said it was a nice evening and I fancied a stroll, patting my flat stomach to indicate the exercise would do me good. The truth was, I wanted to arrive quietly, under the radar of Jess's older brothers and her mother's boyfriend, the 'step-father'. I left the cottage with my laptop tucked into my jacket; a layer of clothing I hardly needed. I was already sweating profusely.

I turned into Jess's road and loitered for a while, watching her front door, hoping she might emerge, but that felt too conspicuous, my furtive glances up to the bedroom windows yielding no result, other than an increase in my blood pressure every time a car passed by. There was nothing for it but to knock on the door.

The letter box was loose and almost came away in my hand. I stepped back, avoiding the dismantled motorbike spread across the *front garden and spilling on to the path, praying it would be Jess who answered. The sound of loud music playing inside drifted towards me, something heavy and metallic, and shouts from within as a male voice demanded, 'Someone answer the fucking door, for fuck's sake!' The voice was deep and coarse, a man in his forties or fifties, at a guess. I took a step back, then another, but to my great relief it was Jess who eventually answered, her skin devoid of make-up, a childish dressing gown cinched across her waist, her hair pulled back in a tight knot. She looked so young, almost a different person, and my disappointment was hard to conceal. This wasn't the Jess I knew, cared for, had risked so much to protect, but then her expression changed, a wide grin spreading from her lips to her eyes, lighting them up, extracting a smile from me, despite my nerves.*

I must have jumped when the voice within demanded again, 'Who the fuck is it?', as Jess placed a finger to her lips to indicate silence before she shouted back into the house, 'Someone collecting for charity, I've told them to fuck off.' Then she closed the door on me.

Unsure whether I should wait, I dithered for a minute or two. It was as I turned to go that I noticed an upstairs window was open and Jess, now dressed in jeans and a tee shirt, was clambering out. Her trainers found the tiles on the roof of the porch beneath, a practised move which she executed with panache, jumping from the porch to land elegantly in the long grass beside me, narrowly avoiding the motor parts scattered around us. When she looked up, I saw her face was hastily made up, her hair now wild and free. Back to the Jess I knew.

We walked to the park in silence. The summer evening was long, but now almost ending, the sun dipping on the horizon so the empty swings and roundabout took on a shadowy quality, obliterating the graffitied profanities. Jess sat down on a bench and lit a cigarette, offering me one which I vehemently declined, remaining standing, as though the physical distance between us would grant me some impunity. It was ridiculous to be with her at all, but the cigarette seemed to raise the most objection in me. 'I only came to ask you why you haven't been in school, Jess. Not to share a cigarette.'

She laughed as I recall, drawing on the filter, the red tip fizzing in the twilight, before she coughed and threw it on the ground, stamping it out with her trainer. 'Bit out of your way, isn't it?' she replied, a smile in her voice as she looked up from the trampled cigarette. 'Was there something else you wanted?'

'No, of course not. I was worried, that's all. You didn't return my messages or calls, and you've been missing from school for days. I don't want you to give up your studies, Jess, not when we've worked so hard. Is it something I've done?'

'Nah, not really. I was a bit fed up with you after what you said, but that's not really it.'

I was almost afraid to ask, but I was there as her protector, I had no choice. 'Is it him, the man I heard?'

Jess nodded. 'I try to keep away from him as much as I can. He doesn't like it, says I need to pay my keep, one way or another.'

I offered her money, not much, just what I had in my wallet, but she shook her head.

'Jess, this man—'

'I really don't want to talk about it,' she said, then she stood up and taking a few slow steps towards me, her head down, she whispered, 'I was going to reply to your messages, but then I thought maybe if I didn't, you'd . . .' the last few words were delivered as *she looked up, '. . . come and find me.' I could see the intent in her eye, smell the smoke on her breath.*

It happened quickly, her mouth was on mine, her arms around my waist. I pushed her away and she laughed, then she was running back towards her house, and I didn't know whether to go after her, or let her go. Either seemed to make it worse. Instead I stood in the fading light, touching my lips with my fingertips. She'd felt soft. Her lips on mine; like cherry juice—

'Karen? Where are you?'

I start at the sound of Mark's voice. I hadn't heard him. I was so engrossed, so appalled. He's running up the stairs, his footfall quick as he reaches the door.

'I didn't hear you come in,' I tell him, springing from his chair.

'What are you doing?' He's staring past me to the computer screen.

'Buying clothes.' I look behind me to the page of Christmas dresses, sparkles and velvet, nothing I'd ever need. 'Is that OK?'

'Oh, I—' He sounds out of breath, pausing to lean against the doorframe. 'Sorry, I thought you might have . . . I didn't know you used the computer. How did you . . . ?'

'You left it on, Mark, or I'd never have been able to log in, would I?' My voice conveys a confidence I don't feel. 'Don't worry, I haven't bought anything. I don't need clothes like that, *do I?*'

He shakes his head, taking a seat as I leave the room.

I linger outside the closed door, listening for signs he's typing again, but the air is silent, undisturbed. Maybe that will be the end of it, the terror of discovery forcing him to delete everything he's written, as if it were never there, but it doesn't matter what he decides, not really, because it's already too late. I know what he's done. He kissed Jess Tidy.

A Month Before . . .

Supervision Session #10 – Jessica Tidy – Tuesday, November 15th, 2016

Full notes in client file ref: 718/16

Meeting taped, transcript of relevant section below (abridged)

Me: Please, don't worry, pay me next time. And I wanted to apologise for having to cancel our last appointment.

Jess: That's fine, I've been busy too. More referrals coming in and finally my boss seems to trust me enough to hand over some of the trickier cases.

Me: You said he's a difficult character.

Jess: Yeah, although maybe it's me, I've always had a problem with authority . . . school, work . . . I tend to—

Me: Kick against it?

Jess: Yes, absolutely. I guess it was drilled into me from a young age that Tidys don't involve 'the authorities'.

Me: It must have taken a lot of courage to report Mark Winter to the police, knowing how your family would react.

Jess: Don't get me wrong, I wanted him to pay for what he'd done, but I didn't ask the headmistress to call the police, she made that decision herself.

Me: How did you feel about that intervention, Jess?

Jess: Are you asking if I would rather have walked away? Because I can't answer that, it's impossible to say.

Me: A lot for a girl of sixteen to deal with.

Jess: I wasn't a typical sixteen-year-old. I'd had to grow up. *Fast.*

Me: Of course, but emotionally you still had a lot of maturing to do, would you agree?

Jess: I'm not sure what you're saying?

Me: I'm not saying anything, just that we always seem to come back to that time in your life.

Jess: Is that a problem?

Me: Maybe. I've been thinking about this a lot since I last saw you, and I don't want you to react badly, because I know we've built up a lot of trust, which is great, but I don't think I can continue to act as your supervisor until you've addressed what happened between you and Mark Winter. I've been in touch with an old colleague of mine. She specialises in this kind of trauma therapy; her name is Marion Gotall.

Jess: But you're the specialist, I don't understand.

Me: Not in this area, I'm afraid. Dr Gotall is the best I know.

Jess: You said I was qualified to deal with anything, so you must be too!

Me: Jess, please don't see this as a rejection. I only have your best interests at heart.

Jess: But I'm happy talking to you, you said it was OK, that you didn't mind.

Me: I don't mind, not at all, but I don't feel I can go any further as your supervisor until you deal with this, Jess. It's long overdue. I think you know that.

Jess: You're sick of me, and you're palming me off like everyone does.

Me: No, not at all. That's not it. Jess, wait! Please, Jess!

Karen

Sunday, 11th December 2016 (Late Afternoon)

Mark barely acknowledges me as I tap on his study door and peer in. 'I'm going out now, won't be too long.'

It should be a relief, no awkward questions about that message, but his indifference sharpens my mood, the kiss in the park replayed in my head each time I look at my husband. I keep imagining him with Jess, how he'd touched his lips afterwards, savoured the taste of her; 'like cherry juice'.

I glance at the computer, Mark's essay on the screen, although he's stopped typing. The title alone is three lines long, but there doesn't seem to be much else on the page, a few bullet points and notes. I pick out the words 'Fitzgerald' and 'Gatsby' and for a second doubt my own memory, but I know what I read, and I also know how easy it is to close down one page to reveal another. 'You're writing again?'

He shrugs, asks me to close the door.

'I'm taking the car, is that OK?'

He says that's fine, his acceptance feeling like another dismissal as he pushes the door closed with an outstretched foot.

I drive out of the village too fast, but I slow down as I near the turning, waiting in my car until Will's van pulls into the lay-by a few minutes later, our vehicles parked nose-to-nose so we're looking straight at one another. The low glare of the setting sun blinds me at first, then a passing cloud reveals Will's smile as he walks towards me. The sight of him causes a jolt in my stomach, a lurch inside. This wasn't meant to be anything more than an affair, but now it is, or could be, and I find the attraction is stronger and deeper for that change. I hadn't planned to move my reliance from Mark to Will, but it seems to be happening anyway, and although I should be able to face a future without either of them, I'm realistic enough to know I don't want to be alone. I wipe away the image of Mark with Jess, and replace it with the reality of Will as I lean across to open the passenger side door. Will's presence fills the cramped space with tobacco smoke and something organic and unique to him, pushing out the stale scent of my life with Mark. He kisses me on the cheek, an unfamiliar move. He's constantly surprising me these days. His declaration of love coming out of nowhere, and now this tender respect, but I'm enjoying the next phase of our relationship, the solidity of it reassuring now we've ridden out the turbulence of Jess's return.

'All right?' He takes out one of his roll-ups.

I tell him I can't go home stinking of smoke and he places it back where he found it, in his shirt pocket, but even without a firm plan to be together I feel the pull of a new life, and my

need to conceal our affair starts to dull by comparison, a reck-
lessness taking over. I stroke his arm, and he smiles across at
me. 'Don't normally hear from you on a Sunday, Kar. Not that
I'm complaining.'

I tell him a little of my concerns over Frey, just general stuff
about her growing up, needing me less. He nods, as if he
knows there's more to it, but I can't mention what happened
between Frey and Jess in the café on Friday, his loyalties certain
to be with his sister. The stuff about Tris feels irrelevant to
him, and, although the thought is disloyal, also none of his
business. It concerns me how we might negotiate all these
divisive issues when we're together permanently, *if* that
happens, but then he runs a rough-skinned hand up my inner
thigh, catching my tights as he moves higher, and I immediately
forget the myriad reasons why we can't be together, and instead
allow myself to drown in the one reason why we can.

'Will, listen,' I force myself to push his hand away; before
intent and desire become confused and I run out of time to
talk to him. 'You know what you said . . . about us . . .' I
hesitate, waiting until he settles back into his seat. 'Did you
mean it?'

'Giving us a proper go, you mean?' He removes the unlit
cigarette from his shirt pocket to spin it between the thumb
and forefinger of his right hand. 'Sorry I lost my temper,
stormed off iike that. But you know I meant it, every word.'

I study him for clues to his true feelings, the light now
fading, but he seems entirely genuine. It had shocked me when
he first suggested we should go away together, the ramifications
too enormous to contemplate, but since then I haven't been

able to put the idea out of my mind. Every day I stay with Mark I'm losing my grip on reality a little more, taking extra pills, terrifying myself with my husband's account of his time with Jess. I need to make some drastic changes, for my sanity if nothing else. And Will cares for me, and he's kind and sexy. It's been a strange kind of affair, but it's lasted, the intensity still there – for both of us, it would seem.

'What about your family?' I ask him.

'What about yours?' he replies. Then he takes my hand and kisses it, says sorry, it was unfair of him to ask.

'Not really, I asked you first, but there's no easy answer, is there? I know I can't go on like this. Mark almost saw your message this morning.'

'God, sorry, Kar.'

'No, it was my fault, but that's what I mean. It feels like it's only a matter of time.'

He pulls me towards him. 'Then let's do it, you and I.'

'Where would we go?' I ask, watching for anything that might warn me he's as uncertain as I am.

'A friend I know, he rents out log cabins, holiday homes, but they're empty this time of year. Just for a few days, then we can find somewhere more permanent and look for work. I can build up my business, give it a real go.'

The reality of leaving my home, living somewhere else, a bloody log cabin of all places, not that different from fucking in a shed, petrifies me. Quickly, before I turn back into the woman who stays only because she's afraid to leave, I ask, 'When?'

Will falters, just for a second, and I think my heart might

break if he backs out now, but then he says, 'I have to be around for Jess until the funeral, and to pay my respects, of course.'

'Of course.'

'The day after, first thing Wednesday.' He smiles, leans across and kisses me, a lover's kiss, and the ridiculous idea of simply walking out of my own life in three days' time seems entirely possible.

As I climb across to his side, the arrangement of limbs awkward in the confined space, it crosses my mind, but only briefly, that perhaps the excitement of our liaisons will be lost when we legitimise our relationship, but for now all I feel is our connection: physical, emotional, visceral. He adjusts himself to me as we rock back and forth, and I lose myself in the moment, which is bliss.

As we drive away, careful to stagger our journeys, I try to envisage how I might leave Mark. What I'll tell him, and the practicalities of selling the cottage, my childhood home, and worse, breaking the news to Frey. If it were anyone other than Will, maybe she'd understand, even Mark might accept that after everything he's subjected me to it would be difficult not to look elsewhere. But with Jess's brother; it's unforgivable. The plan begins to fall apart in my head, crumbling to dust as I drive towards my husband, another man's passion held within me, but there's still a nugget of hope, a terrifying, life-affirming glimmer.

Jess

Monday, 12th December 2016 (Afternoon)

The carpet smells of wet dog, although there hasn't been a pet of any kind in the house for years. At least, not one that I know of. I walk into the kitchen, the only uncarpeted room, and Will's voicemail kicks in, again.

'All done,' the jump-suited cleaner tells me, leaning his head around the kitchen door. 'I've left the invoice on the table by the door.'

'Thanks.' I stare at the brown hall carpet.

'Yeah, well, like I said . . .' He shrugs. 'I've done my best.'

I watch him carry the bulky cleaning equipment to his van, the invoice fluttering from the console table as I close the front door. I should try to find the money to pay him, he was a nice guy, said he has three small kids, but it's two hundred pounds. I push the paper bill into my jeans' pocket and try Will's number again, my socks dampening as I pace the hallway listening to the start of his greeting, a long message about the gardening and home maintenance services he offers. It's our mother's funeral tomorrow, he should be here, at the house, supporting me, and he should have been here yesterday, and the day before, and every day of the last week. I kick at the pile of boxes I brought down earlier, the last few things from Mum's room stacked by the front door, mementoes I thought Will might want to keep. The topmost box topples, the sound of broken glass crunching in the bottom as I pick it up. I slip on my trainers, the cut on my heel now much better, and take everything outside, throwing the boxes one on top of another, adding to the collection of crap.

I'm in the kitchen, wet socks removed, pacing out my fury barefoot, when Will finally returns my call. Now I have his attention I don't know where to start. Then it all tumbles out: the spray-painted messages, how I'd chased after the culprit, retrieved the dropped can, how scared I was. Still am.

Will tells me to slow down, explain again, *'What did you say? Friday night? Why didn't you tell me straight away?'*

'You're not very available, are you?'

There's silence, but then Will snaps back, 'I'm sorry, but that's not fair, is it? I said I'd be there if you needed me. Did you even try to call me when it happened?'

'Yes, I did. I tried you first. Then I called the police. That's what most people do when they chase someone out of their garden. And I'm not most people, am I? I'm the victim of previous attacks!'

The words hang between us, Will's deep sigh his only response.

'I was frightened, Will. James had to stay with me until I felt better.'

'He *stayed* with you?'

'Not like that, but yes, he slept in Mum's chair for a few hours, so I'd feel safe.'

'Look, Jess, I'm really sorry I haven't been there for you as much as I should, but it was you who cut me out of your life. You can't have it both ways.'

'You think I wanted to lose touch with you for the last two years? You think I want to feel like I don't know you any more, that you don't have any time for me?'

'Yes, I do! You moved away, changed your number.'

'I'm here now, aren't I? You asked me to come back, and I did.'

'Yes, you did, and I'm really grateful for that . . . Jess, you still there?'

'I'm still here.' I slide my back down the tall cupboard behind me until I'm sitting on the kitchen floor. 'Where are you?' I ask, steadying my voice as I brush away the dampness from my cheeks.

'The big house at the end of the village. Do you remember it?'

'Which one do you mean?'

'Long gravel drive, tall trees. I love it here.' I say nothing and again there's silence until Will asks, 'Can I come over, tonight? Around seven? I'll bring a takeaway.'

'I'd like that,' I reply, telling him I need to go.

I run to the skip and pull out the last box I threw in, sprinting towards the house as Speedy Ken jumps out of his truck and calls after me, 'Need a hand with that, love?'

Karen

Monday, 12th December 2016 (Afternoon)

The moment I read Will's message, it's as though a switch has been flicked on, my anger immediate. I slam one cupboard door shut and kick another, although it's already closed. A heavy bowl, plastic fortunately, springs from my hand to bounce off the kitchen floor, the noise endless as it careers across the floor.

'Karen?' I look round to see Mark standing in the doorway. He's wearing his coat, and Walter is beside him. 'You OK?' He's wrapping a scarf around his neck. 'Lots of crashing and banging going on down here.'

'This evening's meeting has just been cancelled,' I tell him, looking at the dog rather than Mark.

'That's a shame,' Mark replies, and the air in the kitchen thickens for a moment.

'It's a bloody shame.' I turn away to stare out the window. 'Especially if the development plans are approved.'

I look back to see a smug smile playing on my husband's lips. A surge of fury crests the back of my throat, threatening to spill out as a caustic comment.

'Better make the most of those fields then,' he tells Walter, smiling at the excitable dog.

Mark is whistling as he leaves, a cheery activity for a man in his position, and not something I've heard him do for a long time. It always irritated me. I pick up the bowl from the floor, then watch from the kitchen window as Mark crosses the back garden, pushing his way through the overgrown grass. My temper fixes itself on an old resentment, muttering under my breath how he never even cuts the fucking lawn. He pauses to bend down, opening the low gate then closing it behind him as he joins the lane which curves towards the open countryside, the fields stretching out before him. He pauses, taking in the view, then he disappears into the distance.

My feet take the stairs quickly. I don't even bother with my usual soul-searching, the document open in a flash. I've nothing better to do now that Will's cancelled on me.

Chapter Nine – May 2006

I didn't see Jess for a while after the kiss in the park. She'd given up on her studies, so the opportunities for us to meet up at school had also slipped away. My disappointment was palpable, and for the first time I stood back and realised what I'd done. My classes were neglected, my home life too, all given up to help one student, and it had come to nothing, except that kiss. Panicked, I decided to get my life back on track, and the first thing to do was retract my offer to chaperone at the prom.

'We need more, not fewer helpers, Mark,' the headmistress told me, distracted by whatever she was studying on her laptop. 'You do realise you're on a knife-edge with me already?' She looked up, her reading glasses removed. 'The things I've heard . . . keep hearing, in fact. If I wasn't so busy—'

'Look, I know I may have concentrated too much on my mentoring role,' I replied, shifting from foot to foot under her scrutiny. 'But surely that just shows how much I need a new challenge, something I can really get my teeth into, maybe the high achievers' programme?'

'How about chaperoning? That should be quite a challenge.' She stood up behind her desk to indicate the meeting was over, her sardonic comment her final word on the matter, but as she ushered me out she added, 'But Mark, as I said before when you so kindly offered your help, please stay away from the Tidy girl. I can't keep turning a blind eye.'

'I doubt she'll be there, she seems to have given up on school,' I replied, but the headmistress was muttering something about how it was probably all for the best.

I should have made an excuse the night of the prom, a last-minute but utterly compelling reason not to go: a stomach bug, a family emergency, anything. But I didn't, because contrary to what I'd said, I knew Jess would be there, and I'd made her a promise I was now determined to keep. Everyone else might have written off Jess Tidy, but I hadn't, not quite yet.

I close the document and stand up from Mark's desk to look outside, the red orb of the setting sun blistering the fields. I need Will now more than ever, but despite our plans to go away together, tonight it seems I am not his priority. There's a reasonable part of me that completely understands why he's cancelled on me so he can spend the evening with his sister, but my bitter disappointment has been enflamed by Mark's blinkered stupidity. Time after time my husband threw away opportunities to save himself, and us, from this torment, and whatever may or may not have happened that night at the prom, it's hard to forgive those lost chances.

Jess

Monday, 12th December 2016 (Evening)

'I see the skip's been collected,' Will says, holding up a bag of Chinese food and four beers, a bottle of wine tucked under his elbow as he comes inside.

I take the food as he shakes the cold night from his shoulders and back, then he bends to pull off his work boots. His phone pings, and he hands me the pack of beers so he can read the message. 'They seem to think I'm not allowed any time with my sister,' he tells me.

'Who?' I ask but he ignores my question, screwing up his face and commenting on the smell instead. 'Wet carpets, I'd keep your boots on, if I were you.'

He wriggles his socked feet back inside his unlaced boots, knocking the worst of the mud on to the doormat before we go through to the kitchen.

The scent of sweet-and-sour chicken and egg-fried rice transports me back to the last time Will treated me to a takeaway.

We ate it in his bedroom, away from the others, the first food I'd managed to keep down in days. It was barely a week after the prom, and Will begged me to at least try a bite, smiling when I did just that. I'd then demolished all of mine, and half of his, each mouthful rewarded with a huge grin from my darling brother.

'You OK?' he asks, pointing at the empty serving spoon I'm holding.

'Yeah, sorry, just daydreaming. It's this place, so many memories.'

He grabs the spoon to take over the dishing-up, plating half for me and half for him, even though he's probably twice my size. I open the wine and pour myself a large glass, leaning round him with one hand on his shoulder to steal a piece of chicken. Will tells me off, but he's laughing, easing the cap off his beer and half-draining it, thirsty after a day's work.

'You should look round upstairs, it's virtually empty now,' I tell him, rubbing at the sticky sauce which has dripped down my chin. 'Oh, and there's a box of stuff by the front door, some photos, few bits and pieces, don't know if you want to keep anything?'

'I won't.' He catches my eye. 'Come on, Jess. Mum never bothered with either of us, it was all about the twins.'

We sit side by side at the dining table, eating the greasy food in silence. I've stayed out of the front room since the brick, but it feels OK with Will here. My wine slips down nicely, the meal settling in my stomach beside it, filling me up. The first proper meal I've had since I arrived.

'Can't believe how different it looks in here,' he says, wiping his mouth with the back of his hand and pushing his plate away. 'You've done a great job getting rid of all the rubbish. I really appreciate it.'

'You've dealt with Mum for the last ten years,' I reply, spearing the last piece of chicken with my fork. 'It was probably my turn.'

'It was home for a long time, wasn't it?' Will is staring at Mum's chair.

I push my empty plate away too, sitting back, my stomach so full. 'You really thought of it as home?'

'Yeah, course,' he replies, then he tells me off for rushing my food. 'Good to see you eating though, sis.' He nudges my shoulder with his fist. 'You're far too thin.'

'Haven't had you around to look after me, have I?' I steal a prawn from the side of his plate, picking it up with my fingers. He never liked them, but he knows they're my favourite.

'Yeah, well,' he says, standing up. 'Not sure I was that great at it. Anyway, you're all grown-up now with a job in London and your own flat. Don't need me any more.' He looks at me with sad eyes, then he smiles and starts clearing the table, his fork clattering to the floor. He curses and picks it up.

I watch him carry the plates out, wishing I'd stopped him before he left the table, a hand to his arm to tell him how much I still need him, how sometimes it feels like he's the only one I can trust, the only family I've ever had. I've no idea why I pushed him away, and I wish now that I hadn't. I call after him that he should mind his language in front of a 'London Lady', and he swears again, much worse this time, to make me laugh, then he sticks his head back round the door and says, 'I'm so proud of you, Jess. You know that.'

I shrug, unable to speak, and when I look up again he's gone. I follow him out, opening the fridge to pour myself another glass of wine as he runs the kitchen taps to wash the dishes in the old porcelain sink.

'Can I ask you something?' I say to his back, his hands covered in suds.

He picks up a tea towel and throws it at me. 'Make yourself useful then.'

I catch it one-handed then put my wine down, circling a plate with the cloth. 'You and Becky?'

'What about us?'

'Ten years is a long time.' I hold my breath for his reply, but he says nothing. 'I know you only moved in together a few months before Jackson was born, but you were seeing each other on-and-off for years, weren't you? Pretty much since that night at the prom. You kept it quiet, but I'm right, aren't I?'

He turns to look at me. 'She was pregnant, Jess.'

'Yeah, I know, but before Jackson, what kept you together all that time? Sorry, that sounds awful, but you know what I mean.'

'She was pregnant the night of the prom.'

'*What?* I don't understand . . . ?' I stop talking as he takes the plate from me and places it down on the counter, then he uses the tea towel to dry his hands slowly, each finger individually wiped.

'It wasn't planned,' he says, looking down at the cloth now scrunched in his hands.

'When did . . . I mean . . . *when?*' I ask, my voice cracking.

He brings me my wine and we sit together on the sofa. I try hard to listen without interrupting, but I have so many questions.

'She came here looking for you,' he says, explaining it was a couple of months before the prom, in the March. 'You weren't home. No one was, except me. Mum and the twins were down the school with you. I don't know where *he* was, probably the pub, but he wasn't here.'

I nod, looking down at my wine, the glass filled with an image of my step-father staggering in from the pub later that night. Mum already asleep, my brothers all out.

'It was almost tea-time,' Will says. 'I was peeling spuds. I told her to come back later, when you'd be here, it would be all sorted by then, the twins could be very persuasive, but she was really upset, said it was her fault you were going to be excluded.'

'I remember she kept calling, but it *was* her stupid idea that got me in trouble.'

'She was really sorry, and her mum was being particularly difficult, so she had no one else to talk to.' He looks up.

'I only blanked her for a few days.'

'I'd noticed her around, you know, with you, but she was so young, and your best friend.' He looks away. 'We agreed it was best to leave it at that, just a one-time thing, but then she found out she was pregnant.'

'She got rid of it?' I ask, but then I see Will's face, how hard this is for him and I shut up, placing my palm over my mouth.

'Becky wanted to tell you she was pregnant straight away, but you were always with . . .'

'You can say his name, Will.'

'You were spending most of your time with Mark Winter,' he says, glancing at me. 'I'm not blaming you, Jess, and neither was she, but she couldn't find the right time to tell you. She was hoping to say something the night of the prom, when it would be just the two of you, but you didn't give her a chance. I know Becky lost her temper too, probably the drink, but—'

'Exactly!' I reply, interrupting. 'If she was pregnant, why was she drinking vodka?' I stop talking, realising what an idiot I'm being. 'She didn't want the baby?'

'Broke my bloody heart,' he pauses to rub his hands over his face and shakes his head. 'I persuaded her to wait a while, think it over. Turns out it wasn't the first time she'd, you know. Anyway, then she lost it and she realised, well we both did . . . don't know what you've got till it's gone and all that.' He covers his eyes, but they're dry when he looks up. 'They said it was just one of those things, probably nothing to do with the alcohol, but she blamed herself.'

'Oh, God, Will. I'm so sorry. If I hadn't—'

'There's no point, Jess. It wasn't your fault, or hers. It just happens, to lots of people, all the time.'

'Why didn't you say something at the time?'

'She made me promise. Said you had enough to cope with.'

I slump further down on the sofa as I recall how self-absorbed I'd been, assuming the worst of my best friend – then, and ever since – when she'd only thought of my feelings, despite what she was going through. I think of the vodka, a lost baby, that terrible night, everything merging into a dark mass of emotion and pain.

'Thing is,' Will says, 'it brought us closer for a while. Bex has this hard edge, you know, to protect herself, but underneath she's very different.'

I know exactly what he means, and my guilt deepens.

'We thought we'd wait a while before we tried again, but we both knew we wanted to.' He sits forward, his hands clasped across his lap. 'We were being sensible, putting some money by, to get a place of our own first; a proper home, proper family.' He exchanges a look of resignation with me and I think of him and Becky forced to live with her difficult mother when that longed-for baby finally came along. 'Becky was still so young, we thought we had plenty of time, but then it just didn't happen. Well, that's not quite true. Bex could always get pregnant easy enough.'

'God, I'm so sorry, Will. For both of you.' I reach out to pat his arm, a stupid, inadequate gesture, but he smiles anyway.

'It killed us both. Every time. No one talks about miscarriage, but it's so common, and that just makes it worse, like you're supposed to forget they were your children too. I don't know if it kept us together or pulled us apart, a bit of both at times. I was ready to give up, but then Jackson came along, like some kind of bloody miracle. We're not perfect, Becky and I, neither of us, but we love our boy.' He laughs, and I grin back. 'To be honest, if it hadn't been for him—'

'It can't be easy living with her mother.'

'No, but we couldn't come here, and money just gets eaten up when you've got a kid.'

'You've given him a great start in life, Will. You and Becky.'

'All I ever wanted was to be a good dad. God, what a mess.'

'You are a good dad,' I tell him, taking his hand and squeezing it. 'And he's definitely the cutest nephew I've got.'

Will smiles and points out he's the *only* nephew I've got.

'You don't know that. There may be a few mini Tonys or Micks running around the village for all we know.'

We continue to talk, but not about Becky, or Jackson, or the night of the prom. Instead, Will and I replay a better version of our shared childhood than it probably deserves, flicking through one of Mum's old photo albums, retrieved from the box I'd saved from the skip.

'I've missed this,' I tell him as he gets up to make us both a coffee.

'Missed what?' he asks, turning back.

'Being with my big brother.'

He looks at me for a long time before he says, 'I can't bear what he's done to you.'

'You mean Mark Winter?'

'Yes, of course.' He rubs his hands over his eyes and sniffs. 'Who else?'

'No one,' I tell him, but he's looking away, deep in thought.

'If I've stayed away,' Will says. 'It's not just because you told me to. Or because I'm busy. It's because I feel like I let you down.'

I get up and pull him into a hug. 'Don't you dare blame yourself. You're my brother and you were always there for me. I was the one who pushed you away.'

Will gently removes himself from my embrace and takes a step back. 'Why did you do that, Jess? Why cut me out like that? I was only young myself. I did my best.'

'Of course you did. I never blamed you. I thought you blamed me. All those questions the last time you visited me in London, it felt like you didn't believe me.'

Will shakes his head. 'I was just trying to make sense of it, in my stupid clumsy way.' He makes a joke about what a rubbish brother he is, then his phone distracts him, another message arriving, and he says he should probably get going.

'What about that coffee?' I ask, following him to the door.

'Sorry,' he replies, offering no further explanation. 'I'll be here in plenty of time in the morning. About half-ten, OK?'

'Will!' He stops on the path and looks back. 'Tell Becky I said hi.'

After he leaves, I close the door quickly, then I cry, knowing not one tear is for Mum. I pick up the bottle of wine from the table and drink straight from the neck, greedy gulps until it's all gone. Like my brother said . . . what a mess.

Karen

Monday, 12th December 2016 (Evening)

I tap lightly on the study door and the clicking of fingers on keys stops. 'Can I come in, Mark?'

I wait, allowing him a moment before I turn the handle. The BBC home page is displayed on the computer, Mark's back to me as he stares at the screen.

'Anything interesting happening in the world?' I ask, stepping in.

He says no, he doesn't think so, then he reads a few headlines to me: Trump, Brexit, Christmas Sales. 'You look nice,' he remarks, turning to look at me. 'Have I seen that top before?'

There's a beat or two of silence before I explain the steering committee have decided to meet up after all, a hastily reconvened meeting at the chairwoman's house. 'I shouldn't be long.'

'Strange time to meet.' He looks at the clock above his desk. 'It's almost nine.'

'Yes, well it's panic stations over there. Sue rang—'

'*Sue?*'

'She's in charge of the steering committee. I've told you that.'

'And it can't wait?'

'No, not really,' I reply, backing out again. 'Not if we want to keep those fields you two always tramp across.' I glance at Walter who hasn't bothered to get up from the rug.

'I'll drive you.' Mark stands up and Walter lifts his head from the rug, his ears pricked up. 'Ages since I've taken the car out, do me good.'

'I've already got a lift arranged,' I tell him. 'Sue's picking me up at the end of the lane.'

I close the study door, but then it opens again, Mark calling after me, running to catch up as I fly down the stairs. I grab my coat from the hook in the hallway and slip it on, my hand already turning the handle on the front door as he says, 'Karen! Wait!'

I pause, glancing over my shoulder, a forced smile as I tell him I need to go, I'll miss my lift.

'Please don't,' he says, but I'm already pulling the door closed behind me.

I walk fast, glancing back to make certain Mark isn't following me, but the lane is the darkest I've seen it all winter and it soon requires my full attention. I'm almost at the main road when the van's headlights shine towards me, flashing on and off just once. I walk round to the passenger side and climb in, treading on emptied packets of tobacco and cigarette papers as I clamber into the seat.

'Thanks for coming,' I say, as Will starts the engine. 'How's your sister?'

He doesn't reply or return my glances, driving away as I click the seat belt into place and straighten my coat in my lap. We're heading away from the village, into the countryside, the van speeding up as Will swings it around the bends. I cling on to the door handle to brace myself as I ask where we're going, and why the hurry? He shakes his head, but doesn't answer.

'Will, I mean it, where are we going?' I wait, but no response is forthcoming other than a sharp exhalation of breath. 'Are you annoyed with me? I know you said you were too busy to meet up this evening, but Mark has been acting really strangely, and with us planning to go away so soon I thought . . . Will?'

He maintains his silence, staring ahead at the empty road, lighting a pre-rolled cigarette with a disposable lighter, then cracking his window an inch to allow the smoke to escape into the darkness which flashes by. I complain, telling him the smell will settle in my clothes and hair. 'Will, please. What's wrong? Tell me!'

He turns sharp right into a narrow lane. 'I told you I needed to see my sister tonight,' he replies at last. 'But you had to keep messaging me, demanding I—'

'I didn't demand, and I only sent two messages.'

Branches scrape noisily along the side of the van as he pulls in to park beside a hedge. He looks at me briefly, then opens his window and snaps the end from a bramble. He curses, sucking blood from his thumb, scraping at the pad with his teeth. I watch him, waiting for him to speak.

'You can't treat me like this, Kar.' He's still dragging his front teeth across the inside tip of his right thumb. 'Demanding I—'

'I thought you cared about me, Will? I thought we were going away in two days' time? Or am I wrong about that?'

'Is this about Jess?' He looks straight at me. 'We're burying our mother tomorrow, in case you forgot. I thought I owed my sister a bit of my time before she leaves. I've hardly seen her, or done much to help. I did explain that, didn't I? I thought you understood.'

'I'm sorry, I didn't think—'

'I just wanted this one evening to let her know how much she means to me. To tell her how sorry I am for everything she's been through. I'm all she's got, Kar.'

I lean back in my seat, closing my eyes.

'You jealous?' he asks when I still don't respond. '*Is that it?* Jealous I want to spend time with my sister? Don't make me choose, Kar.'

'I don't give a fuck what you do!' I tell him, unstrapping myself. 'Spend every bloody moment with your precious sister for all I care!' I open the van door and jump down into an icy puddle.

I swear to myself and stamp my soaking feet, then I stride off, deeper into the darkness, the high hedges towering at either side of the unlit road, only the pale moon to illuminate my way. I have no idea what I'll do if Will doesn't follow me. I don't even know exactly how far we've come, but my temper urges me on.

'Kar! I'm sorry, I shouldn't have said that. Kar! Wait!' I hear his heavy boots on the wet road behind me. He grabs my arm and spins me round to face him, pressing his mouth to mine. 'Don't you leave me!' he says, releasing me. 'I love you, Kar.

You know I do. But I love my sister too, and my son, and my bloody awful mother that I'm burying tomorrow, so don't make me choose.'

He wraps me up in his arms, the pair of us almost falling over as we walk back to the van together, then he pushes aside the mess to make enough room for us to lie down.

As we drive back he talks about the funeral, how he's dreading it. 'Did I tell you the twins are allowed out of prison for the burial service? It's going to be a right circus. Sometimes I think I was born to the wrong family.'

I look across at him, but don't know what to say.

'Can you be there?' he asks, animated now, as though the idea has just struck him. 'It would really help to know you're at the church, supporting me.'

'I can't, Will. If Jess were to see me, or the twins – and what about Becky?'

'I don't mean by my side, but if I know you're there, somewhere, I think I can cope.'

'I suppose I could sit at the back, if it's that important to you.'

He smiles, says that means the world. Then he tells me Jess is going back to London straight after the wake. 'I could come get you tomorrow instead, if you like? You'll have time to tell Mark before I arrive? Be ready to go?'

'Tomorrow? I don't know, Will.'

'Listen,' he says, turning the final bend towards the village. 'It's never going to be easy, but the longer we leave it, the more chance there is someone will find out. Better we tell everyone tomorrow, then leave straight away. I want to be with you, Kar.'

I nod, wondering when Will plans to tell Becky: before the funeral, or more likely later, after the wake. Maybe he's hoping to just slip away, but I doubt it, not with Jackson to consider.

'Don't think I'll see much of Jess after tomorrow anyway,' he tells me, no edge to his voice this time, only regret. 'She's busy in London with a new job; she's a counsellor.'

'Well done, Jess,' I say, trying hard to say her name without conveying my true feelings. 'A fresh start for all of us.' I reach for his hand, mine trembling at the thought of the promises I've just made.

He squeezes my hand, then drops it to change gear. 'What do you think Mark will say?'

I shake my head, no idea when or how I will break the news to Mark, let alone Frey. Maybe it would be better to leave without a word, let the pieces fall as they may.

'You still believe him?' Will asks.

'You still believe her?' I reply, but neither of us answer. *How can we?*

He stops the van in the same spot where he waited for me an hour ago; the distant lights of the cottage a faint glimmer at the end of the lane. It no longer feels like home, but I can't fashion a replacement from Will's vague plans for our future either. Tomorrow feels much too soon to leave, and I almost tell him I've changed my mind, I can't go away with him, not yet, but then he kisses me and says he loves me.

'I love you too, Will.'

'You know I'll take good care of you. We're going to be happy together, I promise.'

I kiss him back, passionately, desperate to convince myself

266

we have a real chance at happiness. It's only as he drives away, the van roaring off, that I realise there's someone standing in the lane waiting for me, a dog at their side.

Mark walks towards me as I try to rearrange my expression into an uneasy smile, the receding lights of the van washing over my husband's cold stare.

'How long have you been standing there in the dark?' I ask.

'Long enough,' he says, pulling Walter to his side so he doesn't jump up at me, muddy paws threatening my coat. 'It's getting late. I was worried.'

'Sorry.' I draw level with him, scanning his face for clues as I try to regulate my breathing. The cold air hurts my lungs as I drag it in and out.

'Whose van was that?' Mark asks, following me back towards the cottage.

'Sue's husband,' I say, walking ahead.

'He couldn't have driven you up the lane?' Mark falls into step with me. 'Dropped you at the door on a cold night like this? Nice friend, leaving you to walk up here alone.'

I pick my way around the frozen puddles, but I'm able to walk faster than Mark, the dog dragging him in the opposite direction, away from the cottage.

'Stop!' Mark shouts as I reach our front path and turn in. 'Please don't go inside, Karen.' He runs to catch me up. 'I'm begging you. Stay with me here. Don't go inside.'

'Mark, I—' My voice cracks, and I fall silent.

'I saw you,' he says, his voice strange. 'I saw you kiss him, Karen.'

'No, you're wrong,' I tell him, although I don't know why I persist in the lie.

'Do you love him?' Mark asks, then before I can answer he says, 'Are you leaving me? Please don't leave me, Karen. I'll forgive you anything, I just can't lose you. You're all I've got.'

'I'm so sorry,' is all I manage. Then I walk up the path and go inside.

I expect him to follow – wondering what I've admitted in that apology, *everything, nothing, did he see it was Will, or just that his wife shared a kiss with another man?* – but when I walk back to the open front door Mark is already a distance away, his head torch guiding him back the way we came.

I slam the door and go upstairs, quickly opening up the document where I'd last left it. I need more than a kiss to damn him now. I need to know what happened the night of the prom, because if he did rape Jess Tidy, then I've wasted enough time already, and tomorrow cannot come soon enough.

Chapter Ten – May 2006 (The Night of the Prom)

I anticipated her arrival for almost an hour, positioning myself across the far side of the cheaply decorated hall, where I had the best view of everyone arriving. 'An American theme, apparently,' Barry Johnson informed me, staring up at the homemade flags and star-spangled paper chains criss-crossing the large room. His unshakeable presence at my side was an annoyance, but at least I could still see past him to the entrance lobby.

The other chaperones were grouped around the buffet table next to the disco, throwing back crisps and warm soft drinks, occasionally moving in time with the thumping music amid outbreaks of raucous laughter. Barry was optimistically suggesting we might join them when Jess and her best friend Becky staggered in, distracting us both. In fact, it seemed the whole room turned to watch the two drunk girls, their tightly fitted dresses and high heels adding to their precarious progress. They were loud too, drawing even more attention to themselves as they disappeared into the Ladies toilet. Barry lost interest then, tossed a peanut into his mouth and wandered off 'for a sneaky smoke', but I remained focused on the bathroom door, waiting for Jess's reappearance. Becky emerged a few minutes later, on her own this time, and looking more dishevelled than before she went in. I thought the point was to tidy themselves up, wasn't that what girls did when they went to the bathroom together? But I was more concerned why Jess hadn't come out. I was debating how I might legitimately investigate, when the door was flung open for a second time. Jess looked around her, flushed and clearly disorientated, her friend gone. Then she spotted me, her face opening into a wide smile as she made her way over, calling ahead, 'Mark! Mark!'

Quite an audience gathered, and so quickly. Kids laughing, pointing, chanting Jess's name as she came stumbling towards me, but no one tried to assist her. The crowd simply parted to allow her through. Even the other chaperones seemed reluctant to step forward, feigning distraction as they corralled the swelling crowd of onlookers towards the disco and buffet, although most people's interest remained with Jess.

I caught her mid-slide, her knees crashing towards the parquet flooring as she lunged at me. It was like propping up cooked spaghetti, spindly legs bending beneath her, but she was a tiny thing, easy to hold up. I supported her with one arm around her waist, guiding her to the edge of the room, then out of the hall in search of some-where a bit less public, hoping to save her some of the humiliation she would surely feel when she sobered up.

'Why do this to yourself, Jess?'

She said nothing, just laughed, but she seemed to rally a little, more in control of her movements as we turned into a dark corridor.

'All right there, old chap?' Barry asked, appearing from nowhere. 'Need a hand?' His tone was mocking rather than concerned, his question rhetorical as he puffed on his pipe.

'No, I don't. And put that thing out!' I told him, pointing to his pipe, the smoke choking us as Jess leant against me heavily. 'I'm helping her walk it off.'

'She's a Tidy, Mark, bound to be trouble; drunk or sober. Anyway, aren't you supposed to keep your distance, after all those rumours?'

'I know it was you who reported me, Barry,' I hissed at him, 'so don't pretend it wasn't.'

It was hard holding on to Jess, her limbs slackening again, but Barry wouldn't let us pass, leering at Jess in the gloom and telling me he could think of something better to do with her than carry her around. Jess said nothing, but I felt her stiffen at his onslaught. That's when I flipped, lowering her to the floor before I pushed a startled Johnson up against the wall, holding him there by the lapels of his odorous tweed jacket until my point was made, his teeth rattling in his head as I shook him harder and harder. I surprised myself with my show of strength, but it had been building for some time.

The moment I released him, Johnson trotted back in the direction of the hall, calling behind him that he'd be reporting me to the headmistress, or maybe the police, but I had no time to worry about *his ridiculous allegations, for when I turned back to where I'd left Jess, she was gone.*

I ran down long windowless corridors, calling out to her, sometimes catching what I thought might be the sound of her ahead of me, laughing and singing, although I couldn't be sure. Then I noticed an open door, a slice of moonlight filling the gap and stretching across the corridor like an invitation. I'd assumed she was running without aim, but she must have always been headed there; the Exclusion Unit. Her place of safety. Our place.

It was too dark to see her at first, but then she said my name, softly but with clarity this time, the slur gone from her voice, her intention clear—

I stop reading, breathless, looking for more, but that's where the page ends.

Jess

Monday, 12th December 2016 (Late Evening)

Sluggish from the wine, and still half-asleep, I stagger from the chair to the hallway. 'Will, is that you? Don't you have a key?'

I notice the dog first, a wet nose poking inside as I open the door an inch to see who's out there. Mark barges in and kicks the door behind him, grabs my hand to drag me along the hall and into the front room. I pull away, but he grips the tops of my arms and pushes me down into Mum's chair, my body bouncing back from the force of the shove as I scream at him to get off me. The dog barks wildly, Mark looping its lead around the table leg before he turns again to me, spittle forming in the corners of his mouth as he says, 'I'm going nowhere, Jess. Not until you've listened to what I came here to say.'

'They'll arrest you just for being here, you know that,' I reply, unsteady as I try to stand up.

'You're drunk!'

He pushes me back down, then paces between the sofa and the chair, his hands balled into fists. The dog watches him too, and when it whines he shouts its name, which silences it but startles me.

'Go home, Mark! Go home to your wife and leave me alone!' My challenge is braver than I feel. 'I won't tell the police if you leave now, I promise.'

He laughs, moving in so close I can smell his sour breath. 'I'm not stupid, Jess. You'll ring Facey the second I'm out the door.'

He steps back and rubs his hands through his thinning hair, the moonlight shining in through the tissue-paper curtains to highlight his forehead. I've hated him for so many years, but never more so than right now, everything about him repulsing me.

'The thing is, Jess, I've nothing left to lose.' He pushes his face into mine to whisper, 'You were fine when I left you that night, so what changed?'

'I was far from fine, Mark. You know that.'

'But to say those things about me, those terrible lies. Was it spite, or revenge?' He straightens up. 'You ruined my life. Why would you do that?'

I scream at him to get away from me, kicking out, towards his legs, his crotch, but he's stronger than I am, his hands around my wrists as I fight him, his palms sticky with sweat. It makes me retch, but I force myself to stop, holding my breath, thinking he might try to kiss me, or worse, but instead he releases his hold on me, and I fall back into the chair.

'So you didn't know what you were saying until it was too late, or you knew *exactly* what were you saying, Jess?'

I shake my head, but he doesn't seem to notice, pacing again as he talks to the wall, the dog, looking anywhere but me. 'I really wanted to help you, give you a chance. I was the only one who did. Why would you do that to me after everything I risked for you?' He looks so pathetic for a moment I think he's going to fall to his knees in front of me and beg.

'Mark, please—'

'I won't hurt you, and I will go, I promise, but please, Jess, I have to know what was in your head that night, why you did it. I protected you—'

'Don't!' I tell him. 'Don't say it! It's not true! You didn't protect me.'

'Jess,' he reaches out to touch my face, and I kick him hard between the legs. He crumples, his knees giving way beneath him until he's sitting on the damp carpet at my feet. The dog whines and tries to pull closer to him, but Mark ignores it, groaning and holding his hands between his legs.

I edge forwards in my chair. 'If you leave now, without any trouble—'

He looks up at me, his eyes bright. 'You lying bitch!'

I close my eyes, shutting him out, pushing myself deep into Mum's chair, my bare feet pulled up beneath me, my breaths shallow. I'm aware of him beside me, watching me and when I dare to look again he's right there, kneeling up and staring at me, the pain now forgotten. I want to hit him again, a hard thump on his head this time, bring him down, but I force

274

myself to speak evenly. 'Mark, I know in your head you probably have some other version of that night, but—'

'*Version?*' He stands up and walks towards the window, parting the curtain to look out at the empty street. 'The truth, you mean?'

It must be late, maybe almost eleven. The house next to this one is unoccupied. My neighbours the other side separated from me by two brick walls and a decade of ugly rumours. No one to hear me if I scream.

'Whatever you think of me now,' he says, glancing back at me, 'you must know how much I cared about you, Jess.'

'Is that what you tell yourself?'

He drops the curtain and walks over, pulling me up to stand in front of him, his eyes shining, then he shakes me like a rag doll, his whole body wired with desperation. 'That's not true, is it? You've rebuilt your life, it's mine that's been destroyed.' He lets go of me. 'Mine and my family's. Because of you!'

'You need to leave,' I warn him, backing away. My head is clearing now, my fear sobering me up. If only I could find my phone . . . I drop down into the chair, lowering my hands into the gaps along the sides of the cushion.

'All I want to do is talk to you,' he says, his voice composed now. 'Get it clear in both our minds. It's been awful, for all of us, I can see that, but if we can talk it through together, rationally, we can make sense of it. It's not too late, Jess.'

He moves to the sofa, outwardly calm, although his eyes are wild, his limbs unsteady as he lowers himself to sit down. I push my hands deeper into the chair, my movements subtle, but my fingers find nothing except dust, and what feels like an old sock.

'I admit I let you down,' he tells me. 'You were young, vulnerable. But to make up those awful lies about me, it's unforgivable.'

I feel around for my phone again, then I remember where it is and almost gasp at my stupidity, fumbling in the back pocket of my jeans, my fingers around it. I press the screen, hoping Mark won't notice as it lights up my pocket. He's still talking, looking down at his hands, worrying at one with the other. I take a chance, quickly pulling the phone out and holding it at my side as I unlock the screen and tap on James's last message, sending a three-word reply. **Mark is here**

'What are you doing?' Mark asks, looking straight at me. 'Put that away!'

He lunges forward, snatching the phone from my hand then throwing it to the carpet where it lands face up, James's reply immediate. We both stare at the screen then Mark shouts, 'Tell me before Facey arrives! Just admit it to yourself, to me, to the wall! I don't care. Just tell the bloody truth this time!'

Two Weeks Before . . .

Supervision Session #11 – Jessica Tidy – Tuesday, November 29th, 2016

Full notes in client file ref: 718/16

Meeting taped, transcript 1/2 of relevant section below (abridged)

Me: I'll send all my notes over to Marion, Dr Gotall. So you won't need to go over everything again, at least, not in the same way.

Jess: It's funny, isn't it?

Me: What's that?

Jess: Oh, nothing. I was just thinking . . . all these years I've locked it up, told no one, thought the sky would fall in if I did, but all I needed was to find the right person to unlock it.

Me: Just doing my job.

Jess: Yes, just doing your job. Asking questions, listening. Do you like it, hearing all those terrible things?

Me: I'm not sure I—

Jess: Sorry, ignore me, always playing the counsellor; guess I'm in the right job.

Me: Yes, you are, but that comment, Jess. Can we just—

Jess: I like listening to people, you see. Always have. They come in and I put them at their ease, then they tell me their secrets. And if I listen to theirs, I don't have to share mine. That's how it works, isn't it? A storyteller and the listener. It's not really a conversation, is it? Not like life, that's a constant back-and-forth. Always a bloody negotiation, quid pro quo, that's what he said, and I knew what he meant.

Me: Jess, you seem—

Jess: Angry? Disappointed? I am a bit, to be honest. I've come here every few weeks for the last, what . . . five, six, months? Told you my story, and you've listened, professionally, I mean. Not friends, of course. Nooo, not friends. And now it's time for me to move on. I get it. But, the thing is, I trusted you. It's just so fucking disappointing.

Me: Jess, if I've offended you—

Jess: I've never trusted anyone else, you see. Not since . . . Tried, but it never worked out. You were my last hope. Then you pass me along, to the next person. Move along, please!

Me: I'm sorry you feel that way, but I promise you, this is for the best. The best for you, I mean. The start of better things to come. A fresh start. And the fact that you've managed to share so much with me will stand you in such good stead with Marion.

Jess: You think you know everything about me, about Mark, about what happened that night? That we're done?

Me: No, not everything, but that's why it's important you see a specialist, someone who can help you more than I can. Then afterwards—

Jess: So you're not interested in the truth?

Me: Very much so.

Jess: How much time do we have left today?

Me: As long as you need, Jess.

Jess

Monday, 12th December 2016 (Late Evening)

A loud knock at the door startles me. I abandon my search the cupboards for alcohol and run down the hall into the front room, checking from the window this time, as I should have before.

'It was stupid of me to let Mark in,' I say as soon as I open the door. 'But I was disoriented. I'd been asleep. In Mum's chair. I didn't know who it was at first, and he barged in, then he grabbed me.' I hold up my wrists to demonstrate. 'He probably would have kicked the door in if I hadn't opened it.'

James comes inside. 'Which is it, Jess? You let him in, or he barged past?'

'You don't believe me?'

'I'm not saying that.' He's looking past me into the front room, the bottle of wine Will brought now empty and on its side by the chair. 'Why don't you make us both a strong coffee, perk us up, then we can talk?'

'I thought you'd want to speak to Mark straight away?'

He glances at his watch. 'Let's have that coffee first.'

James is seated at the dining table, coat undone, his body language conveying no sense of urgency as he thanks me for the hot drink. I stare, then pace with my tea in my hand, waiting for him to say something, but he sips his black coffee in silence. I imagine Mark running home along deserted streets, the dog at his side, warning his wife to expect a knock at their door any moment, or maybe already in his car, disappearing, but when I ask James directly, he tells me Mark won't be going anywhere, he's not the type. There's something in James's answer I don't like, but when I frown at him, he says, 'Tell me again what happened.'

'He frightened the hell out of me, don't you get that?'

James looks at the wine bottle and picks it up, placing it on the table beside his empty mug, then asks me exactly how much I've had to drink this evening.

'Is that relevant?' I ask, and he says it's his job to question and I have been particularly obstructive in the last few days, withholding information. He needs to be certain of his facts before he speaks to the Winters. The consequences for Mark are very serious. He will most likely be recalled to prison straight away.

James is so involved in his lecture he doesn't question why I move across to the table and pick up the bottle, walking back to the window before I turn round and hurl it towards him. It hits the wall directly above his head, an explosion of green glass, swiftly followed by my mug of tepid tea. He ducks, twice, although neither missile was aimed at him, nowhere near. There's a second or two of of silence as we stare at one another, then he stands up and brushes the shards from his coat. I run at him, my fists raised, but he grabs me and holds me at arm's-length, moving me away from the broken glass and jagged bits of mug to guide me into Mum's chair. I tell him to let go of me and he does, walking out to the kitchen. I hear him opening and closing cupboard doors, then he returns empty-handed, collecting the glass and pieces of mug in his palm and ferrying them to the kitchen bin.

'I'm sorry,' I say as he's clearing up. 'I wasn't trying to hurt you.'

'I know that,' he replies, looking at me. 'But this isn't accept-able, Jess. I don't need to tell you that, do I?'

I follow him into the kitchen, saying over and over how sorry I am as he drops the last few pieces into the bin, then he washes his hands, a glint of glass on his back, a cut to his hand which he rinses as the blood swells.

'Are you going to arrest me?' I ask as he shakes the excess water into the sink, his palm cleaned, although a new line of red immediately returns. 'I wouldn't blame you.'

'Listen, Jess,' he's wrapping a tissue from his coat pocket around his hand. 'I'm on your side, don't think I'm not, but you can't behave like this.'

'I'm sorry, I don't know why I did that. I didn't want to hurt you, James. I would never want to do that.'

'I know, and I want to help you, but I need proper evidence. And I need you to cooperate with me, not get in the way. You have to be completely honest, about everything. Then I'll do all I can, I promise.'

282

I ask about the paint can he took away, but he says it only had my prints on. I open my mouth to explain again how I'd dropped it in a puddle, but I know there's no point. I should have let him do his job at the time, given him the brick, the note, told him everything, all my suspicions. Now James doesn't trust me, and who can blame him?

'Mark Winter was here, I promise you. He threatened me, shook me hard. I'm asking you to protect me from him. I'm scared, James.'

He looks out of the kitchen window, parting the slats of the blind to peer at the darkness. 'I've said I'll do all I can,' he replies, scrunching the tissue in his hand as he turns back to face me. 'But I need to be certain of the facts before I speak to Mark. It's a breach of his licence conditions, a violation of the Sexual Harm Prevention Order imposed on his release. Mark will be in an enormous amount of trouble. If you're mistaken, or even deliberately trying to pervert the course of justice—'

'*Mistaken?* So you don't believe me!' He pushes back his fringe and avoids my gaze. 'James, look at me!'

'It's just—'

'*What?* Tell me!'

'Don't take me for a fool, OK? Because I'm not one.'

I tell him he should go, and he says I'm right, but he promises he'll be in touch after he's spoken to Mark.

'So, you're going to?' I ask, following him to the door. 'Speak to him, I mean.'

'Lock the door behind me. I'll be in touch tomorrow, but call me if you have any concerns at all, OK?'

I grab the door and swing it towards him, forcing him to jump out of the way as it slams in his face. The letter box rattles so violently on its remaining hinge I'm afraid this time it will fall off, although somehow it hangs on.

Karen

Monday, 12th December 2016 (Late)

I sit up in bed and look at the clock. Eleven-twenty. Mark's been out for at least an hour, perhaps a little more, but now he's back, Walter's claws tapping on the hall floor. The kitchen door opens and closes, then Mark climbs the stairs slowly, almost silently. He must have removed his shoes to avoid waking me, putting off the inevitable confrontation; much as I did when I chose to feign sleep in the darkness. There's a change in my husband's pace as he crosses the landing, then the bathroom door closes. I lie down, listening as the toilet flushes, then a tap runs. I hold my breath, pulling the duvet over me, but when I look again, the sliver of light under the door has disappeared, and there's the soft click of a door closing somewhere across the landing.

I push back the duvet and place one foot then the other on the cold floor. The room is in almost total darkness, my hands in front of me as I walk towards the door. I press my ear to the wood and listen, but there's no clue, nothing out there but silence. Whatever he's doing, my husband clearly isn't going to join me in our bed.

I feel my way back, then reach for my sleeping pills on the bedside cabinet, swallowing one with a sip of water. I need some rest, then I can face him, but even as I slide into a fitful sleep the thought of what tomorrow might bring opens my eyes. I try to imagine attending the funeral, then somehow telling Mark and Frey about my plans to leave with Will. Maybe by phone, although that seems too cowardly. None of it feels real, but soon it will be. It's almost midnight now. Almost tomorrow.

Jess

Tuesday, 13th December 2016 (Morning)

Will is here early as promised, the throaty sound of the van alerting me to his arrival. I'm dressed for the funeral, my navy suit jacket draped over the back of a dining chair, my bag packed and placed by the door, ready for the drive to the station after the wake. I move it aside as I open the door, watching as Will parks his van down the road, although there's space directly outside. 'For the funeral cars,' he says as he notices my confusion.

I remind him not to take off his boots, the carpets are still damp, and he comments how it smells even worse today.

'I must be getting used to it,' I say, sniffing the damp air.

He smiles at me as we go into the front room, sitting next to one another on the sofa. 'So, big day, sis.'

'Yeah, big day.'

'Becky's meeting us at the church. She wanted to double-check all the arrangements first, and the landlord at the pub has agreed to be the other pallbearer with me and the twins. I guess that's OK. As long as he keeps off the whisky until the wake.'

'You must be very proud of her,' I reply, then noticing his confusion I say, 'Becky, I mean. Oh, and she mentioned something about the bill.'

'We can talk about that later,' he says, commenting how smart I look. 'How are you doing? You look tired.'

'I'm OK.' I get up, walking to the window to look out.

'*Jess?* Has something happened?'

I turn round to face him, his expression full of concern. 'Please don't go mad, Will. Mark Winter was here last night, after you left. Barged his way in.'

'Bloody hell!' His hands fly to the sides of his head, his scruffy work-shirt pulling free of his waistband as he gets up. 'He didn't hurt you, did he? If he's—'

'I'm fine, honestly.' I hold up my open palms as he moves towards me. 'Please, I don't want a fuss; I might cry if you're too nice.'

'Why didn't you call me?' He steps back. 'I thought we'd been through this.'

'Yes, I know, but Facey's number was—'

'You contacted Facey again?' Will's eyes narrow as he turns away. '*Shit!* Why did you have to call Facey?'

'I didn't have much time to decide whilst my attacker was three feet away from me. Anyway, I thought you'd be pleased. Mark will almost certainly be on his way back to prison by now.'

'Yeah, sorry,' Will replies, looking at me again. 'But you should have told me last night. I should have known.'

I had thought about it, but James's obvious distrust had rattled me. I couldn't have coped if Will had questioned me too.

'Well I'm telling you now. Do you believe me?'

'Of course I believe you. You sure you're OK?'

'I'm fine, honestly.'

'Tell me everything that happened,' he says, sitting down again and patting the cushion beside him.

I want to share a thousand things, mainly how much it means to me that he cares so much, but I content myself with a smile and a shake of my head. 'Can we leave it for now? Today should be about saying goodbye to Mum. Let James deal with the Winters. I'm with you all day, then you're taking me to the station, so there's really no need to panic.'

He rubs the back of his hand across his nose and sniffs. 'Yeah, about that . . . I'm sorry, but I won't be able to take you to the station after all.' He kicks the toe of one boot against the heel of the other, pellets of dried mud landing on the carpet. 'I have to be somewhere after the wake.'

'Where?' I ask, but he says it doesn't matter, as if that's a proper answer. I tell him it's fine, I can order a taxi, but he offers to change his plans, make sure I'm safely delivered to the station first.

'I'm a grown woman, Will. I can look after myself; have been for years.'

'What time are the cars arriving?' he asks, changing the subject.

'Don't you and Becky ever talk to each other?' I regret the question as soon as it's out of my mouth. 'Sorry. They're due at twelve. You should get changed, it's almost time.'

I wait in the kitchen, making us hot sweet tea whilst he fetches his bag from the van and then goes upstairs to change. He looks much smarter when he comes back down, but uncomfortable. He's not used to wearing a suit, and it's a bit tight on him. We lean against the wiped counter tops, the last two mugs in our hands, a reflection of one another, our feet almost touching, mine tiny compared to his. He's wearing dark grey socks which look new, the bottoms darkened from the damp carpets, his jacket open, the collar of his shirt done up with difficulty. I try to swallow some of my tea, but the hot liquid explodes from my mouth as I cough and cry, my brother reaching out to take my mug, asking what's wrong, is it Mum, something else? *Mark?*

'I don't want today to be over,' I say, although I know it makes no sense. 'And I've ruined your clean shirt.' I brush at the brown stains.

Will takes my hand in his and asks what I mean, why wouldn't I want today to be over? I tell him I've missed him so much, and now Mum's gone we'll have even less reason to keep in touch.

'I just don't get you, Jess.' He throws his tea down the sink after mine. 'You said you wanted to move on, that this place, and me,' he catches my eye, 'were just a reminder of bad times. Now you say you don't want today to be over.'

'I'm so sorry,' I sob. 'I don't know what's wrong with me.'

'There's nothing wrong with you.' He pulls me into a tight hug.

'Will you visit me in London?' I sniff. 'Like you used to?'

'I'll try my best,' he replies, as if London was Mars.

'It's fine.' I pull away.

'Don't be like that, I will come. I promise.'

He walks to the mirror in the hall, straightening his tie which is a mangled mess. 'You look very smart,' I say, helping him with the knot, then stepping back to admire my big brother, so handsome, his nails scrubbed, red hair combed back.

He kicks at the last remaining box by the door: a few pictures, a chipped vase. I run and collect the kettle and mugs and drop them in, asking if he can let the clearance company in tomorrow. 'They're taking the heavy stuff: sofa, bed, anything else that's left. I've given them your mobile number. They said they'll call ahead, but probably be here around midday, so keep an eye on your phone!'

Will says he's not sure he'll be available, and I'm about to tell him off for never helping, when the shadow of a long dark car pulls up outside. He takes my hand tightly in his and we look up at the mirror above Mum's beloved console table, the surface still littered with her lipsticks. Will and I smile at each other's reflections as he squeezes my hand tighter. We are cut from the same cloth, no one can take that away from us, and for a moment I revel in our shared heritage as we incline our heads towards one another, our hair merging so I can't tell where his ends and mine begins. Will tells me to lean on him today, I'm his sole priority.

'We are the Tidy family, and maybe just for today, we can be proud of that fact,' he says.

'I expect we'll be the only mourners, other than the twins,'

I reply, but he tells me he's managed to track down quite a few cousins and distant relatives, should be a decent turnout.

'Come on, let's give Mum a proper send-off,' he says, opening the door to the sunny, but bitterly cold day.

I hesitate, picking up one of Mum's cheap lipsticks to smear the iron red on to my lips, as if she'd planted a big kiss on them herself. Then Will leads me along the front path, towards our dead mother.

Karen

Tuesday, 13th December 2016 (Lare Morning)

I walk briskly away from the cottage, relieved I've escaped without waking Mark. I thought Walter might have disturbed him, scratching at the spare room door to be let in, but there was no sound from within. Mark's always been a sound sleeper. I envy him that. I slow my pace as I negotiate the treacherous lane, last night's rain still frozen in puddles beneath the overhanging branches, but once I reach the main road the going is easier.

The village is unusually busy, and there's a sense of anticipation in the air, like the arrival of snow, transforming the usual dreariness to create a very different atmosphere. Perhaps the bright crispness of the morning has shifted the winter malaise, but I think there's more to it than the rare appearance of sunshine on a December day. People are milling around, talking in hushed but animated tones, a frenetic excitement to their whispered exchanges.

The slowness of the vehicles draws immediate attention, a ripple of murmurs crossing from one side of the High Street to the other when the cortege is spotted, but as the hearse slides by, silence falls. I stare at the slim coffin which is topped with a single floral tribute, craning my neck to see who's seated in the back of the car following behind, but it's impossible to tell, the windows are tinted. I watch until both cars have turned in to the church then I select an apple from the display beside me, weighing it in my palm. I made a promise, but it might be wiser not to keep it. I return the apple and look around me before I cross the road, falling in with a group of sombrely dressed but inappropriately jovial mourners.

Progress is slow, the bottleneck caused by the necessity to siphon through the narrow lychgate. I take the chance to slip a tiny pill under my tongue where it partially dissolves, intensely bitter and dry as chalk. Almost impossible to swallow.

A taxi cuts the corner and pulls in at speed, forcing everyone to move aside. I lose my balance and bump into the man beside me, the tablet caught in my throat.

'You all right, love?'

I nod, a fragment of tablet spat on to his dark coat as I clear my throat. He huffs and brushes at his chest, the taxi ticking over beside us.

The first passenger is tall, red-headed, stretching out long limbs in an exaggerated manner as he emerges from the back seat. He's swiftly followed by a shorter, but equally broad man, zipping up a fleece jacket which strains across his midriff. The guard instructs his charge to stand still as he pays the fare, then the taxi reverses away. The gathering mourners part to allow the men through, a glint of metal between them which catches the sunlight as they pass by, the tall man glancing over his shoulder and grinning at his audience. I drop my gaze, but I can't imagine he'd recognise me after all these years. Mark was always the focus. I was a pace or two behind; other than one time in court when lost control, but I don't recall Jess's twin brothers being there that day, or any other. It crosses my mind that if Will and I do end up together, the handcuffed twin could one day be my brother-in-law, and I stumble again as we move forward. This time the man at my side looks away. I shuffle along, looking around to make sure there's no one I know, but I'm surrounded by people I've never seen in the village before today.

'Mick's already in there,' the woman to my right says to her companion, adding, 'That must have been Tony. He's the real psycho.' I chance a quick look at her, taking in the distinctive shade of red hair. She notices me, no recognition in the warm smile she offers, asking if I knew Lisa well. I shrug, turning away. We're almost at the huge oak door now, open to invite us in, unease stirring in my stomach. 'You go ahead,' I tell the red-headed woman as she waves me through. 'I need to catch my breath.'

'Karen!' I look up to see a familiar face, although I can't immediately place it. 'Are you all right, my dear? You look very pale.'

'I'm fine, thank you.' I'm looking beyond her to the packed church.

'Amazing turnout, considering,' she says. 'But are you sure you want to be here? I thought you said . . . ?'

Her displacement continues to confuse me, then I remember those enquiring eyes, searching mine as they do now, but from behind the post office counter. I take an order of service from her bony hand and step inside the chucrh.

The nearest pews are full, and no one seems keen to make room as I wander slowly past. I turn around, then spot someone I know coming in, the mother of a friend of Frey's from school, a governor, or she used to be. She's always loud, over-compensating with effusive greetings as if we were the best of friends when I know she was never a supporter of Mark, quite the reverse. She hasn't noticed me, but she will if I try to leave now. I walk further into the church, searching up and down for a space, just a tiny opening, that's all I need. Somewhere I can tuck myself away, bend my head to the order of service and become invisible, but every seat is taken.

'Karen? Over here!'

I can't work out where the voice is coming from, and I want it to stop. I scan the sea of unfamiliar faces until I notice a raised hand near the back of the church, beckoning me over. A friendly face, or at least, not an unfriendly one; Sue from the steering committee.

'Couldn't be more surprised to see *you* here,' she says, squeezing over to make room for me on the end, by the aisle. 'How are you, Karen?' She inclines her head as she speaks. 'We've barely seen you at the meetings lately, or any of the steering committee get-togethers.'

'Yes, sorry, I haven't . . .' I drop my gaze. 'I haven't been feeling so good.'

Her breath is hot as she whispers close to my ear, 'It's OK, I'd assumed you were—'

'Assumed what?' I ask, leaning away.

'I thought maybe you were keeping your head down whilst this pantomime was going on, but you're here now, so I guess . . . ?'

'I'm feeling much better today,' I reply, studying the order of service but taking little in, especially as the card is shaking so much. 'I wanted to pay my respects.'

I place my hands in my lap, then tuck them in my pockets, the card floating to my feet. Sue is still talking, her voice like nails down a blackboard, earworming its way into my thoughts, although I try to ignore her constant babble. 'Very decent of you, but isn't it a bit . . . ? I mean after what that family put yours through, I'd have thought—'

'*Thought what?*' My demand rings out across the packed church.

Sue laughs loudly, pats my arm and tells me to talk quietly, people are looking. I colour, glancing around me, but we're seated way back. The family, I assume, will be in the front pews, the noise of the voluble chatter in the rows between us hopefully covering my outburst. Sue reads her order of service, then starts fanning her flushed face with it, but the flimsy card flutters to the floor like mine. 'Oh dear, what are we like?' she asks, scrabbling to her knees to pick them both up. She manoeuvres herself around the confined space with some difficulty, apologising to the man to her right as she knocks into him.

Whilst she's distracted, I look around for Will. If I can just see him, let him know I'm here, then I'll be free to go, my obligation fulfilled. I rise from my seat, then up on to my toes, spotting Jess in the front pew, the mass of red hair a giveaway. Becky is down the front too, wandering around, stuffed into a skirt-suit, but I can't see Will. Sue pops back up, handing me my order of service as I reluctantly sit down. I study the thumbnail picture of Lisa Tidy, taken a good few years ago judging by her line-free smile and the dyed blonde hair. She's painfully thin with dark red lips, possibly a faint smudge on her middle tooth as she grins back at me, and there's definitely a strong resemblance to Jess, although it's hard to tell, the photo is small and poor quality, cropped from a larger shot, headless shoulders either side of her grainy face. I have the idea of expanding it with my thumb and forefinger, trying it out before I realise I'm being idiotic, it's a piece of card, not a touch screen. I shake my head to clear the nonsense, but the move attracts Sue's attention, and she starts talking again.

'Seriously, though, why *did* you come? I'd have thought it was the last place—'

I'm saved from answering as the organ strikes up, everyone standing and turning to the back of the church as the coffin arrives, held high on the shoulders of four men, three of whom bear the hallmark Tidy hair. I stretch my neck as they carry the polished wood slowly down the aisle, the same aisle I once glided along in a white dress, then nursed a crying baby down, carrot regurgitated all over her christening gown. Strange I should think of those times, not Mum's funeral, but then I remember that day too, Mum's coffin so small like Lisa Tidy's, as if there wouldn't be enough room inside for the sleeping occupant.

The slender box is easily supported by the sturdy shoulders

of the twins at the front, the guard keeping pace beside Tony, his focus entirely on his charge. Mick is similarly monitored, the handcuffs unlocked from both twins, but still attached to their wrists, the empty halves swinging free. The twins look identical, apart from their expressions; Mick's impassive, Tony's less so as he scans the church, his nervous energy discomforting. I turn my attention to Will, at the back of the coffin behind Mick. His hair is slicked back, his bulk packed into a dark suit, his eyes cast down. Next to Will is a man I've never seen before, older, perhaps one of the three fathers? I breathe deeply as Will passes the end of our pew, his jacket so close I imagine brushing it with my fingertips. If only I could reach out to touch him, feel the solidity of him beneath the formal clothing, but then he's gone, the moment passed.

The vicar welcomes us with a booming voice, his words rattling around my head, rising and falling, loud and clear, but with no meaning; at least, not for me. All I can see of Will is the top of his head, those slicked back curls moving into the front pew as he joins his family. I should probably slip out now, under the radar, whilst everyone's focused on the action at the front of the church, but the ache to be with Will grows inside me, a painful sensation, and difficult to contain. I stand on my tiptoes and can just about see Jess, the mass of unruly hair, and Becky the other side of Will, but I still can't see Will's face. I hadn't expected him to publicly acknowledge me, but I'd burned for a moment between us, some recognition of my presence, the effort it took. He was so close; he must have sensed me beside him, could have offered something tangible in return: a raised eyebrow, a darting look, anything.

I fall into my seat and reach inside my bag for my pills, popping one into my mouth and just about managing to swallow it dry. Sue asks me if I'm unwell and I nod, tapping my forehead as if that's the problem. It's so hot in here, I say, and she agrees, but the church is freezing, cold breath on lips as we'd arrived. She's probably menopausal, hot flushes in her cheeks, fanning herself with the order of service again now we're seated, but I'm burning up for a different reason. Sue pushes up against me, her mauve coat giving off a powerful scent of camphor, and a waft of perspiration. I need to take mine off, but find it's impossible in the confined space. Then everyone's standing again, except me, my legs incompliant, my head woozy. Sue grabs me and helps me up, but I feel detached from my surroundings, and yet everything is amplified: the music, the singing, the smell of mothballs, and the overpowering headiness of the white lilies that swept by on top of the coffin. I lean heavily against Sue and she frowns, righting me with her formidable grasp, a clammy palm touching my hand. I grimace and snatch my hand away.

I shouldn't have come, it was a huge mistake.

I must have said it out loud for Sue is responding, her words mouthed, no sound to them, everything muted, as if the church and the congregation were underwater, or perhaps I am, swimming away from them to the strains of a childish hymn, the words nonsensical, *'Kum-bay-ya, my Lord'*. I need to get out of here. Sue's right, this is the last place—

The odd sensation of impending unconsciousness washes over me. I've only felt it once before. I was in the kitchen, late at night, that terrible night, after Mark came back from the police station. Frey and I had waited up, desperate to hear him say it was all over, a huge mistake, the worst night of our lives, but just one night. Instead he broke down, sobbed in my arms. It was as I made us cups of tea, the ridiculous refuge of the lost and tragic, that I felt as I do now, everything slipping from my grasp. Not just the china cup, one of Mum's favourites which smashed on the hard floor, but everything I thought was true. *And what now? A new life with Will?* He didn't even notice me. He walked straight past to join Jess and Becky. I reach out to save myself, but there's nothing to hold on to, nothing but space to fall into.

Karen

Tuesday, 13th December 2016 (Afternoon)

It's Frey I see first, her face above mine, as if she were part of the ornate ceiling. I have no idea where we might be, but she's kneeling beside me, supporting one of my hands, smiling down, her mouth moving, although at first the words are jumbled up. 'Mum, can you hear me?'

'Yes, Frey. Am I—?'

'It's OK, Mum, try to relax.'

I'm on my back, a paramedic in a dark green uniform tending me, another uniform standing behind her, the same green trousers and tunic. I lift my head, just a little, and regard my parted legs, my modesty preserved by my black opaque tights. My skirt, knee-length, has ridden up to barely cover my thighs, and I'm missing a shoe. My winter coat has been undone, the buttons on my blouse also unfastened to allow the sensors which are stuck to my chest, although the black lace bra I'd selected, with Will in mind, is thankfully still tucked away. Around us, the congregation are oddly mute, and still seated, every face turned to me. There are whispers, but no movement other than a lone figure I hadn't noticed until now. He's standing a few feet away from me, next to a thick pillar, half his body behind it, his face full of concern. I smile at him and he smiles back, looks around him, then mouths, 'I love you, Kar.'

'Karen!' Mark rushes in and runs towards me, blocking my view. 'Oh my God, what happened? Freya?'

Frey begins explaining to her father, then they are both talking to Sue, her voice louder than theirs as she congratulates herself on her quick thinking. Mark says something about a bad night, he can't believe he missed Sue's calls, thank God Frey rang the house phone, then Sue hands my mobile to Frey with a sympathetic smile.

I rest my head back on the carpet, the paramedic insisting I must relax as she asks me to describe the pain, where is it? Mark kneels beside her, whispering something I'm struggling to hear above the voices growing louder behind us. I move my eyes slowly down to my chest, noting the rise and fall, the calmness of the paramedic's movements as she exchanges technical jargon with her note-taking colleague. I don't think I can be dying, no one seems to have much sense of urgency, except perhaps Mark.

'She fainted,' Frey tells him across me, lifting her voice to be heard above the background noise. 'Just a few bruises, hopefully. She fell back, cracked her head on the wooden bench thing, so there might be a concussion. She was out for a while. They definitely want to take her to hospital, get her checked. Maybe keep her in overnight. I'll go with her.'

Frey's expression is infused with a forced cheerfulness as she smiles at me, but my focus is blurred and nausea is creeping in, swelling and falling. A sweaty, red-faced Sue tells Mark she tried to save me, but there was no warning. Boom, and I was on the floor. Then more shouts come from behind us, at the front of the church, covering her words.

'Did you know your mother was coming to the funeral?' Mark asks Frey, as if I was still unconscious. 'I can't understand why she'd be here.'

Frey says she has no idea, then James Facey's profile partially covers my daughter's face as he leans in to ask if he can get us out of the building ASAP, before there's any trouble. The paramedic tending me tells him not yet, they need to finish their checks before I can be moved.

'Mark, can we have a word outside?' Facey asks, something in his tone alarming me, although my husband seems not to care, his refusal adamant. 'Mark, we need to get you out of here.'

I try to sit up, aware of how vulnerable I am lying prone on the red carpet, but I don't have the strength.

'Mark, now!' Facey shouts, lifting my husband's elbow to drag him to his feet, his hold urgent, pulling him up and out of my view. I manage to raise my head and shoulders enough to see Facey struggling with Mark further along the aisle, trying to persuade him out, then hands press me gently back down, reassuring me.

'Mum, listen,' Frey says. 'You have to stay still.' She glances up, but only briefly, her attention remaining on me. 'Let them—'

I have a sense of movement, somewhere behind, but I'm

unprepared for the boot that lands an inch from my face. Frey moves fast, her arm thrown across me before another set of heavy footfalls runs past, and I hear Facey shout, 'Mark, look out!'

I push Frey off, sitting up in time to witness the blow that hits the back of Mark's head, sending him crashing forwards. Mark stumbles, then drops to his knees, holding on to what he must have thought was the end of a solid wooden pew but turns out to be a flower arrangement, the petals dripping white on to the crimson runner beneath. I clutch at my head, pounding now, watching as Mark takes a few more paces, before he pitches over on the carpet near the door. Facey and the guard are restraining Tony Tidy by lying on top of him, only yards away from us, the guard slipping his wrist into the empty side of the cuff swinging from Tony's flaying arm. Tony is screaming expletives, but he stops thrashing around, submitting at last. I'm calling out for someone to help Mark, blood flowing from my husband's head on to the carpet, but no one seems sure what to do. He's lying completely still.

'Frey!' I look for her and find she hasn't left my side, her hand in mine. 'Oh my God, Frey, do something.'

'Lie down, Mum. You need to rest,' she says, her voice so calm, it's chilling.

We wait inside the church, my head now resting on a kneeler whilst final medical checks are completed. The congregation file past as Facey crouches beside me to explain the eagerness of the Tidys' extended family to get involved was causing concern, so they've locked the main door and everyone has been asked to leave by the side exit, through the graveyard.

'Where's Mark?' I ask Facey and although I get the impression he's told me before, he explains again that Mark is outside, out of harm's way, on a bench just by the main door.

'He's fine,' Facey says, his voice echoing around the emptying pews. 'The wound is deep, but the bleeding is reduced enough for it to be cleaned. He'll need stitches, but honestly, it could have been a lot worse. He's sitting up and talking.'

'Thanks for keeping an eye on him,' I say, wishing I could ask about Will. Has anyone seen him? Is he OK? I guess he's already left with the rest of the family, ushered out of the side door.

The blonde paramedic, *'Call me Jules!'*, addresses Facey. 'Must be cold outside, though. No sign of the other ambulance yet?'

Facey shakes his head, says he'll check again, but the last he'd heard it was being rerouted to a major RTA on the motorway.

'I'll need to get Karen to hospital as soon as I can,' she tells him and the detective nods.

Facey disappears again, then returns a few minutes later to suggest it would probably be a good time for Mark to come back inside; the church is almost cleared, and it's getting much colder out there. I shake my head a little and the detective takes the hint, tells me it's probably best not to move him, although I notice he exchanges a look with Jules who is helping me to my feet.

'It was the metal that did the most damage,' Facey tells us as he supports my other arm. 'Tony used the handcuffs as a weapon. Nasty piece of work he is. Always has been.'

I take a few steps to the nearest pew, my shoe retrieved on the way. Jules reminds me to keep the gauze pressed tightly to the cut I sustained, my arm aching with the effort of holding it to the back of my head. She smiles at me, telling me it'll build up my muscles, but Frey takes over, gently holding it in place. Jules sits beside me and feels down my spine again, asking if there's any pain as she presses her fingers gently in.

'No, I told you, I'm fine. I just want to get home.'

'Not quite yet,' she replies, smiling but there's a firmness to her tone.

I watch as Facey's colleagues lead the last of the congregation out through the side door, a nod to the detective as they go. Mick and Tony have already been taken from the church in a police van, sirens blaring according to Frey, although I have no recollection of it.

'Are you sure you're OK out there?' Jules asks Facey, glancing at me. 'It must be literally freezing now.'

He tells her it's a chance for him to have a smoke, and I notice them exchange a wry smile, her gaze following him as he returns to my husband.

'So, let's get you off to A&E!' Jules says, taking my arm.

I allow her to help me up, my head spinning as she steadies me, Frey the other side, but I've already made up my mind. 'I'm not going,' I tell her. 'I just want to go home.'

'You'll have to sign a refusal,' Jules tells me. 'But I'd strongly advise your mum to come with us,' she says to Frey. 'She may well have a concussion.'

'Use the ambulance for Mark,' I tell Jules, still unsteady on my feet, although I shake free of her, leaning on Frey instead. 'My daughter will take care of me, won't you?'

'Quite a funeral,' Jules observes, reluctantly handing me the paperwork to sign as Frey searches her pockets for her car keys.

Jess

Tuesday, 13th December 2016 (Afternoon)

I n the hour we've waited at the pub, the bright winter sun
has disappeared, replaced by a dank and dull day. I nurse
my glass of wine, red today, the bottle on the table beside me.
I've chosen a quiet spot in the corner, with a good view of
the church. I look out again and spot James walking to his car,
parked on the road outside. He glances over, but doesn't appear
to notice me. He's probably wise to give the wake a wide
berth, it's getting pretty raucous in here, the drink flowing,
but I am disappointed not to see him. I wanted to ask him
about Karen, what the fuck she thought she was doing turning
up at my mother's funeral like that, and why Mark is still a
free man. James's car pulls out, then stops to allow an ambulance through, blue light flashing as it emerges from the church.
A second vehicle is following behind, although that turns in
the other direction, away from the village.

I drain my glass and push through the packed bodies to

find my brother. He's on his phone, his brows knotted, startled when I tap his arm. He looks around the room and makes an announcement, but no one seems interested, so we leave the free-loaders to hoover up the cheap buffet and neck pints, just the two of us crossing the road to walk back up to the church.

The light is fading fast, an early twilight descending as we reach the graveyard. I stumble on the uneven ground and Will grabs me, asks how much I've had to drink. I shake my head as if I don't know what he means, weaving my way towards the vicar's white robes which are billowing in the rain and wind.

The chill air bites into every inch of exposed flesh on our hands and faces as we witness the coffin's descent. I look across at my brother, his forehead furrowed as he checks his phone for the hundredth time. He won't say why Becky stormed out of the church after Karen fainted, or what happened when he chased after her, but it's obvious their relationship is in even more trouble than he's admitted. Anyway, I'm glad we've been left in peace to say our final goodbyes. Will takes my hand and I feel the prick of tears, hot salty reminders of how much goes with that tiny coffin. Not just a body, that's not important any more, but a past, a shared history that will be most likely forgotten, a head full of sketchy memories buried too.

'Come on.' Will touches my back, then walks a pace or two, turning to say, 'It's time to leave, Jess.'

'No, not yet,' I tell him.

The vicar is talking to me. He's a hook-nosed man, stooped, but younger than you might expect, his voice carrying across the gaping hole between us, a monotonous drone of nothingness.

He's saying how hard today must have been for us, especially as . . . but I don't hear him, not really, my thoughts too overwhelming to worry about how awful this day has been. It doesn't matter that yet again our family were a spectacle to be gossiped about. None of that is important because I'm losing my past; can't anyone see that? I thought that's what I wanted, to run away, leave my old life behind, but this is brutal. It's tumbling into the earth, walking away from me in the half-light as Will retreats. I'll be left here alone and I'm not ready. Not anywhere near prepared. How did this happen? I'm not a grown-up. I'm still that child who tried to pretend it was all OK, that I could cope, that my life was normal. But I can't cope, not on my own, not then, not now. Not any more. Not without my mum and my brother, a home to come back to one day. 'Will! Don't leave me! Please. Don't leave me!'

He turns back and takes my hand, leading me away.

We drive through the village, Christmas lights strung above our heads from lamppost to lamppost, the van whizzing past the pub, still buzzing with the gathering Becky arranged and didn't attend. Then we turn the corner towards Mum's house, empty and dark. It's only as I climb out I remember Will said he had somewhere to go straight after the wake. 'Is this OK, you've got time?' I ask, leaning back into the van.

He rubs his hands over his face, looks at his phone again, then throws it into the door well, telling me he's trying to sort out a million things.

'Is everything OK?' I ask him, and he nods, says hopefully it will be.

'Nothing's gone as planned today, has it?' he says with a shrug.

I open my handbag and take out the keys. 'Are you coming in? An hour till my taxi arrives.'

He hesitates, then grabs his phone and follows me along the front path, but he stops at the door, his hand to the frame as I fiddle with the stupid lock. 'I won't come in, Jess. You have a safe journey, and let me know when you get home.'

'It's so cold, Will,' I say, my voice childish, imploring. 'Let's go inside for a minute, try and warm up. We might not see each other for ages, and after last night I really don't want to be here on my own.'

We sit in the front room, me in Mum's chair, Will at the dining table, a tot of whisky before him; the half bottle and shot glasses retrieved from under his mattress after I'd decided we should raise a toast Mum, then realised there was nothing in the house. He keeps checking his phone, sending more messages, then he looks up and apologises, putting it away in his jacket pocket. He's taken off his tie and undone his collar, but he still looks uncomfortable.

'Why do you think Karen Winter was there?' I ask, knocking back my drink. 'She must hate us all, even Mum. Do you think it was deliberate, some kind of protest? James told me she's doped up to the eyeballs, doesn't know what she's doing half the time.'

'I'm not sure that's true,' he replies, looking down at his glass.

'But to turn up like that, sabotage Mum's funeral. Pretty shitty thing to do.'

'I don't suppose she planned to pass out.'

'No, but . . .' I pause, about to challenge him, but there's something odd about the way he's defending her. I look at Will and raise my glass. 'Anyway, to Mum!'

Will raises his glass in response to mine, but he's tightly wound, unsmiling. He pours me another shot, takes out his phone and says to it, 'Why isn't anyone replying?'

'Who?' I ask, but he shakes his head.

'Look, Jess, I really need to get going, but I wanted to tell you myself, before you leave. I won't be around here much longer. I'm moving away, not far, I still want to be close by for Jackson.' He's twisting his glass round and round on the table. 'Thing is . . . there's someone else . . . someone I care a lot about; *love*, in fact. She feels the same. We're going away together, at least that's the plan, but after what happened at the funeral—'

'*Love?* Who?'

'It doesn't matter who she is,' he replies. 'I'm only telling you, so you heard it from me, first-hand.'

'You can't leave!'

'Why not? You won't be here, and now Mum's gone too . . .' He looks up from his whisky. 'I know it's been hard for you since . . . well, I don't blame you for being a bit clingy with me—'

'*Clingy?* Is that what you think?'

He tries to backtrack, says it was a bad choice of word, but it has been a strain on him.

'Sorry if I've leant on you as I grieved for our mother!' I grab the bottle of whisky from the table. 'But I don't have anyone else.'

'You know I didn't mean it like that.'

I fall back into the chair and I try to pour another shot, but I miss, whisky showering my legs and skirt, the shock of it making me stand up quickly, my balance not great. I stagger towards Will who reaches out to steady me.

'Jess, don't do this. We've had enough drama today.' He guides me back to the chair. 'I promise I'll keep in touch, and I won't be any further away from you than I was here. Anyway, nothing's definite, not now. I need to speak to her, make sure.'

'Who is she, Will?' I down my drink, the strong taste of neat alcohol unpleasant, but I swallow it quickly, along with a suspicion I already know the answer.

'Look, it doesn't matter who she is, Jess. Just someone, OK?' He stands up to go.

'If it doesn't matter, then tell me!' I stand up too and make a grab for his arm. 'Tell me who she is!' He shakes me off, but says nothing. 'It's *her*, isn't it? It's Karen Winter.'

Even as I say it, I'm desperate for him to laugh it off, tell me I'm wrong, of course it's not her. She's too old, too crazy. I convinced myself at the wake that I was mistaken, I must have misread the way Will looked at her as she lay on the floor of the church, imagined the words he mouthed, my grief making me paranoid, but now it all makes sense. I stare at him, but he refuses to meet my eye.

'She's married to Mark Winter for fuck's sake!'

'I should go,' he says, walking out.

I run after him into the hallway, then out on to the wet front lawn, clutching at his jacket, pulling him back through the darkness. 'Will, you can't leave me now. We need to talk.

You're making a huge mistake. Have you forgotten what Mark did to me? She stood by him all those years. You can't love her!'

'I know I can't, Jess, but I can't help it!' I step back, staring at him as he says he's sorry, but he has to go. 'I have to get to the hospital. I shouldn't have left her at the church. I thought I was doing the right thing, giving us all time to calm down, but I should be with her.' He walks towards his van, and this time I don't try to stop him.

I'd had a good view from the pub, watching as Mark Winter climbed into the back of the ambulance, lights flashing as it turned out of the church, then right towards town, sirens blaring. But it was the small red car following behind that held my attention. Freya Winter was driving, her mother in the passenger seat, Karen's face pressed to the window, her eyes finding mine as they passed by, something in them that alarmed me.

The car had turned left at the top of the road, towards the far side of the village, where the lane runs down to the Winters' cottage. Frey was taking her mother home.

Karen

Tuesday, 13th December 2016 (Late Afternoon)

That was quick, *wasn't it?* Or maybe I've lost track of time, lying here. Sofa, darkness, pain. Time elastic. An hour or a minute since Frey left; who knows? There's a split, it feels like, across the back of my skull, into which heat drives. Another knock. I can't move. Don't they know that? 'Frey, use your key!'

Where did she go? Oh yes, neither of us had the stomach to leave him there. He could get a taxi home? No, that would be too spiteful. He's been stitched up, a nasty wound. Needs collecting from the hospital, bringing home. *Please, Frey, he's your father!* Another knock, louder, rat-tat-tat, echoing around my head. Walter barks, somewhere upstairs. Shut away. Why is that? *Frey, make him stop.*

Limbs ache, head groggy, throat scratchy. A hand to the wall, then another. Need to answer the door. No light. Switch it on. So tired. A moment's rest dissolving into this. Am I drugged? Forms to fill in, before I could come home. So tired in the car, Frey's car. Jess at the pub window looking out. Why didn't Will notice me? Or did he? Was he there at the church, telling me he loved me? Did I really see that?

Another knock, so loud it shakes me. I stagger, feeling my way, holding on, my head too heavy. 'Who is it?'

'Let me in, you fucking bitch!' Jess's voice is loud, screaming at me, fists thumping so hard against the door I'm afraid it might break. 'I'll kick this fucking door in, Karen!'

'Go away,' I reply, my voice rasping, my breaths shallow as I lean my back against the wall. 'Please go away.'

'I know about you and my brother!' She's shouting through the letter box, holding it open to look inside. 'I can see you in there, Karen. I see you! I know you're on your own. I watched Freya leave.'

I close my eyes to try and focus. I should do something, call someone, get help, but I can't think. My skull feels like it's about to snap in two. 'I'm calling the police,' I tell her, but she can see I haven't moved, her eyes framed in the open letter box, fixed on me. 'Mark will be back soon,' I tell the eyes. 'With Frey. They'll call the police. They'll arrest you, Jess.'

'They'll arrest him, not me!' she replies. 'They always believe me, Karen. *Me*, not your liar husband!'

She straightens up, her nose pressed to the glass as she thumps at the door again, then she kicks the frame, somewhere near the bottom, the sound of splintering wood on the other side making me cry out. She yells my name over and over, louder and louder, but there's no one to hear her but me, her shouts blasting into my pain, exploding around my head. I

317

close my eyes, try to squeeze out everything except the need to remain conscious. I can't let myself pass out again. I have to hold on. Then it stops. Silence. Jess's dark shadow gone from the other side of the glass. I wait, the anticipation almost worse than the bangs and the shouts. Where is she? I lurch from the hall towards the sitting room, unsteady but buoyed by adrenalin, faster now, looking for my mobile. Where is it? I grab the home phone from the coffee table instead, determined to call the police, but then I hesitate, wondering if she's right. Would they arrest her, or would they believe her lies as they always do? I need time to think.

I drop the handset on the sofa and listen for Jess. Nothing. I chance a glance outside, standing to the side of the window to look up and down the dark lane, my heart stamping in my ribcage. I check the front door as I pass, sliding the bolt across, then I stumble into the kitchen, grabbing the counter to steady myself. There's a pan upturned on the hob, a chopping board by the sink, a knife across it, diced vegetables beside. I listen again. Nothing. Perhaps Jess has given up and gone home, back to Will. He must have told her about us. A confession, but why? Because she guessed, or because he was coming for me? But he hasn't. I'm still here. Alone. I cup my hand under the running tap and try to remember if it was me that left the water on, the sink overflowing. I scoop up the cold water, splashing it over my face and neck. I'm so hot, burning up, but it's cold in here. And there's water all over the floor, so slippy, but I can't think what to do about it. And where's my mobile phone?

Movement in the back garden. Someone is climbing over the

low gate. The thought focuses me, the pain forgotten, my senses sharpened. Jess is still wearing a suit, the skirt restricting her strides, although she's barrelling through the long grass towards the cottage, her wild hair streaming out behind her as she runs, trainers on feet. I run too, into the hall, hurling myself at the back door. We rarely lock it, the dog always in and out, but we leave the key in the door, just in case. I try to turn it, but instead manage to dislodge it. I drop to my knees, fumbling to pick up the slippery metal with wet hands as the door flies open, Jess falling inside. The impact hits me hard: first the edge of the door, then Jess. I push her away and run to the kitchen as she rights herself, trying to slam that door on her instead, but she's too quick, pushing me aside as she charges in. The key is still in my hand, slick, like a fish. I grip it tight, the pointed end sticking out, my only weapon, but as I lash out she knocks me to the sopping wet floor, the key lost. I crawl into the space between the table and the wall, my knees pulled up to my chest where I hug them tight. Jess is telling me that I'm a fucking bitch, I need to leave her brother alone. She hates Mark. Hates me. Haven't we already taken away everything she had, do I have to take Will too? What kind of scheming bitch am I? She looks terrible, her hair matted, her eyes unfocused, an overpowering smell of alcohol when she gets too close. She circles the kitchen, picking things up, pawing them before she throws them back down: a cup, a tea towel, the dishcloth.

'Jess, is Will OK?'

'Shut up!' she screams. 'Shut up about Will. He's *my* brother, nothing to do with you! Do you hear me? *Do you*? Stay away from him. You're the last person he needs. The last!'

I don't reply, horrified by what she's now holding. In her right hand, gripped tight, is the knife I was using to chop vegetables. The same knife I once ran along my palm to draw blood. I pull myself up, using the table for support as I say, 'Give me that!'

She stops her pacing, glancing down at the knife. 'Why did you stay with Mark?' She's looking straight at me. 'How could you believe him, and be with Will? What kind of twisted . . . ?' She stares at me wide-eyed. 'Oh my God, you don't believe Mark, do you? Even his own wife—'

'Shut up!' I shout. There's a pause, then I shout again, 'You're a liar!'

I run, making a dash for the open back door, then out into the garden, calling for help, Jess at my heels. She's fast, and I'm so clumsy, my movements laboured, my brain disengaged. I slip on the greasy stones of the patio, almost falling, Jess close behind. I'm screaming for Mark now, for Frey, anyone, then I trip again, landing heavily on the lawn. I get up and hurl myself through the untamed patch of grass, desperate to reach the gate before her. I know the paths through the fields, I stand a chance out there, but she overtakes me. When she reaches the gate she turns around, smiling, knowing she has me trapped.

'Don't call me a liar!' She slips the knife behind her back as I lunge forwards to make a grab for it.

Her foot lands a blow against my thigh, sending me backwards. I land with a thud, my back hitting the lawn, winding me. She takes a pace or two to stand over me, her legs scratched and bleeding, her tights laddered. She looks a mess, but it's her eyes that terrify me. 'You know what really happened that night at the prom, don't you, Karen? You *know*.'

I dig my bare heels into the ground and push myself away, ready to fight back, but as I get up the garden is swaying around me. Jess has backed towards the gate again, her right arm behind her. I can't see the knife, but I know it's still there. I step towards her, reaching out, trying to keep my voice steady as I ask her to hand it over, my palm upturned. I can help her, I say, or get Will, anything she likes; it's her call. She bristles at the mention of Will's name, and I know I've played it all wrong.

It happens fast, a shadowy figure behind Jess, forcing the gate open with a hefty kick. Jess loses her footing as she's propelled towards me, her elbow crashing into my cheekbone. I don't understand what's happened, why she's fallen so heavily, and why she's writhing beside me, both of us on the ground. Then I see the blood, so much of it. On hands and faces and clothes, even the grass, dark stains in the dark night.

Jess

Tuesday, 13th December 2016 (Late Afternoon)

My head is cushioned by the frosted grass, my eyes looking up at the navy sky. I'm part of it: the stars, the moon, the endless dark. Mark is shouting, telling us he's going to get help, but I don't look at him, focusing on the slow-moving clouds as he runs towards the house, talking fast into his phone. Then at last it's just Karen and me. I turn my head to look at her, but her eyes are closed, although the eyelids flutter a little, the lashes whispering to me. I slide nearer, lifting one of her cold hands to press it between mine, begging her to please wake up. I need her to listen, before it's too late. I wrap her arms around me, rocking us gently as I talk, hoping she can hear. 'He told me he cared, Karen. He told me he loved me, on the night of the prom. Did you know that? Of course you did. You were in court, listening to it all. Every day you were there to support him, the devoted wife. But sometimes I thought I spotted it in your eyes, a moment of doubt. I wasn't sure, but now I am. You know what really happened, don't you? Did he tell you, or did you guess?'

Karen stirs, and I soothe her, holding her tighter, telling her none of that matters right now. We can sort it out later, the truth from the lies, but I can feel the slow ebb of a life slipping away and I panic, pulling her to me, saying her name over and over. She wriggles free of my embrace, kneeling up, then she takes my hand in hers. That's when I know I'm dying. I thought I'd be afraid, but my only fear is I won't have enough time to tell her everything. She takes me in her arms and talks to me. 'Shush now, Jess. Try to stay calm. I'll stay with you. I promise. Don't give up, Jess. Keep talking.'

I close my eyes, shutting out the night. I don't want Mark Winter's face to be the last thing I see. Instead I imagine I'm with Mum, one of her better days, her fingers running through my hair, teasing out the curls, the scratch of her nails against my scalp soothing me.

Freya Winter

Tuesday, 13th December 2016 (Late Afternoon)

It's so cold, my hands wet and shaking, the steering wheel sliding in my hands. I rub my palms against the woollen fabric of my grey work trousers, red smudges down my thighs, like paint splashes. *Oh my God, oh my God, oh my God.* I force myself to focus on the bumps and crevices in the lane, but all I can see is Mum's face, smeared in Jess's blood as she cradled *that girl.* I wanted to push Jess aside, tell her she has no claim on my mum, but Dad told me to get out of there. He would sort everything, but I had to go.

My tyre hits a pothole and I cry out, correcting the steering just in time so I narrowly miss another dip in the lane. I need to stay calm, get home. Get my story straight. We had so little time, but I know what Dad's going to do. The question is, *can I let him?*

I catch sight of myself in the driver mirror as I turn left into the main road, my panic reflected back. I haven't been this scared in years, but the feeling is familiar, everything around me an affront to my senses, the rain that's arrived too loud, the lights of the oncoming traffic too bright. It was a different kind of night when I last felt like this, a warm spring evening.

Everyone was going to be at the prom, the whole of my year, except me, of course. Even Jess Tidy had plans to turn up. *That girl*, as Mum always called her, long before the night of the prom; although she insisted she never listened to village gossip, and neither should I. But Mum didn't have to deal with it every day; jibes as I walked to lessons, giggles behind my back in class, until no one wanted to be my friend, or even be seen with me. *'Jess Tidy shagged your dad yet?'* I was asked it ten times a day, even by kids from lower years who probably had no idea what 'shagged' meant, parroting it back and forth like idiots, then laughing as I cried. That's the thing with kids, they're not only cruel, they're relentless. Something had to change, and it would, after the prom. Exams would soon be over, and then the long summer break would clear the air. Sixth form would separate out the wheat from the chaff, and Jess would be where she belonged, behind a checkout or pushing a brat in a second-hand pram. The ultimate revenge; a life well-lived. For me, not her. Mum and I just had to survive the night of the prom. We were going to watch a film and eat a giant bag of popcorn, but even as we laughed at the stupid rom-com, I thought of Dad with Jess, and I hated them both with such force I thought I might be sick.

A car horn blares behind me and I press my foot against the accelerator, faster now, the speed good. I was driving too slowly, my memories clearer than the task in hand. I need to get home without attracting any more attention. Quickly, before—

I clip the kerb, the tyre bouncing off the edge of the road and sending me towards the oncoming traffic. Headlights blind me, another blast of horns and then I'm back on my side of the carriageway, my death that close, then gone. I take a deep breath, gripping the steering wheel tighter as I regulate my speed. I need to concentrate, but all I can see is Jess's squirming body, and blood, so much blood.

It wasn't only Mum who pretended not to notice what had been going on for weeks. I ignored it too, told myself it was ridiculous. But I saw the way Dad looked at Jess, and I knew what it meant. I'd seen that look myself, lain under it a couple of times, listening to grunts and expletives. It was a funny game, if you played it well. A power trip. But he was my dad, for fuck's sake. A grown man. Not some pimply boy with a hard-on who was as scared as the girl he was pressed into. He was my father. And a teacher. Almost forty. It was degrading for all of us. It needed to stop, but it didn't. It just got worse.

Why didn't you leave afterwards, Jess? Why didn't you pack up and go when the whole village talked about you constantly, how you *must* be lying. Or when I threw a brick through your window, daubed paint on your walls? My last desperate attempts to make you see sense before the court case began. But, no, you had stick to your story, make him pay. The thing is, Jess, you made us pay too, me and my mum. Every day. Even now, as I walk around the school where I teach and remember how it felt to be bullied, or when I tell the man I adored that my dad is a sex offender and watch his love for me die. I've seen my mum sleepwalk her way through the last ten years, and every day I blame you. And *him*.

I could see it in his eyes, the deceits required to convince himself, and Mum. I was so scared that night, even before the police came. He looked so odd when he came home early from the prom, pretending to us that he was fine, a stupid excuse about a drunk student who'd thrown up on his shirt as he headed straight for the shower. Mum was already falling for his lies, but I knew. And I saw what it did to Mum, the effort it took to maintain her belief in him through the endless months of the trial, then the prison visits, and afterwards, when the shell of her husband came home. She's been hanging by a thread for years, only the pills keeping her going, desperately clinging to the hope that Dad was the victim, not Jess. How could I destroy that lifeline on a hunch? How could I tell her I wasn't certain what happened that night in the Exclusion Unit, but I'd seen something in him I would always despise, that would stop me from loving him, however hard I tried? Even tonight when he's sacrificed his freedom in return for mine, I loathe him more than ever.

Sirens and blue lights whizz past. It's too late to go back now. Far too late. Over ten years, in fact.

I peel off my clothes as soon as I'm through the door, feeding the evidence into the washing machine just as Dad did that night, my fingers fumbling for the hottest wash. I stand shivering, naked and crying as I watch the red water swish back and forth, but I'm home, if not safe. Not yet. The shower runs reddish-brown at my feet as I lather every speck of skin and hair. I need to clean the car too, inch by inch, as soon as I'm dry. There was so much blood, so quickly. I turn the jets up as high as they will go, hard beads bouncing off my head, my shoulders, my back, but I can still hear Mum's screams, my world changing the moment I opened the car door and stepped into the lane. Something was wrong, voices raised in the back garden; Mum's voice, and another. I had to get to her, Dad somewhere behind me, his wound raw, his head groggy, those two or three seconds all it took. Jess was by the back gate, her hand behind her, holding something that caught the light as I flung myself towards her. It was easy, as if it was nothing, which in a way it was, the knife soon in my hand not hers, the reflex action quick and strong. She fell as soon as I pushed the blade in, landing heavily on Mum. *My* mum, not hers. *Mine.* I wanted to pull Jess away from her, but Dad screamed at me to go, get out of there. *Now!*

I step out of the shower and dry my skin and hair with a soft towel, then I scrub under my nails with a brush tinged a pale rust. Afterwards, I swill out the bristles in the sink, wiping the porcelain clean with a squirt of bleach.

Cleaning the car takes longer, the front seats hard to shampoo in the dark, but I'm afraid to put the light on. I do my best, frozen by the time I'm back inside, rinsing the bucket again and again. My phone rings a few times, but I ignore it, although I jump at every sound, expecting the police to turn up at any moment.

My shoes are still by the door, where I kicked them off. I scrub at the soles, scrubbing and scrubbing, then I dab polish on the scuffed toes and rub hard, just as my Grandmother Elspeth taught me. She showed me how to buff them to such a shine we could see our smiling faces in them, telling me my father was as useless at cleaning shoes as he was everything else. She idolised me, said I could do no wrong, that I would lead a charmed life, and have everything she and my mother had been denied. How mistaken a person can be, only seeing what they want to see, when the truth is there, hidden in plain sight.

Sometimes I'd be talking to Dad and it would be so normal I would doubt myself, wonder if perhaps it was all in Jess Tidy's warped imagination, then I'd remember the way he looked at her that day I saw them in his car, laughing as he turned the corner, too busy to notice his own daughter walking home alone, his eyes shining in a way I've never witnessed before or since. I'd open my mouth to tell him I knew what he'd done, to scream at him that he was a monster, but then Mum would pop another pill, swallow down another lie, and I couldn't be the one to do it. I just couldn't take that risk. I'd already lost one parent.

I pick up my coat from by the door to throw it in the bath, then I remember Mum's mobile is in the pocket, passed to me in the church by that awful woman who'd called us to say Mum had passed out. I glance at the screen, but it's locked, so I see to my coat first, pressing it down in the scalding water, emptying and refilling the bath until it runs clear. Then I add washing liquid, pressing the ballooning fabric deep beneath the suds. The phone is low on charge, but there's enough for me to try a few combinations whilst

I let my coat soak. I only need one, my date of birth. Mum's nothing if not predictable.

The water has turned cold, the phone slipping from my grasp to slide beneath the film of burst bubbles, the screen flickering then gone.

Supervision Session #12 – Jessica Tidy – Wednesday, December 14th, 2016

'OK, Marion, thanks. Yes, I'll let you know if I manage to track her down. I'm so sorry about all of this, she promised me she would contact you to arrange an appointment, but her mother has very recently passed away, so I guess she . . . Yes, of course. I know. Thanks again.'

I drop my mobile in my bag and close the front door behind me, walking briskly to the tube station at the end of the road. I suppose I shouldn't be surprised Jess hasn't turned up for our final appointment, or returned my calls or emails – it *was* her mother's funeral yesterday – but I am disappointed, and concerned. Especially as Marion hasn't had any contact from her either. I can't get an image out of my head from our last appointment, the things Jess said, the way she looked at me, such hurt in her eyes. I drum my nails on the top of my bag and count down the stations to Chancery Lane, the dark tunnels swallowing me up.

The journey clears my head, the bustle of Central London convincing me I will manage to find Jess and persuade her to see Marion. I feel even more positive as I climb the stairs to the practice where Jess works, pleased to have found it so easily. I don't necessarily expect her to be here today, although that would be nice, but it seems the best place to start my search. It's the only address I have for her.

The receptionist, a pinched-face woman behind an overly high counter, silently expresses her irritation at the interruption my arrival has caused, her body language as telling as her perfunctory greeting. Then I mention the name 'Jessica Tidy' and her interest ignites, a wariness in her which immediately alerts me to a problem. It strikes me as she walks towards a closed door that it would have been prudent to hire a receptionist who can conceal her feelings a little better.

'Please, I'd rather you don't disturb your boss,' I call after her, but she's already tapping on the peeling varnish.

I wait on a plastic chair, the tired premises much as Jess had described. I can imagine her here, opening one of the numbered teak doors to welcome a client with that wonderful grin of hers, a ray of sunshine in this drab environment, instantly putting her clients at ease. Her boss emerges with a scowl, exchanging a few words with the receptionist before he approaches.

'I did say I was more than happy to wait,' I tell him, extending a hand to meet his tight grip. He's tall, overbearing. 'I'm a practising integrative counsellor myself,' I explain. 'I understand that client time is sacrosanct.'

'Well it's done now, isn't it?' He releases my hand. 'How can I help you?'

'I'm looking for a colleague of yours,' I explain, although I suspect Jess may no longer work here, the receptionist's narrowed eyes speaking volumes as she returns to her post.

All I hope is they were as accommodating about Jess's need for personal therapy as she led me to believe, although the fact she hasn't made an appointment with Marion indicates they most probably were not.

'A colleague of mine?' He fixes me with a rather condescending stare.

'Yes, I was hoping you might have a home address for her, or know of some other means I might get in touch? I've tried her mobile, and emailed of course . . . I should explain, I'm Jess Tidy's supervisor.' When he says nothing, I add, 'Jessica Tidy, she's been coming to me fortnightly as part of accreditation. She didn't mention me to you?'

A sigh escapes his thin lips, then he rubs his hands over his face. Behind him, his name is listed beneath an eight-by-ten photo, part of a gallery displayed on the wall. I scan up and down the half-dozen dusty frames, but Jess's face and wild curls are missing. If they've let her go, it will be partially my fault. I'm already running ideas in my head how I might make amends, possibly call in a few favours to find her a new position, when he finally responds.

'I'm sure I don't need to tell you that I cannot discuss anything without a client's express permission.' He looks down his long nose at me. 'But I cannot for the life of me imagine why Jess would require supervision . . . from you, or anyone else.' He laughs. 'Unless of course the training programme has shrunk to what . . . a mere seven months since my day?'

I thank him for his time and the inferred information, then leave.

Walking down the steep flights of stairs, I turn over the

facts I've gleaned from that short exchange. Jess was clearly not a counsellor, and due to client confidentiality she remains untraceable. Unless she contacts me, of course, which seems unlikely given the fact she's ignored all my attempts to reach her so far.

Reluctant to give up and go home, but uncertain of my next move, I turn into the café located at street level. I need caffeine, and time to think, although it's not the most salubrious of establishments. I choose a seat by the window, away from the grouped tourists and a screaming child, avoiding the sticky table top as best I can. A waitress approaches and cuts across my thoughts, staring at me impatiently, her Christmas hat and earrings at odds with her lack of humour. She can't be much more than twenty, slim-waisted with dark flicks of eyeliner beneath pencilled eyebrows. For some reason she reminds me of Jess. Not that she looks like her, but her make-up is similar.

'I was a waitress for years, hated it, kids throwing food, rude parents, tourists who can't speak English, or find the right change . . . and the pay is crap!'

'You foreign?' she asks. *'Com-pren-des?'*

'Yes, sorry. Americano, please. No milk.'

She's already walking away when I call after her. 'Sorry, can I . . . ?'

'You want a cake or something?' she asks, reluctantly returning. 'We've got brownies, or some dodgy carrot cake.'

'No, thank you. I just wondered . . . it's a long shot, but I don't suppose someone called Jessica Tidy ever came in here?'

'Yeah, I know Jess. Why?'

Three members of staff now crowd my table: Jess's boss,

who wants to know if she is ever coming back – *'A few days, she told me, a few days!'* – a concerned young man holding a dripping washing-up brush in his hand who asks repeatedly if I think she's OK, and the waitress who served me, a 'for fuck's sake' escaping her dark lips when I say I'm concerned for Jess's safety. She wanders to another table, taking their order with the same wearisome countenance she wore when she'd taken mine. She's clearly tired of Jess's antics and the attention her colleague has attracted, even in absentia. I make my excuses and leave, realising there's little to be gained in thrashing out one hypothesis after another. It would seem they have known Jess for longer than I have, but not as well. They have no address for her, didn't even know she once lived in a village a hundred miles away, the name of which I was never given. They gave me her mobile number, but I've already tried it, many times. She was paid cash in hand, everyone does it, her boss said, telling me she was a good little worker, conscientious and honest, but with a bit of an attitude problem at times. She either loved the customers or hated them, there was no in between.

I'm waiting at a pedestrian crossing when the boy with the washing-up brush runs out into the street, pushing past the crowds to press his contact details into my hand, scribbled on a damp Post-it note. He asks me to call him the second I hear anything, anything at all.

'Do you have any idea where she lives?' I ask.

He shakes his head, said she never invited him back. She was pretty much a loner.

I reverse my journey with a heavier heart, expectation now

replaced with regret. I'd set out seeking answers, and of course to find Jess, but all I've done is dredge up more questions; and drama, plenty of that. I walk up the steps from the tube station and back along my road, imagining Jess doing the same. Eleven times she came to see me. Eleven opportunities to see through the pretence. She sat in the chair opposite me, spinning her tales, and I never suspected, never questioned her once. Why did she lie to me for all those months, pretending she's something she's not, inventing fake qualifications and imaginary clients? I would have helped her if only she told me the truth. *Wouldn't I?*

'People say things because they want to please someone, it's as simple as that.'

I turn the key in the front door, walking straight through the house and out to the back garden where I take a seat beneath the stars. I'm not ready to write up my notes, or contact Marion quite yet. It's cold, but I'm managing to cling on to Jess out here, keeping her with me for as long as possible, the pain of knowing I failed her too awful to admit. Jess needed me, just as she'd needed Mark, James, Will, Becky, her mum, even a missing father . . . she was a lost soul who invented and reinvented, who craved something none of us could offer; our undivided, unquestioning devotion.

Perhaps she contacted me because she wanted to gain some perspective on her life, but couldn't at first face the ordeal of personal, often intense therapy, instead talking about herself in the third person as she told me of her sixteen-year-old 'client'. Maybe it was an elaborate game to her, another way to pretend life was better than she knew it was. Or just a desperate scheme to get the counselling she knew she needed when she could no longer afford to pay the going rate, her last counsellor losing patience with her excuses, his scowl driving her away. Maybe she believed her own lies, that she was one day going to be a counsellor herself, some hope in her bleak life. *'It's depressing to think I haven't moved on in the last decade.'* She told me everything, if only I'd listened, and if I ever see her again, which I doubt, I shall thank her for trusting me enough to share what she could.

I look up, a spectacular view of the supermoon hanging bright in the sky, as if it were closer tonight. I reach out to touch it, my fingers searching for something out there, something just out of reach.

Back in the bright warmth of my consulting room, I go through my notes, scanning them for clues, anything I might have missed, but it's the last entry I'm drawn to most, spreading out the transcript across the open bureau, reading again and again those final words, the only ones I can now trust. The only time, it would seem, she wasn't lying to me.

Two Weeks Before . . .

Supervision Session #11 – Jessica Tidy – Tuesday, November 29th, 2016

Full notes in client file ref: 718/16

Meeting taped, transcript #2/2 of relevant section below (abridged)

Jess: How much time do we have left today?

Me: As long as you need, Jess.

Jess: I wasn't drunk that night at the prom, at least, not that much. I let Becky drink most of the vodka. I just took the odd swig so she wouldn't notice. I wanted to be in control, you see. That's a joke, isn't it? But that was my plan. I was upset, after Becky slapped me, but I still managed to convince everyone I was drunk, staggering across the hall. I *know* drunk. Learnt from watching my darling mother. I told you that, didn't I?

Me: Why would you want to convince everyone you were drunk when you weren't?

Jess: Not everyone, just Mr Winter.

Me: But you said you ran away from him, that it was a game. Why would you go to all that trouble, if . . . ?

Jess: Why do you think?

Me: I don't know, Jess. Do you want to tell me?

Jess: I wasn't sure what my feelings were for Mark, they were complicated. Guess it'll cost me a fortune in therapy to work that one out! But at the time I chose to believe I was in love with him, and that he loved me. I was prepared to do anything to be with him. Whatever it took.

Me: And what did it take, Jess? Your virginity?

Jess: Ah, you're starting to see the whole puzzle now. That's good. *You're* good.

Me: Jess, if you're angry, let's discuss that first.

Jess: Another thing Mum taught me was that the best way to keep a man is to give him what he wants in the bedroom. She said it is the only time you ever feel in control. But I didn't feel in control, not at all. I wanted it to stop. I was out of my depth, knew straight away I'd made a huge mistake. The second I saw his skin beneath the clothes, the hairs, parts of his body that appalled me, revolted me. He was old and married and he scared me. IT scared me, the whole thing, the noises, the smells, the intensity and urgency, and it hurt like hell, but I held on to him, hoping it would make sense, that . . . that he'd stay with me, look after me. I thought it would mean . . . I thought I'd be safe after that. He said he loved me, he said we could be together, but I knew how wrong it was, even as it was happening. I knew. Afterwards I felt sick, and I started screaming. It was the shock, I suppose. He left, ran out in a panic, then there were so many people, all asking me what had happened. I didn't know what to say. I didn't say much, but once I said it, I couldn't seem to take it back. I knew I should, and I kept trying to, like I did before, with Johnson, but it felt like it was true . . . in a way.

Me: Jess, listen to me. Please. This is important. None of this is your fault. He was your teacher, you were a vulnerable child. Regardless . . . no, listen . . . regardless of what you said or did, the fact remains it was his responsibility to stop it happening. He took advantage of you, he thought you were drunk, and even if he realised you weren't, you were his student.

Jess: But I lied about what happened.

Me: So did he, Jess. So did he.

Five Months Later . . .

Mark

May 2017

I've been expecting him, nothing happens in this place without multiple layers of prior approval, but it's still a shock when I spot DS Facey walking across the crowded visitors' hall. He sits down opposite me and smiles, as though we were old acquaintances, meeting up for a beer at our local; but that was never my style, or his as far as I know. His hair is a little longer, the fringe falling into his eyes. He brushes it back, asks how I am and I spout some meaningless platitude in response. The detective's trademark dark coat is missing, the collar and tie too, replaced by a casual jacket, jeans and tee shirt. He tells me it's been a few months since he retired, although he stumbles on the last word and I wonder if there's more to it than he's admitted to in our limited correspondence. He's far too young to be pensioned off. I'm guessing he's been placed on gardening leave at the very least. I wonder if I should apologise, but I didn't ask for his lenience, it was his choice not to report my visit to Jess straight away. I don't know why he gave me that final chance, maybe some doubt in his mind, but it's irrelevant now. I'm back here anyway. I ask him what he's been up to since he left the force, and he says he sees more of his daughters these days, which is nice. He checks himself, apologises for his clumsiness, asks me how I'm coping. I tell him it's OK. Karen visits when she can, although it's been a while. She's been poorly the last few weeks, a bit run-down. He nods, as if he already knows my wife is even frailer than before, her skin pale, her lips colourless. 'But Freya comes every week,' I say, thinking of the last time she was here, how she'd said so much whilst telling me almost nothing. She clearly wants to hate me, as she has for many years, but feels she must now be grateful. A conundrum I did not envisage. I told her not to come back. She has no news of her mother, and that's what I crave and miss more than anything.

'What happened there?' He points to the criss-cross cuts up my forearms from the wrists to the elbows.

I tell him it's scratches from brambles, gardening duty, and he says it's good to keep busy, the trial will likely be a few months yet, or so he's heard; it's impossible to know for sure, sometimes the wheels grind much more quickly than others. He thinks he's done me a favour, brought me some precious information via his contacts, but it's immaterial now, although I thank him anyway.

'Why did you want to see me?' I ask, aware we don't have that much time together so the niceties should be kept to a minimum.

'Stupid, really.' He pushes his fringe back then looks directly at me. 'I just want to satisfy my own curiosity, I suppose. Do you mind?'

'No, not at all, but there's nothing new I can tell you.'

'Why did you do it?' he asks, looking around him, then he lowers his voice. 'I'd have thought you'd do anything to avoid coming back here.'

'Jess was threatening Karen with a knife.' I look down at my hands and pull my shirt over my cuts. 'I had no choice.'

'Oh, come on, Mark. The truth, please. It's just you and me. I'm not on this case, not even a detective any more, and even if I was . . .' He waits for me to speak and when I don't he says, 'I read the report, a mate of mine . . . it doesn't matter how . . . the point is, it was Karen who stabbed Jess, wasn't it?'

I look up. 'Is that what the police think?'

'No, but if Karen were to plead—'

'No, you're wrong. It was me. I killed Jess.'

'You don't have it in you, Mark.'

'You're wrong,' I tell him again, holding eye contact.

'I know how it looks, how you made it look.'

'How it was,' I reply.

'Your daughter drove you home from the hospital, is that right?'

'Yes, but as I'm sure you also know, she dropped me at the end of the lane and went straight back to her flat in town.'

'And as you know, the investigation was then dominated by your confession. But the thing I don't understand is, you were concussed, a head wound recently stitched, and yet your daughter dropped you at the end of an icy lane, didn't even come in to see how her mother was?'

'Where are you going with this?'

'Nowhere, Mark. Just wondered if Freya might have seen something. Maybe if I talked to her—'

'No, she didn't. Read her statement, ask your mate for that.'

'Quite something, to take the blame when you know what to expect,' Facey says. 'True love, I guess. I always thought you and Karen had something special, not many couples survive an accusation like that.'

It takes me a moment to realise what he's referring to this time, then he's on his feet, saying he really should get going. I watch as he leaves, wanting to call after him, to clarify his comments, to tell him my wife hasn't visited in almost two months, that I've given up hope I'll ever see her again, does he know why?

He walks to the door, but then he turns back, and at the insistence of the closest prison officer Facey sits down, leaning in as far as he dare under watchful eyes as he whispers, 'I've heard people say all kinds of things over the years. They tell a story, and then that's the one they have to stick to.'

'Are you talking about me, or Jess?'

Facey sighs, his breath reaching me across the table, a scent of peppermint. 'I'm not saying anything, Mark. It's never that simple, is it? I did my job at the time, I know that. You want to elaborate?'

I shake my head and Facey nods. 'As far as Karen is concerned, if she were to admit to killing Jess, in self-defence, of course, I think you would stand a good chance of—'

I cut across his words, telling him there's no point trying to convince me Karen should confess instead of me. 'I don't want you to stir things up, please. Just let it all take its course. I've made my choice.'

He looks up, a flicker of something in his eyes. 'Well, it's out of my hands now.'

He stands, and I think he's going to leave this time, but he shoves his hands in his jeans pockets, transferring his weight from one foot to the other, clearly something else on his mind. 'I noticed the "For Sale" sign outside the cottage. Is Karen moving on?'

I don't ask him why he drove up the lane, although there's little else that would take him there other than a visit to my wife. I assume she refused to talk, which is why he's here.

'She's put a deposit on a two-bed on the new estate,' I tell him. 'Fresh start.'

I should perhaps explain that it's only a fresh start for Karen, but then Facey offers his congratulations to us both.

'It's important to have something to look forward to in here, isn't it?' He glances up at me, holding eye contact for a moment too long. 'Oh, don't look like that, Mark. I'm not here to judge. Plenty of people have babies at your age, and in worse circumstances. You'll work it out, between you. And don't blame Karen, she didn't say anything. She must be what, five, six months by the look of her? My wife was bigger with our second one . . .' He trails off, perhaps imagining how hard it must be having a pregnant wife when you're a convicted sex offender locked up for murder.

He has no idea.

Karen

January 2018

The sound of the postman feeding the mail through our shiny letter box wakes us after a restless night. Downstairs in the kitchen Walter barks, and from the bedroom next door come the unmistakable sounds of children stirring after another broken night's sleep. Jackson never settles when he stays over, but it's only twice a week; a small price to pay for his father's happiness. Will kisses me, then gets up to see to the kids, telling me to stay in bed, I must be shattered. 'Four-month-olds are no fun!' he says, grinning as he pulls on a pair of boxers and a tee shirt, throwing me my robe.

I smile, tell him two-year-olds aren't exactly a picnic either. I'm wide awake, despite the jet-lagged feeling I've grown used to since the baby arrived, that strange nocturnal existence I thought I'd left behind half a lifetime ago. It reminds me of the drug-induced stupor I used to accept as normal, before the pregnancy and my need to protect the bud of new life growing within me. I catch sight of Will as I go downstairs, his movements gentle for a man of his size. He picks up the baby from her cot then cradles her one-handed, her red curls corkscrewing like a halo around her sleepy face. He's distracting Jackson with the other hand, thick fingers tickling his giggling son's soft neck. If only Frey were as easy to placate as the little ones.

The thought dulls my previous good mood, a pang of sadness shifting my momentum so I almost stumble, the thick carpet sliding under my bare foot. I grasp the bannister and steady myself, imagining Frey's smile as she walks through the front door. 'She'll come round eventually,' Will always says, but it's been more than a year now. No contact since the night Jess died.

Only Frey and I now know what really happened that night, and I assume that's what keeps her away, the spectre of truth. Maybe she can't face Will, but she must know I'll never tell him it was her that killed his sister, not, as he believes, Mark. For Will's sake as much as hers. I worried James Facey might have guessed, the 'retired' detective fishing for information for a while after Mark was arrested, but it never came to anything and now I doubt it will. The last time I saw James he'd been the one to make the tea, my hands shaking too much. He'd said he wanted to tell me himself, had pulled in a favour so he could be the one to break the terrible news. It wouldn't have mattered who said those words, their meaning incomprehensible, although I thanked him for his kindness. He wasn't a detective any more, but he said if I ever needed anything, I was to call. When I waved him off I noticed he was driving a different car, something much less impressive, although he'd grown in my estimation that day. There have been many people I've misjudged, but I think I'm finally making some good decisions.

The letter lies amongst the leaflets and flyers on our doormat, Walter looking at them intently as I release him from the kitchen. 'Good boy,' I tell him, smoothing the velvet fur on the dome of his head as I pick up the post. It's mainly junk mail, the proliferation of it a gripe we share good-naturedly with our new neighbours. I guess they must talk about Will and me when we're not around: the big difference in our ages, and how old I was when I gave birth for the second time, only a few weeks after we'd moved in, and of course, our shared and chequered history. I find I care much less about the gossip than I did before. What's happened in the past year has changed my priorities, reaffirming how unimportant most problems are. All that matters is protecting your family. Nothing else.

I stoop to pick up the envelope I've left behind, my back aching, my breasts heavy with milk, laughing as Walter nudges his head against mine. He's such a sweet dog, devoted to the baby, sitting with me when I feed her, his head resting in my lap. He must miss Mark and Frey, but he seems perfectly content. The envelope has a London postmark, addressed to me at the cottage and forwarded on by the new owners, a couple with money to burn who have big plans and fake smiles. It wouldn't surprise me if they knock the cottage down and build three or four houses in its place, although they assured me they wouldn't. I have no feelings either way; I've moved on.

I take the letter through to the kitchen, slitting it open with a sharp knife. Walter settles at my feet, and I lean against the worktop to read. It's beautifully written, the words formed in a softly sloping hand, the grey ink unusual and expensive-looking, as is the creamy paper.

Dear Mrs Winter,

Apologies for the intrusion. I have thought long and hard how I might best approach you, and decided a handwritten letter would be the most appropriate method. I'm sure you are wondering how I came by your contact details as I doubt you know who I am. Please let me explain.

In December of 2016, your late husband wrote to me via email enclosing the first three chapters of his book. It was, I was led to believe, a fictional story about a man accused of an attack against one of his students. Indeed, Mark had stated that it was a 'novel' he was writing, a work of fiction, for which he was seeking representation, his full contact details provided in the covering page of the manuscript. With that information, it was simple enough to discover, as I'm sure you can imagine, that he was documenting real events. His own story.

There was something compelling about the writing, and I asked him to send me more, any that he had, which he did as he wrote. As the story unfolded, at an alarming pace, I became increasingly concerned by his (please forgive me) delusional version of the well-documented events surrounding his case. I decided the manuscript would never be publishable and told him this, but he continued to send his work, even an unfinished chapter, although I repeatedly asked him not to contact me again, advice he eventually

heeded, the final chapter promised, but, to my relief, never
delivered. I filed away the emails and thought little of it,
until I learnt of your husband's death.

Since then I have often wondered what might be the
best course of action, deciding in the end to wait a good
time and then send your husband's correspondence to you.
It is, after all, yours now to do with as you see fit. If I
have misjudged the situation, please accept my profound
apologies.

Louis Hart, LJH Literary Agency

I turn over the letter, unclipping the printed pages attached.
Walter looks up at me, his head inclined. 'Later,' I tell him,
reminded of those times when Mark would say the same,
preferring to type away in his study until the light had faded,
striding across the fields in the dark, a head torch to guide
him. I twist my hip to rest it more comfortably against the
glossy worktop, the thumps of Jackson's tiny feet mixing with
Will's heavier tread overhead as I spread out Mark's words
across the counter. Then I scan the pages, as I once did on
screen, but there's nothing new here, and I wonder, as Louis
Hart did, why Mark decided to send it for consideration in the
first place. What was he hoping to achieve? Did he really think
anyone would be interested in publishing his side of the story?
Again, the heat of betrayal rises within me. He can't have
given a thought to the effect on Frey and me if it ever was
published, his ego seemingly having no conscience. I haven't
looked at the chapters Mark typed on the computer for over
a year now, but seeing them as hard copies, and knowing he

sent them out into the world, to a stranger who could have instigated their publication, the same sense of unease washes over me. Just as it did when I would sneak into his study and torture myself with doubt. I've managed to push down those feelings, concentrate on the future, not the past, but now, seeing the chapters again, my thoughts spin away from me, my head light.

The old computer is in the lounge. The only one we have, funds tight since the move, although with the change in weather business is starting to pick up again. Will uses Mark's computer for his accounts, but I haven't touched it since the night before Jess died. I take a seat at Will's untidy desk and manage to tap in the familiar combination, although I'm out of practice, my fingers awkward on the clunky keyboard. Even as I open the folder, I'm telling myself there won't be the promised 'final chapter'. Mark never wrote again after that night, events over-taking us when he was arrested the next day for Jess's murder.

But there it is.

I draw breath, checking when it was saved, Monday 12th December at 11.45 p.m. I recall him coming in late that night. He'd been to see Jess, confronted her, although I didn't know it at the time. When he didn't join me in our bed, I assumed he'd gone to the spare room to sleep – that was where he was the next morning when I left for Lisa Tidy's funeral – but he must have slipped into the study first.

Upstairs, Will is placating his son who is demanding they set up his wooden train track, Jackson's shrieks piercing my thoughts. I sit back, looking at the screen. I could delete the entire folder and switch off the computer, tear up the letter and go back upstairs to join Will and the children. It's tempting – Will's choo-choo sounds making me smile despite my dilemma. I take a few seconds before I read, sensing life is about to change; again.

Chapter Eleven

The lies we tell ourselves are the worst kind, for we have all the time in the world to convince ourselves they are true. Ten years, in my case.

Jess wanted me to follow her to the Exclusion Unit, we both knew that. She pulled me to her in the darkness, kissed me, held me, begged me to stay. 'You're the only one who cares,' she told me, kissing me again. 'The only one.'

I pushed her away, said she was drunk, it would be wrong of me, but she confessed it was all an act, a way of getting me alone. 'I knew you'd be the one to save me, Mark.'

No one had ever looked at me as she did that night. She was so full of adoration.

Maybe it was that which I found impossible to resist, or her vulnerability that spoke to me, a perfect innocence. Have you ever wanted something so much it made it impossible to resist? Have you ever felt that madness, a complete abandonment of self, of sense, of consequence? I held her then, felt her body against mine, told her I loved her as much as she did me. And in those few precious moments we both felt anything might be possible. I know we did.

But afterwards, I sensed a change in her. She turned away from me, adjusted her dress, said she was fine, but could I go? She wanted to be alone. Had I missed something, misread her? She said, no, she was fine, but I felt a prickle of fear. I promised I'd message her, but she said she would contact me, and when I reached out she recoiled, began crying. I tried to comfort her, but she pushed me away, raised her voice, told me to get out, screamed for help.

I ran home, showered, washed my clothes, covered my tracks, but still I held on to the hope that once she'd calmed down, she would see sense. How far we were away from that scenario already, I had no idea.

I saw her tonight, went over to her dead mother's house, looked into her eyes, begged her to admit it was her idea, that she wanted it as much as I did, that she was the one who manufactured a way for it to happen. That it was something beautiful, something precious; not what she had turned it into with her lies. It's always been my hope I'm torturing myself for no reason, that what we shared that night was tarnished by her out of spite, or even regret, but not fear. I begged her for that release, some impunity. Then I saw what I have tried so hard to dismiss, to explain, to justify. I saw the devastation of a life, a young life, barely begun, and I knew then that I'd taken away something it was impossible to atone for, something innocent and precious – her trust.

I stop reading to wipe away the tears. All those wasted years. All the times he swore to me she was a liar, that they never had sex, and I chose to believe him. All the months of grief and guilt since his death, whilst his confession was right here, waiting for me. Would Mark have told me, had he lived? Admitted how he took a child's innocence that night, betraying not only her trust, but mine and his daughter's too? He wrote it all down, so there must have been some kind of rationale.

Or would he have kept his confession a secret, locked away like the truth, convincing himself once more that he was the victim of her treachery, his lies necessary to protect us, his family?

I think of all the times he stared into my eyes and perjured himself. In court too. And the years in prison, as I waited at home. He was a man of thirty-nine, a teacher, a family man, and Jess was a child, a damaged, vulnerable girl—

'Kar?' Will calls down to me. 'Could do with some help up here; I think it's time for another feed.'

My breasts leak milk on to my robe as I call up, 'Be right there.' I close the document and shut down the computer, but I don't get up, exhaustion and a long-forgotten feeling of inertia taking over.

'I've changed her nappy, but Jackson . . . Jackson, stop it! You okay, Kar?'

'Sorry, just coming.' I walk the letter to the bin, collecting up the printed pages and pushing them beneath the dirty nappies. Then I check my face in the hall mirror, rubbing at the dark circles under my eyes before I climb the stairs.

The last time I visited Mark, before the pregnancy was too obvious to hide, he said he was looking forward to coming home. This home. The one I chose when he suggested we start over, somewhere new. To make better memories. I couldn't bring myself to tell him about the baby, going along with his plans as I always did, pretending to him and me that there truly was a future for us. Perhaps he was pretending too, his epiphany sitting too heavily on his conscience, his intention to end his suffering already decided. Maybe he wanted me to choose a new home so he could imagine me there, a fresh start. But he'd hung on for two more months, prison somehow more attractive than the alternative – decisive action never his style, or so I'd thought. Maybe it simply took time to procure the blade and steel himself for those final cuts. The reason as prosaic as that. But he left no note, no confession. Or so I'd thought.

James visited him the day before he died, still blames himself for mentioning the pregnancy. I've tried to convince him that what Mark chose to do could have been for any number of reasons, but perhaps it was James's revelation which finally decided my cowardly husband, a point of no return. Mark told me I was all he had left, all he needed, and his only reason for carrying on, but guilt eats away at you if you let it, poisoning everything. You can tell a lie over and over, convince those who love you, who are desperate to believe you, but can you ever convince yourself? Maybe now I can assuage some of Frey's guilt for her part in all this, if she'll let me.

I always suspected it was my daughter who threw the bricks, daubed messages, wreaked an ineffectual revenge. She often goaded her father for his apathy, it seemed logical to conclude she might have taken matters into her own hands. I suppose subconsciously I allowed her that release. We all need one. I hope, in time, she can remember the good things her father did, how he chose to save her because he wanted her to have a better life, be happy. There's no shame in loving a parent, even a bad one, and she needs to move on, begin the next chapter in her life, as I have.

In the months following Jess's death, Will and I kept our

distance. Despite the pregnancy, impossible to keep secret in our gossip-fuelled village, the division between us was so deep I thought it would never be breached.

Then Mark took his own life.

Maybe it was too soon after my husband's death, or perhaps I'd already waited far too long, but each moment we were apart felt like another wasted chance, the ache to be with Will building inside me until I drove to the deserted campsite so fast it's a miracle I didn't crash. The holiday park was a surreal setting for our reunion, the log cabin much as I'd imagined it when Will had made plans for us both to move there; almost six months before. Side-by-side in his unmade bed, Will pulled my bump to rest against his stomach, his head inclined to mine as he told me yes, we would move into this house together. I'd chosen it after all, and the sale on the cottage was already going through, but there was one condition . . . I must never mention Mark's name again.

I may be about to go back on my word.

Will is sitting on the carpet between the crib and Jackson's bed, holding Jessica in his lap whilst he and Jackson assemble the train track. What an amazing man, to still love me after everything my family has done to his, but he won't countenance any such talk. *'It's not your fault, Kar, none of it.'* He's still grieving for his lost sister, and for a moment I hesitate, unsure of my decision and questioning his loyalty, although I know I shouldn't.

He looks up at me. 'Kar, what is it?'

Three faces wait for my reply, a rare moment of silence, and I know what I must do. For them. For me. But most of all for Jess Tidy.

Acknowledgements

Writing this book has been a wonderful experience, more so because I now have the talented team at Wildfire behind me. My editor, Kate Stephenson, is a genius, and I simply could not have written this book without her. Also to Ella Gordon, for whom nothing is ever too much trouble, and Alex Clark for heading up the best team in publishing. Wildfire is one big family because of you, Alex. Also thanks to Claire Baldwin who added her brilliance to a later draft and Siobhan Hooper for my amazing cover. Big thanks in fact to everyone at Headline, from marketing to publicity and everything in between, especially Jo Liddiard, Katie Brown and Georgina Moore.

And thanks of course to the incredible team at Sophie Hicks: Sophie, Sarah and Morag. But especially Sarah Williams. She's clever, kind and always has my back. I am so fortunate to have found her. No one could ask for a better agent.

The themes of *Lying To You* are ones I wanted to handle responsibly. A huge debt of thanks therefore goes to Detective Sergeant Nigel Hatten, who has steered me well with his advice on all police-related matters. Being a writer is a dream job, but I'm aware that there are many people, like Nigel, who do the real work: important, humane, and often unrecognised. Thank you. And thank you to Julie Swain for her generous advice regarding paramedic procedures.

My family have been endlessly supportive with their interest, as well as their time. Thanks to my husband, Chris, for his patience and love. He is fortunately more level-headed that I am. And to my grown-up children, Beth and Dan, who always share in my excitement at being a published author. Also, my mum, dad, mother-in-law, and all my extended family, especially George who is now one of us, and Clare, David, Hannah, Morgan and Olivia.

Also thanks to the loyal members of Cotswold Creative Writing, and all my other friends, old and new: writers, readers, bloggers, and those for whom this is an alien world. Thanks for embracing my books by reading, blogging, Tweeting, and turning up to support me at events. It's so appreciated.

Special mention to my best writing-buds, Hayley Hoskins and Kate Riordan. Can't thank you enough for every message, coffee, lunch, email, emoji, retweet and just being there for me...I love you both. And to Alison Tait, an early and encouraging reader, and Jess Earl who is my constant cheerleader.

I'd also like to thank the writing community who have welcomed me and made me feel entirely at home. Inclusiveness is their mantra, and I have learnt so much.

If you have read this book, you are also thanked, because readers bring books to life. Without you, there is no story.